I
DREAMED
OF
FALLING

ALSO BY JULIA DAHL

STANDALONES
The Missing Hours

REBEKAH ROBERTS NOVELS
Conviction

Run You Down

Invisible City

I DREAMED OF FALLING

A Novel

JULIA DAHL

MINOTAUR
BOOKS
NEW YORK

First published in the United States by Minotaur Books,
an imprint of St. Martin's Publishing Group

I DREAMED OF FALLING. Copyright © 2024 by Julia Dahl.
All rights reserved. Printed in the United States of America. For information,
address St. Martin's Publishing Group, 120 Broadway, New York, NY 10271.

www.minotaurbooks.com

Designed by Omar Chapa

The Library of Congress Cataloging-in-Publication Data is available upon request.

ISBN 978-1-250-86597-7 (hardcover)
ISBN 978-1-250-86598-4 (ebook)

Our books may be purchased in bulk for promotional, educational, or
business use. Please contact your local bookseller or the Macmillan Corporate and
Premium Sales Department at 1-800-221-7945, extension 5442, or by email at
MacmillanSpecialMarkets@macmillan.com.

First Edition: 2024

10 9 8 7 6 5 4 3 2 1

For my parents

CHAPTER ONE

I hadn't planned to go anywhere that night. Tara made mac and cheese on the stove and I watched Octonauts with Mason until she called us in for dinner. It was just the three of us: me, my son, and his grandma. Mason's dad, Roman, was in the city, and Tara's fiancé, John, was working late. We finished eating and I washed the dishes while Mason and Tara built Lego spaceships in the living room. I opened a beer and scrolled through my phone.

When I heard Tara say, "Time for bed," I met them at the bottom of the stairs.

"I'll do bedtime," I offered.

"I want Gerty to do bedtime," said Mason, touching Tara's leg.

"Mommy can do tonight," Tara said.

"No."

I wasn't going to make him say more. I knelt and opened my arms. "Can I have a good night?"

Mason gave me a big hug, both arms.

"Good night, Mommy," he said. He kissed me on the cheek.

"Sweet dreams, baby. I love you."

"I love you, too."

I watched them walk up the stairs, his rejection scratching at my heart. In the kitchen, I finished my beer and was about to open another when the text came in. What else did I have to do? It was eight o'clock on a summer Friday night. Why not distract myself from the fact that my child loved his grandmother more than he loved me?

It wouldn't always be like this, I told myself as I put on my new sandals. The ones I bought because I knew Roman thought ankle straps were sexy. Soon, everything would be different.

CHAPTER TWO

Roman answered the call reluctantly. He was hungover and hungry and squinting into the sunlight as he sat in traffic on the Palisades headed north from Manhattan.

"I'm so glad you picked up!" said Daniel. "Ash is an hour late and she's not answering her phone. Can you tell her to get her ass in here? I've got to pick up my mom."

"I'm not home," said Roman. "I left early."

It wasn't exactly a lie. He'd left yesterday and was just now driving back. Daniel could be a gossip, and he didn't need the whole town wondering why he hadn't slept at home last night.

"Are you sure she's on?" Roman asked. His longtime girlfriend and the mother of his four-year-old son, Ashley Lillian, rarely worked at the local coffee shop anymore, though the owner did occasionally ask her to cover shifts.

"She's supposed to fill in for Bobby and train this new girl. I guess it was last-minute. But it's not like her to forget."

If Ashley had forgotten her shift, or slept through it, she had probably been out the night before. She'd been going out more the last few months. Not that he could judge: he'd vomited in a trash can outside a Starbucks on Lexington Avenue this morning.

"I don't know what to tell you, man," Roman said. "You could go by the house."

Koffee was on the town's main street and the Grady house, where Roman and Ashley and Mason lived with Roman's mom, Tara, and her fiancé, was barely a quarter-mile east toward the Hudson River.

"I don't think I can leave the new girl alone."

"I'll be home in a half hour, forty-five minutes."

Daniel sighed dramatically. "Tell Ash I said she's too old for this shit."

Roman hung up. He checked the GPS—bloodred for the next three miles. The app indicated an accident. He pressed his fingers to his eyes. The air-conditioning in his 2007 Accord was spotty, blowing cold out of one vent, hot out of the other three. They'd paid $600 to have it fixed two years ago, and he wasn't going to do that again.

He inched forward, surrounded by city couples and families with kids and dogs in their rented Smart cars, mountain bikes or kayaks attached to the roof racks. They were all headed out to enjoy their summer weekend in the mountains or on the river. They were smiling. At least some of them were. He felt like ass, but looking at those weekenders Roman Grady decided that he was going to do his best to enjoy his family this weekend, too. Tonight was the monthly town-sponsored outdoor movie. They'd all go with a picnic. They'd watch the fireworks and carry Mason home to bed, asleep.

He texted Ashley:

you up? call daniel

He added a goofy face emoji. Ashley had been prickly and distracted lately, and instead of allowing her the space to work out whatever needed working out, he'd used it as an excuse to be exasperated. On Thursday night, he picked a fight while she put the dishes in the dishwasher and he prepped coffee for the morning.

"Did you forget to get half-and-half?" He knew she had. It wasn't in the fridge.

"Was it on the list?"

Ashley was in charge of grocery shopping, which had been challenging lately because her car was acting up.

"I don't know," he said, though probably he'd forgotten to add it to the little notepad on the counter.

"You have to put it on the list."

"You didn't see we were out?"

"I don't drink half-and-half."

"Yeah, but you look in the fridge."

Ashley said nothing, which enraged him. He'd lived with this woman for years and she knew he drank his coffee with half-and-half every morning, but she couldn't be bothered to check if there was a carton in the refrigerator door before she went shopping? She checked for Mason's snacks; she checked for Tara's tea; she checked for John's fucking energy drinks. His heart withered in his chest as he thought about her disregard. *She doesn't see me. She doesn't know me. She doesn't love me.*

"I'm going to bed," she said.

"I'm just saying that it would be great if you remembered what I like to drink. And if I forget to put it on the list, when you pass it in the store, you could pick it up."

She met his eyes. Roman was ready to have it out. He was ready to defend his grievance. But all she said was, "Okay."

Thinking about it now, he cringed. He'd been an asshole. He would apologize and he would make it up to her. As the traffic cleared and he passed the Bear Mountain Bridge, headed up the mountain, he felt ready to make real changes.

Connor was hammering at the roof when Roman finally got home. Classic rock trickled weakly down from a speaker balanced on the gutter. Roman's grandparents had bought the circa-1875 house in the 1980s, paid it off, and when they died—in a car accident when Roman was seven—Tara inherited it. After Roman left for college, his mom had taken out a home equity loan, and created a suite on the first floor to use as an Airbnb. But she should have spent the money shoring up the house. Two weeks ago, the ceiling in the suite collapsed and his mom had to refund $800 to the couple who'd had it booked in order to save her "superhost" designation.

Tara's fiancé, John, was in charge of fixing the ceiling and the leak that had felled it in time for the mother-daughter pair who were scheduled to arrive next weekend. John was a handyman. He'd worked construction crews in his twenties and thirties, and after his divorce started picking up freelance jobs. John could do everything from carpentry to HVAC to tile, but he'd had to enlist his friend Connor for a couple days while he finished a job for a client up in New Paltz.

Roman parked along the curb. With Connor's tools and the detritus he'd dropped spread across the lawn, their house showed its age. The porch needed sweeping, the hanging flower needed water, the shutters needed straightening, and the whole thing needed paint. Ashley's PT Cruiser was in the driveway but his mom's car was gone. Tara must have taken Mason on some outing.

Bang bang bang. Connor's hammer echoed down the street. How could Ash sleep through this? He entered through the kitchen door and called for her.

"Hello?"

Was it possible Ashley crashed somewhere else last night?

Bang bang bang.

Roman opened the refrigerator and drank from the carton of milk. He grabbed a cheese stick and walked up the stairs to the third floor. Technically, Mason lived in the apartment upstairs with Roman and Ashley, but their kitchen was an afterthought, leftover from when the house was a duplex in the 1970s, and the family mostly ate meals downstairs together with Tara and John. Roman often worked evenings. He was the sole reporter for the local paper—the *Adamsville Advocate*, circulation 8,000—and he covered meetings and retirements and dedications and graduations in three towns over a ten-mile radius.

Tara, who Mason called "Gerty"—the "g" sound for Grandma and "tee" for Tara—was nineteen years old when she had Roman, so she was just forty when Ashley gave birth to her grandson in the middle of Covid lockdown: April 12, 2020. None of the family were allowed in the hospital, and there were complications. When Ash and Mason finally came home, she was barely recovered, and Tara became the boy's caretaker.

Roman peeled off the plastic wrapper and pulled down a string of white cheese, pleased with the symmetry of the strip. He folded it into his mouth. If Ash was here and not in a terrible mood, he'd walk to work with her and get a free bagel.

"Ash?"

He pushed open their bedroom door. The bed was empty, coverlet tossed over the pillows. Her toothbrush was dry in the bathroom.

Roman went back to the refrigerator downstairs and the first thing he saw this time was a jar of strawberry jam. His son's favorite meal these days was "jammich," and damn if that didn't sound good. He spread a thick layer between two slices of bread, and as the banging on the roof started up again, he called his mom. The call went to voicemail. Tara had a whole life on Facebook, but she was fastidious about not using her phone around Mason, or while she was driving.

He texted:

> call me pls

Roman's phone rang. Daniel again.

"Is she on her way?"

"She's not here," said Roman. "I'm sorry, dude, she must have forgotten. Maybe her phone is dead. I'll have her call as soon as I see her."

Roman stepped back outside to check on the progress of the roof, and his phone rang again. This time it was his boss, Larry Mullins, the sixty-eight-year-old editor, publisher, and opinion columnist of the *Advocate*.

"Hi, Larry."

"Did you forget about the bench?"

Shit. Yes, Roman had forgotten that he was supposed to cover the unveiling of a plaque on a bench in the town park that morning.

"They're waiting for you to start," said Larry.

It was the curse of working at a small-town paper: pretty much every event was important enough to cover, yet almost nothing was so important they couldn't wait for the reporter.

"This is our bread and butter, kid," said Larry. "You can't be making podcasts if you can't remember the important stuff."

Roman knew better than to try to create some Mason-centered emergency as an excuse. Larry didn't care. Although his boss had to pretend to embrace the family-friendly nature of the town whose newspaper he ran, privately he was a man with a heart as atrophied as his calf muscles. Recently Roman had asked if he could watch the live stream of a school board meeting instead of attending in person so he could take Mason to gymnastics class. Larry almost laughed: *he's got two moms, doesn't he?* Thinking back, Roman marveled at Larry's ability to cut straight to the throbbing heart of the situation. Crudely articulating Roman's silent, chronic fear: *my son doesn't need me.*

"I'm on my way."

CHAPTER THREE

Roman rolled up to the town park ten minutes later—forty-five minutes after the ceremony had been scheduled to start. About a dozen people gathered around the cloth-draped bench. It wasn't even a new bench; it had been installed by a local Eagle Scout when Roman was in elementary school.

The mayor waved as Roman approached.

"We knew you'd make it!" exclaimed Mayor Elizabeth "Bitsy" Sloane. Bitsy was breathless, sweating in a pantsuit, smiling too broadly. Roman guessed she'd been performing a small-talk song-and-dance while impatient relatives clucked and clicked at their phones.

"All right," said the mayor. "Let's get started."

Roman turned on his recorder and snapped a few photos with his phone. The mayor read from a piece of paper that whipped against the breeze and finally flew off, tumbling toward the algae-choked pond. Matt Biaggi, who'd been a year ahead of Roman and Ash in high school, rushed after it in his Birkenstocks. Roman took pictures of everything: the fluttering paper, the wreath of red, white, and blue silk flowers on the flimsy aluminum stand, the yawning family, the reveal (*Martin Michaelson, 1941–2023, Veteran, volunteer: "I just want to help."*), and the whole group gathered around the bench.

Roman had enough information to write the piece from what the mayor had said, but he approached the widow anyway and asked how she hoped her husband would be remembered.

"Marty loved this town," said Mary Michaelson. "He felt lucky to have raised his family here. It's not the same as it was. But even so, he really did say that. 'I just want to help.' He said it all the time. Didn't matter who. I hope people remember that."

Not the same as it was. Roman heard that constantly from the town's older residents. He knew it meant people from New York City—though most of his grandparents' generation had moved up from Brooklyn or Queens themselves, albeit fifty years ago—and specifically nonwhite people. The town was still something like 80 percent white and Christian, but apparently that wasn't quite enough.

"He was a good man," Mary added. "A good husband."

Matt walked up, reeking of weed. It was nearly ninety degrees, but he wore a gray knit cap over his ever-expanding cotton candy hair.

"Matthew, you smell terrible," said Mary.

"It's legal now, Grandma," said Matt, grinning.

Mary excused herself.

"Wanna smoke?" Matt asked once she was out of earshot.

"Absolutely."

The mourners dispersed and Roman and Matt walked up the

hill from the bench, past the library, toward the Little League
fields. Adamsville teens had been getting high in those dugouts
for generations. John told a story about his dad, a linebacker for
the high school football team, leading the then–police chief on
a mile-long foot chase after they found him with a freshman
girl and a joint in 1968. *Never caught him,* John said, shaking his
head. *Or at least that's how my dad told it.*

Matt pulled a big square vape from his pocket and took a hit,
then passed it to Roman. He thought back to the early days of
Covid, when every tiny thing they'd taken for granted—opening
the mail, obtaining groceries, the very act of breathing around
other people—was suddenly terrifying. But here he was, back
to swapping saliva with whoever had pot. And it was going to be
fine. It was breathtaking how quickly things had changed—then
and now.

He and Matt stood together without talking, taking in the
breeze, the geese arrowing in from the river, the slightly rancid
smell off the pond. The first time Roman and Ash had snuck
out to meet up, they came to this park. They were thirteen, in
the same math class, and Ash had missed three days of school.
Roman texted asking if she needed the homework, and if she
wanted to talk. She texted back:

> *swings at midnight?*

It turned out she'd missed school because her grandma had
died and they had to drive to Pennsylvania for the funeral. Roman told her about his grandparents, and listened while Ashley

worried that this was going to make her mom even more anxious and superstitious, which was how she saw her mom's increasing religiosity. They had their first kiss a week later, in Roman's bedroom. All those years in middle school and high school, meeting at the swings in the middle of the night, and they never encountered anyone else. Lighter now, from the weed, Roman smiled thinking about it. Did the whole town know it was their place?

"How's Ash?" asked Matt.

Roman was momentarily surprised to hear his voice.

"Oh, she's good."

"I saw her at Bella's last night."

"Bella's?"

As far as Roman knew, Ashley and Bella Abernathy hadn't seen each other since Mason was born. They'd all been close in high school, but after graduation, while everyone else went off pursuing their various paths, Bella got stuck. Her mom had died of cancer when Bella was fourteen, and her dad, a commercial airline pilot, was away for long stretches. Bella's house had been the party house, which was fun in high school, but grew darker when Bella suddenly had nowhere to go every day, no one to expect anything from her; no one to notice if she didn't eat, or started taking pills. She stole from Ashley more than once before she and Roman cut her out of their lives.

Since, they'd heard only rumors. Bella's dad had decamped to Florida; she'd gotten behind on the taxes; gotten a job at Walmart; caught an early case of Covid. Roman wasn't sure, but he heard she'd been on a ventilator. Bella didn't reach out when

Mason was born, and they didn't reach out either. They lived half a mile apart, but somehow they'd gone years without seeing Bella.

At least Roman had.

"What was going on at Bella's?" he asked Matt.

"Nothing much when I stopped by. It was just her and Ash in the backyard. Bella called me the day before for some weed and I was dropping it off. They seemed good. It was cool to see them hanging again."

Roman had more questions, but he didn't want Matt to know he was surprised Ashley was at Bella's. He didn't want Matt to think he didn't know what was going on with the woman he lived with. But he did want information.

"What time was that?" he asking, trying to sound casual.

"Maybe eight? Bella's cousin—you know Kevin? He texted asking if I'd make a beer run around eleven. He's only nineteen. Nice kid. I was headed home and it wasn't too out of the way so I said sure. Didn't see Ashley or Bella when I dropped it off. But things had gotten rowdy."

CHAPTER FOUR

Tara didn't even look at her phone until after she strapped Mason into his backseat booster. They'd been on one of their day trips. Tara Grady wasn't a stay-in-and-color kind of grandma; if it was above twenty degrees outside, she and Mason were on an adventure. He'd be cooped up in a classroom for twelve years; now was the time to learn from the outside world. Today, they'd hiked to a waterfall just outside Beacon.

"Can we listen to my playlist?" Mason asked as Tara threw her backpack onto the passenger seat of the RAV4.

"Sure, sweetie," she said, digging around for her sunglasses.

"Put it on shuffle, please."

"Thanks for that 'please,'" she said, smiling back at him. "We have to call your daddy first. Looks like he was trying to get ahold of us."

She dialed Roman and he answered after the first ring.

"Hi, you okay?"

"Am I on speaker?" he asked.

"Yeah," said Tara. "What's up?"

"Can you take me off speaker?"

"Hi, Daddy!" Mason shouted from the backseat.

"Mom?"

"Mason says hi."

"Hi, mister," said Roman. Tara wondered if Mason registered the lack of enthusiasm in his father's voice. Was that what she'd sounded like when Roman was young?

"We saw a dead fish!" said Mason.

"Mom, please."

Tara picked up the device and put it to her ear.

"Did you hear Mason? He said we saw—"

"Do you know where Ash is?"

"No." Tara knew better than to ask what was wrong. What was wrong—what was always wrong—was that her son was in a shitty mood. He'd been in a shitty mood for four years. He refused to call it depression—which it clearly was—and she'd given up trying to get him to see it that way. But more and more she was allowing herself to be angry and short with him when he was like this. He needed to know that she noticed, that his mood seeped into their home like gas. It seeped through the fucking phone.

"She was supposed to do a shift at Koffee, but she's not there and she's not at home," he said. "Did you see her get home last night? Or this morning?"

Tara hadn't. Mason had come downstairs to the bedroom she and John shared just after sunrise, like he did most mornings. They'd gone upstairs to brush his teeth and get dressed around nine, after breakfast. Tara remembered that Ashley and Roman's bedroom door had been cracked slightly; she assumed Ashley was asleep.

"I didn't see her," said Tara, "but that's not unusual."

"Can you put on my playlist, Gerty?" asked Mason.

"You have to give me a minute to talk to your daddy, mister," she said. "You have your book."

Mason furrowed his brow and shot Tara a side-eye before relenting and picking up the book about the mischievous cat who gives a mean side-eye. It was a small triumph: refocusing the boy's attention from what he wanted but could not immediately have, to what he could have instead. Tara looked for those triumphs, which she took as reassurances. Technically, she was caring for a small child for the second time in her life, but the truth was that her parents had raised Roman until he was seven. When she finally got her shit together and was ready to be a mom, her son was years past the sweetness of his early childhood. Then, four years ago, Roman and Ashley gave her another chance while she was still young enough to take advantage. When Tara lifted baby Mason from the car seat on the day he and Ashley finally got home from the hospital, she touched the boy's face and promised she would show up for him every day. And she had. And she would. *I love you forever,* she told him constantly.

"Have you called the gym?" Tara asked. Ashley taught yoga at one of the local fitness clubs. Maybe she mixed up the shifts.

"No," said Roman. "I guess I can try that."

"Gerty, can we still get donuts?" asked Mason.

"Yes, Mason."

"Yay!"

"I just saw Matt Biaggi and he said he saw her at Bella's last night," said Roman.

Tara closed her eyes. She'd been avoiding telling Roman about the argument she'd had with Ashley last month. She couldn't say anything now, with Mason in the car. But if Ashley was hanging out at Bella's, things probably hadn't gotten better.

"Maybe she stayed there," said Tara.

"Did you know she was hanging out with Bella again?"

"No."

"Okay. Maybe her phone died. If she's not home when I get back, I'll go by Bella's."

"Good luck," said Tara. She ended the call.

"Bye, Daddy!" called Mason.

"I'm sure he meant to say goodbye," said Tara, shaken, imagining Ashley passed out on the floor at Bella Abernathy's. Likely to be hungover until tomorrow. They'd planned to take a picnic to the outdoor movie and fireworks that evening. But Ashley would probably bail.

"Donuts!" shouted Mason, setting his book down.

Tara started the car. She hadn't handled last night well. Why hadn't she just let Ashley do bedtime? She couldn't blame her for not begging her own son to let her do what she should be doing in the first place. The person with the power last night, as usual, was Tara, and she had used that power to stay with Mason because being with Mason made her happier than anything else in her life. His weight on her crossed legs as she read to him in the

rocking chair beside his bed; his little chest beneath her hand
as they lay next to each other before lights out; him holding his
stuffed St. Bernard, eyes on the ceiling fan as she sang him to
sleep. Ashley rarely asked for bedtime, even when she was home;
Tara should have made it happen. Next time.

CHAPTER FIVE

Bella's car wasn't in the driveway, but the side door was unlocked and Roman walked in.

"Hello?"

His voice disappeared into the carpet. The house badly needed air. Bella had lived here more or less alone for ten years. If it hadn't been for him and Ashley—Ashley mostly—she likely wouldn't have made it through high school. At first, after Roman left for NYU and before Ashley went to Hawaii, Bella did okay. She sold some comics and got a couple gigs drawing ads for local businesses, but her ADHD, lack of savings or family support, and general disdain for institutions made the idea of college—even art school—basically unthinkable. She'd have to sell the house, which she wasn't willing to do. It was the only steady thing in her life. Her last connection to her mom. The house itself was a dump, but the land was worth close to half a million dollars. Maybe, Roman thought as he looked around, Bella somehow knew she'd blow through even that much money within a decade or so, then end up forty and homeless.

"Bella?"

Roman walked down the narrow hall to the living room, where a wall of windows looked out over the Hudson. He hadn't been here in years and he'd forgotten how dramatic Bella's panoramic view was. There was literally nothing but air between the edge of her yard and the river.

"Bella, is that you?" called a male voice from one of the bedrooms.

The voice belonged to Kevin Abernathy, Bella's cousin. From what Roman remembered, Kevin's mom and Bella's mom were sisters. Kevin was sometimes around when they were in high school—Bella babysat him while his mom worked—but all Roman could recall of him was that he spent a lot of time in the backyard, kicking a soccer ball against the crumbling wall that separated Bella's cliffside property from her neighbors.

"I don't think she's here," Roman said. "Her car's gone."

"I guess she had a shift," said Kevin. He was shirtless, his basketball shorts hanging below his underwear. "Or maybe a doctor's appointment. She's at the doctor every other day."

"Is Ash here?"

"Ashley? No."

"Was she here last night?"

"I didn't see her, but I didn't get here till late and there were a lot of people."

"She didn't stay over?"

"Not that I know of. You want coffee?"

The kitchen was a sticky mess of empty and half-empty bottles of beer and liquor, juice jugs, Cheetos dust, a pizza box; an aluminum tub of popcorn was overturned by the garbage can. Kevin found the coffee maker in a corner on the peeling Formica countertop and pulled the carafe from the warmer.

"Bella would seriously drink the same pot for a week," he said, pouring the leftover coffee into the sink.

"Are you living here now?" Roman asked.

"No," he said. "I mean, I'm here a lot. My mom's got a new boyfriend and he's an asshole. Bella doesn't mind. I don't think. Did she say something?"

Roman shook his head. "Honestly, I haven't talked to her in ages."

"I heard you and Ashley had a baby."

"He's four now."

"Shit." Kevin filled the carafe and poured it into the coffee maker. "I see your name in the paper. Pretty cool. You know, I take pictures. If you guys ever need some help or something."

"We don't have much of a budget," said Roman. "I pretty much do it all."

Kevin nodded.

"What was the party for?"

"I think it just happened. Honestly, I can use any reason to party these days. I've been working at that new Amazon warehouse and it's killing me." He lifted his bare foot. "Swollen ankles, dude. I'm not even twenty."

"You in school?" asked Roman.

"I should be," said Kevin.

"What time did you get here?"

"Last night? I don't know. Ten, maybe eleven."

"Who else was here?"

"The usuals. Some randoms."

Roman wasn't sure if he should ask Kevin to elaborate. They stood silently for a few moments as the machine percolated. Kevin opened the refrigerator door and peered inside. A smell like bad deli meat drifted out. "I don't think there's any milk in here."

"I'm good," said Roman. His stomach felt sour. Kevin pulled a mug from one of the cabinets. He poured his coffee and sipped.

"I gotta take a piss," he said, headed toward the back door.

"Outside?"

"The pipes are fucked," said Kevin. "The only toilet that flushes is Bella's and we're trying to keep it that way. If it's yellow . . . we go outside."

Roman knew Bella's house had plumbing problems. Some-time after her mom died, her dad made the executive decision to write off one of the three bathrooms entirely. Apparently, they told him they'd have to dig into the foundation to replace the pipes and he was either unable or unwilling to pay the thousands of dollars that would cost. Roman supposed it wasn't surprising that the situation had deteriorated. Bella's capacity for enduring creature discomforts had always been somewhat remarkable.

Roman followed Kevin out back. The Hudson River spar-kled before them. A sailboat coasted along the water. Roman could see the specks he knew were kayakers at the base of Ban-nerman Island. This same panorama, though not as completely unobstructed, helped pay their bills. They could advertise "a spectacular view of the Hudson River." Lots of days—too many days—Roman wanted to give the river his middle finger for be-ing so beautiful when he felt so ugly.

Bella's lawn—90 percent crabgrass and dandelions—stretched maybe thirty feet from the house. To the north, a wall separated her property from the neighbors, but east and south was only a stand of trees and bushes and boulders before the hillside dropped sharply to the road that ran along the freight railway tracks about a hundred feet below. Kevin put his coffee down on a rotting picnic table and whistled his way through the woods to stick his dick into the vista. Roman righted an over-turned metal chair and sat down. He checked his phone. It was 6 p.m. and still nothing from Ash. Roman supposed it was karma: him not knowing where she'd slept last night.

"Holy shit!" yelled Kevin. He started running backward, then tripped and fell. "There's somebody down there!"

Kevin's face was white, his eyes changed. He crept back to the edge and pointed down. "Is that? Oh my God, is that Ashley?"

Roman raced across the lawn and peered over the edge. There she was. Horizontal with her back to him. Her long legs and blond hair. Her white top. She was lying against the dried carcass of a discarded Christmas tree, itself lying against the trunks of three maples growing in a row. They'd caught it—and her—like a fence.

"Ashley!" Roman shouted. He imagined her face pressed into the tree's sharp needles. "Ash!"

No response.

"I'm going down," he said to Kevin. "Call 911."

Roman's first step down the cliffside was sloppy. He slipped, freeing a cascade of stones that tumbled toward Ashley, some hitting her back, some jumping and knocking past her, out of sight, onto the tracks below. It had been a dry summer, and the dust rose around him as he slid down, grabbing onto a jutting root. He turned to face the hillside, crawling backward, shouting, "Ash! I'm coming!" He slid and scraped along the rocks and the brambles and finally reached her. Her blue-painted toenails. One sandal on, one missing.

"Ash! Are you okay?"

But the moment he put his hand on her he knew she was gone.

CHAPTER SIX

"Is she breathing?" called a male voice.

Roman crouched beside Ashley, his hand on her hair. He'd never felt anything so still. So hopelessly, absolutely unmoving. Above him, the EMTs had arrived; Big Mel Rossy and Gwen Yarmuth, two of about a dozen trained local volunteers.

Roman shook his head but couldn't manage a sound.

"Roman?" called Big Mel.

"No!" Roman croaked.

Gwen started to climb down.

"Have you started CPR?" she shouted.

Roman didn't answer.

"Roman?"

She would be here in a minute; she'd see for herself. He closed his eyes against the dust and debris Gwen let loose as she climbed, angling his body to protect Ashley, too. When she arrived beside them, Gwen put her hands on Ashley's shoulders, preparing to turn her and start the assessment and healing she'd been trained to provide. But she must have felt the stiff nothing as surely as he did. She placed two fingers on Ashley's throat, where her heartbeat had been, but was no longer.

Gwen called up to Mel.

"We need a stretcher."

"Roger that," Mel shouted. "What's the status?"

Gwen hesitated. She looked at Roman. "I'm sorry," she said, then called up: "DOA."

"Shit," said Mel. "You sure?"

"Call the chief, Mel," she said, her voice strained and hard.

"Roger that," Mel said again, and disappeared from the edge.

"How long have you been here?" Gwen asked Roman quietly.

"I don't know," he said. "Not long."

He'd interviewed Gwen less than six months ago when she became the youngest fully trained volunteer EMT in town at nineteen. Her older brother had died of an overdose when she was a freshman and she'd told Roman in the interview that she wanted to help people like him. "If someone had gotten to him faster he might still be alive," was one of the quotes he'd used for the paper.

"Did you see what happened?" Gwen asked.

"No," said Roman.

They sat together quietly for what seemed like a long time. Gwen adjusted herself so that her knees were pulled to her chest. Far below them, a car rumbled over the railroad tracks. Roman looked through the trees. The sky was pinking, and the river glistened, water running north and south together. How long had it been since he and Ash had been out there? How long since they'd done anything fun?

His phone, which had fallen from his pocket and was about two feet away in the dirt, rang. It was Larry.

"Do you want me to get it?" Gwen asked.

"No," said Roman. He heard sirens approaching, and then from farther away, the whistle of a train.

"Do you want me to call someone? Your mom?"

"Not yet," he said. What was he going to say to Mason?

At the top of the hill Kevin hollered, "The cops are here!"

Roman looked up and saw Chief Michael Hawkins and Sergeants Scott Kingsley and Felix White. Hawkins was in his sixties and had been chief since his father retired twenty years ago. Kingsley was thirtysomething, another second-generation Adamsville officer, and White was new in town. Mid-forties, if Roman remembered correctly. He'd done a profile when they hired him. Ex-Army, moved from Arizona.

"What's the status?" called the chief.

The cargo train got louder. The rail line on this side of the river had once carried passengers, but now it was oil and gas and waste and lumber: down from Canada, up from the city. The hillside began to tremble, the clang of the crossing bells below them. Roman imagined the blinking lights, the red-and-white-striped barriers coming down. After a few moments, he felt the train roar by. He could hurl himself onto the tracks and never have to face Mason, or life without Ash. He grabbed hold of a root protruding from the ground.

The piercing sound of metal on metal, the wheels wilding over the track, rose like an angry banshee, obliterating all other sound. Sometimes the trains pulled only twenty or thirty cars.

Once, he and Mason had counted ninety-nine. Roman gripped
the root, knuckles white. The tears came as he squeezed against
the desire to obliterate himself. Gwen reached out and put her
hand on his. She had some kind of skin condition, her fingers
scaly and flaking around the nails. When he forced himself to
look at her face, he saw that she was crying, too.

The last car pulled past, and the silence brought a moment
of relief. Sergeant Kingsley started making his way down the
hillside. Roman put his hand on the tattoo on Ashley's leg that
she'd gotten in Hawaii. A simple line drawing of a wave. Her
forever reminder, she'd told him, to "roll with it." He'd been on
FaceTime with her when she got the mark—him lying in his
dorm bed, gazing out the window onto the night creatures who
occupied Union Square after dark; her, six hours west, on a chair
outside, beneath a shade awning, palm trees behind her. She'd
been talking about getting a tattoo for years, but wanted to wait
for the right moment, the right idea, the right image.

"Here we go," she'd said, and Roman heard the high-pitched
whir of the needle start up, saw Ashley flinch.

"Does it hurt?"

Ashley smiled. "No, it's just a little weird. Like a scratch. But
he keeps doing it."

"I love you, baby," he said.

"I love you, too. I wish you were here. They do couples!"

"I'm here," he said. "I'm always here."

She scrunched her nose.

"It hurts?"

"It's fine."

"Can I see?"

Ashley turned the phone. A black-haired man was bent over her bare leg. Roman watched him straighten up, flick his hair out of his eyes, wipe Ashley's leg, and bend over again. He wore black latex gloves but no shirt. The better to show off all his tattoos. He couldn't tell how old the man was, but Roman wondered if he and Ash might hook up. She'd been in Hawaii only a month, and she told him she wanted to establish an identity outside of her sexuality before she started playing around. Roman hadn't been as smart about his desires when he got to college; he traded oral with a girl on his floor the second night on campus, and had intercourse with the girl who happened to sit next to him on the first day of his Intro to American Literature class. Ashley had laughed when he told her, and they made a pact to be available for phone sex at any hour until at least Halloween.

The whirring needle stopped and the black-haired man rolled his stool out of sight, then came back with some clear ointment that he smeared over the ink. Ashley held the phone so Roman could take it in.

"It's simple for now," she said. "But Bella sent me a whole series that would let me fill it in gradually when I have more money."

So Bella had designed the tattoo. He struggled to contain his reaction. It made no sense to be jealous. Bella could draw, but Ash had chosen him to experience the tattoo, not her.

"Awesome," he said.

"Thanks for coming with me," she said, turning the phone back to her face now. "I love you."

"I love you, too."

It was their second year apart. No one gave their relationship any chance of surviving his four years at NYU. But then again, no one gave it a chance when Ashley came out as bisexual and they opened the relationship, either. They'd proved everyone wrong. Even when she fell for Bella, but still loved Roman, and Roman not only understood but loved her more. And she him. Sure, some of it was about sex. Why not? Sex was fun! What they had together was honest, and somehow it was also rarely painful. They never fought like their other teenage friends in relationships did. Roman loved the breadth and depth of Ashley's ability to see the good in people. *You'll love her, too,* she'd said of Bella. And she was right, when he looked through Ashley's eyes. Ash understood desire and the need for adventure and excitement and she begrudged Roman none of it. There was, she always said, enough to go around. Despite, or perhaps because of, the paucity of it in the home where she grew up, Ashley was bottomless with the capacity to love.

When Sergeant Scott Kingsley reached Roman and Gwen, he checked Ashley for a pulse. As he leaned over her, Roman saw something sticking out of Ashley's shorts pocket that he hadn't seen before.

"What's that?" he asked, pointing. But he didn't need to be told. It was a tiny plastic baggie. With little white pills inside.

Scott adjusted his squat to see.

"Let's not touch that," he said. "I'm going to take some pictures. Gwen, why don't you and Roman head back up to the house."

"I want to stay with her," Roman said weakly. *If I leave,* he thought, *she'll be all alone.* She'll be all alone with people who don't love her. She'll never be loved again. When was the last time he told her he loved her?

"There's nothing you can do now," said Scott.

CHAPTER SEVEN

Tara hadn't broken the rule against phone use while driving in ages, but when she saw the screen flash *Roman*, she reached out and pressed the green button. They were just blocks from home, turning left onto Main Street.

"Did you find her?" she asked. No response. "Roman? Can you hear me?"

"Ashley's dead, Mom," sputtered her son.

Tara twisted back to look at Mason—had he heard?—and accidentally turned the wheel with her, sending the car onto the sidewalk and into a utility pole.

When the airbag punched her in the face the first thing she thought was: *Will I blow high?* Because that's what she'd done the last time she'd careened off the road with a child in the backseat. But she was sober now, thank God. The car alarm blared, and she tasted blood.

"Gerty! No phones!" Mason yelled from the back.

She turned around to make sure he was okay. There must

have been blood on her face, because Mason gasped when he saw her and started to cry.

"Are you okay, mister?"

"Gerty!" He held out his arms. He was alive. He was fine. No, he was not fine. His mother was dead and he would maybe never be fine again. Her head felt heavy. What would be his last moment of happiness? The donuts? Splashing in the waterfall? Singing along to the Shania Twain song on his playlist? "Gerty! Do we have to go to the hospital?"

She'd dropped the phone. Roman was saying something, but she couldn't understand him. The airbag began deflating and when she twisted to unlatch her seat belt, her chest hurt. She opened the door and held the handle to steady herself as she climbed out. People were coming toward them. The car had jumped the curb on the corner shared by the sweet shop and the local State Farm rep. The coffee shop where Ashley sometimes worked was twenty yards up. Roman was still on the phone.

"Mom!" His voice was tinny and distant.

"I'm here," she called, kneeling, reaching behind the pedals for the device. Spots of black floated before her eyes. "Hold on."

"Are you okay?" A voice from the sidewalk. It was Bobby, Koffee's owner and one of her oldest friends. Mason was sobbing now, his pitch rising as he called her name.

"I'm fine," she said, her fingers finding the phone. "Roman, hold on. I'm okay. Mason's okay. Where are you?"

"Don't tell Mason, Mom," said Roman. "Don't tell him!"

"Where are you?"

"Don't bring him here!"

Bobby's hand on her shoulder. "Unstrap Mason," Tara instructed.

Bobby ran around the back of the car. More people began approaching. *Are you okay? Are you okay?*

Mason barreled into her and she fell backward with his weight.

"Are you okay?" Bobby's voice was low. He was asking if she was sober. She nodded and he smiled in return: *phew.* The smile, almost kooky, told Tara that he didn't know about Ashley.

"I need to find Roman," she told Bobby, stroking Mason's hair. The boy's legs were wrapped around her waist, hooked on like a barnacle.

"You look scary, Gerty," he said. "I don't like it."

Bobby motioned to Daniel, who was standing with the others from the coffee shop. "Go get some paper towels."

Daniel hurried back toward Koffee. He and Ashley were close; he probably didn't know either. Every single person standing on the sidewalk knew Ashley. Had known her for years. They knew what her tattoos meant; they noticed when she cut her hair. They took for granted that she would always draw every eye in every room she entered. The possibility that Ashley was gone—as gone as Roman's dad, Jason; as gone as her parents—opened like a black hole inside Tara. Everything felt like it was dropping down, sucked away. Her family was cursed. She wanted to scream. But here was Mason, holding her, needing comfort.

"I'm fine, mister," Tara said, forcing a smile. "See? It's just a little blood. Remember when you ran into the tree on the playground?"

Mason nodded. "There was lots of blood."

"But you were okay. Remember what we said?"

"When you hit your head there's lots of blood. Even if it's a little boo-boo."

"Exactly." She hugged him tighter, though it hurt a little. He was so smart. "You're such a good boy. I love you so much. Your mommy and daddy love you so much." Her voice broke.

"I love you, too," said Mason. He was the only person in her life who'd never left her hanging on an "I love you." Not once.

Daniel appeared with the paper towels and a bottle of water, and Bobby began wiping blood off Tara's chin. They'd been close since high school; when Jason died, Bobby had a silly idea he could take his best friend's place. But Bobby was even less cut out for parenthood and monogamy than Jason and Tara; or Ashley and Roman. Twenty years later, his current girlfriend was threatening to leave him for the same reason they all did: they wanted kids and Bobby was never going to go there. The girls—and they all seemed like girls to Tara now, never much older than twenty-five—were always cool with it at first, thinking they'd be the one to bring him around. But what they didn't know—what few people besides Tara knew—was that Bobby had a vasectomy soon after Jason died. They'd never had the conversation, exactly, but Tara suspected he had been traumatized by what happened after his best friend got Tara pregnant, then fell into a depression he couldn't find his way out of. Bobby looked at what happened and determined it wouldn't happen to him, so: snip.

"I need to find Roman," Tara said. "Something's happened."

Before Bobby could ask what, Sergeant Felix White drove up in his town police car. From Tara's perch on the curb, the black nose of the SUV felt aggressive. The needlessly twerking siren and lights. Felix stepped out of the cruiser and rushed to Tara and Mason. His face was ashen; like he'd just seen something terrible.

"Have you talked to Roman?" he asked.

She nodded. "What happened?"

"He's at Bella's."

"What happened?" she asked again, more forcefully.

"She . . . fell."

"Mommy?" Mason loosened his grip on Tara and looked at Felix.

"Is she okay?" asked Tara. Maybe Roman was wrong. Felix shook his head.

"Mommy fell? Where did Mommy fall?"

"Do you want me to take him?" asked Bobby.

"Where's Mommy?"

"Mason," said Bobby, kneeling to get the boy's attention. "You wanna come get a blueberry muffin?"

Tara ignored him. "Come on, Mase," she said, standing up. "We need to go find Daddy."

"Tara," said Bobby, "let me take him. Go see what's going on and call me."

"I'm not letting him out of my sight," she said.

"Tara," said Felix, "I don't know if you want to take him over there."

"I wanna see Mommy!" screamed Mason.

"Are you gonna tell him that?" she asked. Every part of her body hurt, but she took one step and then another, Mason's forty pounds around her middle, toward Felix's cruiser. She gripped the latch and opened the back door. "Come on."

CHAPTER EIGHT

Bella's house was awash in red and blue flashing lights. An ambulance and three cruisers jammed the narrow residential street, and the neighbors were openly gawking. Pia and Will Atkinson and their twins, each on a different wheeled apparatus, lingered on their front walk across the road—despite it likely being a good bit past their bedtimes. Next door, another family who'd moved from Brooklyn during the pandemic were pretending to garden in the gathering dark. The man, bald and aggressively fit, leaned against a rake, though there wasn't a leaf on the grass. The woman, in a peasant-style sundress that probably cost $300, struggled with a hose. The child, a boy with long blond hair, was filling a plastic dump truck with mulch.

Felix stopped his cruiser just past Bella's. Mason was in Tara's lap and all the lights and commotion excited him.

"Is somebody in trouble?" he asked as they stepped out of the car.

"Let's just find Daddy, okay?"

Tara grabbed Mason's hand. The gate to Bella's backyard was ajar but Felix beat them to it. A moment later, Chief Hawkins appeared. Hawkins had been the one who cuffed and booked her all those years ago. He'd been the one who called social services to manage Roman. She'd made up for it as much as she could, but every time she saw him she was suddenly twenty-six years old again, drunk and angry and full of shame.

Hawkins put his hand up, blocking them from walking through the gate.

"Roman called me," Tara said.

"I don't think it's a good idea—"

"Daddy!" called Mason. He let go of her hand and ran around Hawkins's legs into the backyard. Roman turned around.

"No, Mason!" He caught his running son and picked him up, looking angry. "I told you not to come here!"

"Daddy, you're hurting me," Mason wailed. He flailed his arms, reaching back for Tara. "Gerty!"

Roman let the boy go, and he ran back to her. She knelt and let him jump into her arms.

"What is wrong with you?" shouted Roman. "What, can't you listen! Do you want him to see her?"

Tara had never seen Roman like this. She was on the second week of what was supposed to be six weeks in Europe when she found out she was pregnant. It was July 1999; she was eighteen, and when she looked in the mirror of the hostel bathroom in Rome, she saw that her breasts had changed. Her nipples were darker. She and Jason started having sex that February but she'd only gotten on the pill in late May. And she'd definitely forgotten to take it a few times. Tara had been accepted to college at SUNY New Paltz in the fall, and Jason was headed to Binghamton, four hours away. They talked about staying together, but Tara suspected it might be wishful thinking. She called Jason from a pay phone, dialing what seemed like hundreds of numbers to reach him where he was teaching mountain biking to kids in the Catskills.

Jason asked what she wanted to do and she said she didn't know. *Maybe it'll go away,* she thought.

Jason was supposed to have been with her on the trip, but his dad didn't come through with the $500 he'd promised for graduation in time to book the flights. So it was just Tara with her then–best friend Aly, and Aly's boyfriend, Bobby. The plan was another week in Rome, then north into France, where they'd bike through wine country and end up in Paris. Tara didn't tell Aly or Bobby. Every day she prayed for blood. Was she going to have to get an abortion? None of her close friends had ever been pregnant, that she knew of. There was a junior last year who, rumor had it, got an abortion after getting knocked up by a senior after homecoming. But Tara didn't really know her. She knew there was a Planned Parenthood in Newburgh because a family she babysat for protested there on weekends. They kept their signs by the front door and seemed to have new ones routinely, with color-photocopied images of fetuses attached to umbilical cords, floating in yellow and red liquid, screaming "Don't murder me" or some shit. Occasionally the mom asked Tara to help load the signs in the car, and they made her a little bit nauseated.

In Paris, she called Jason again and said she was going to come home early.

"If it's not gone, I'll go to Planned Parenthood."

It was not gone. But when she got to the clinic the sidewalk was crowded with people. She tried to keep her eyes down, to ignore it all, but it was impossible. The signs were for her now. "ABORTION IS MURDER! YOUR BABY FEELS PAIN!" A little boy, barely school age, was among the crowd. Around his neck he wore a sign that said: "Don't kill your baby." Jason grabbed her hand, but Tara couldn't move forward. The people on the sidewalk came toward her. They smelled blood.

"We can help you," said one woman.

"You don't have to do this," said another.

"Take some time to think," said one more.

Jason's tug got weaker. He was stuck, too.

"Don't let her do it," said a male protester. "You can be a dad. Here. Take this." The man gave Jason a pamphlet. "Are you a Christian?" The man didn't wait for Jason to answer. "Abortion is murder, son. You'll both go to hell. And the baby, too."

They stood there, holding hands on the concrete in the August sun, with the men pressing into Jason and the women into Tara. Every second the crowd seemed to get more energy, like they were feeding off the teenagers' fear. They were young and old, Black and white and Hispanic. "Do you know what abortion does to a baby? They stick a spear in its brain. The baby suffers. And you will, too. You'll regret it for the rest of your life. Did you know abortion increases the risk for suicide? And breast cancer. How far along are you? Take some time. We can help you make a plan."

Finally, from inside the clinic, Tara saw a woman in an orange vest come toward her. She had long gray hair tied in two braids and her vest said "ESCORT."

"I'm sorry," she said to Tara. "Everybody back up! Come on, miss, you can come with me." The escort extended her arm and the men and women started yelling.

"Don't pressure her!"

"Baby killer!"

"It's her choice!"

Tara started walking backward. Jason looked at her. "Let's come back later," she whispered, and they both ran for the car. Behind them, the crowd cheered.

At home, her parents could see something was wrong. They hadn't questioned her excuse for coming home from Europe two weeks early. She'd told them she was sick of being third wheel with Aly and Bobby, and that she'd seen Italy and France and wasn't all that excited about Germany or England anyway. Tara assumed they suspected she wanted to get back to Jason.

She broke down in the kitchen and told them where she'd been and why. Once they got over the shock, they told her they'd support whatever she decided to do: have the baby and defer college, or go through with the abortion. Her mother even offered to go with her to the clinic next time. But Tara never called there again. And soon it was too late.

She named him Roman for the city she'd been in when she found out. But those early years, every time anyone said his name, all it did was remind her of what she had missed. It reminded her that she'd made the wrong choice. She could have stayed in Rome forever. She could have gotten a job making espresso or teaching English and had a whole life in a foreign land. Instead, she was a teenage mom in the hometown she'd never leave.

So, she leaned into it. She hated everybody around her: Jason for getting her pregnant; Roman for existing; her parents for making caring for an infant seem easy. She made everyone aware of her pain. But Jason kept his inside. Was he moody? Always. Was he drinking too much? Yes, they both were. But was there a hint that he'd decided their life was a burden that could never be lifted? No. Jason hid that very well—until Roman's second birthday, when he leapt off a fucking bridge into the Hudson River.

After she brought herself out of the fog her first love's death sent her into, Tara began looking hard at Roman. She warned him over and over: your father didn't express his emotions. Please, she'd beg, talk to me. But he never did. She worried and worried and then, when he met Ashley, she saw that he'd found someone to talk to. And she rejoiced. Through all the upheaval of the last four years—their surprise pregnancy, the pandemic—Roman had Ashley.

And now she was gone.

"I thought we should be together, as a family," said Tara, struggling to hold on to Mason. "We just got in a car accident, Roman. Mason's pretty shaken up."

"Take him home, please. Go home." Roman was holding himself now, arms crossed over his chest, bent over slightly.

"I'll have Scott take you," said Chief Hawkins.

"What happened?" asked Tara again.

"Mom!" shouted Roman. His eyes were unfocused. Did he really think he was sparing Mason by creating this scene? It was time to make the best of a terrible situation, a skill she had developed, but not, apparently, passed down to her son. Scott opened his cruiser door and she and Mason slid in.

CHAPTER NINE

"Where are they taking her?" Roman asked as they closed the ambulance door. Big Mel and Gwen pulled away slowly. Without a life to run for, the sirens were silent.

"The county hospital," said Felix. He and Chief Hawkins were the last two of the uniforms left at Bella's. Hawkins was on the phone, standing at the edge of the yard, looking over the cliffside they'd lifted Ashley from. The wind picked up, and in the light of the moon Roman could see storm clouds coming from the west. "Did you know she'd been using?"

"No," said Roman. It wasn't entirely a lie. Before Mason, they'd both occasionally do a line at a party, or take Molly if it was around. And recently, since the pandemic, he knew she sometimes took the pills they'd prescribed for her anxiety in an off-label manner. A little soothing when things were hard for her; when yoga didn't cut it. But like his occasional weed habit, it wasn't something they advertised. They were parents. He was the town reporter; she'd worked on and off at the coffee shop for years. They were familiar faces, lifelong residents of Adamsville. Not addicts. Not "users." Not regularly, anyway.

"Any idea what she was doing here?"

"We were friends with Bella in high school," Roman said, "but they haven't been close in years."

A rumble of thunder. The weather was getting closer. *At least she's inside now.* He shivered, thinking of Ashley lying alone in the dirt, getting soaked by the rain.

"When was the last time you saw Ashley?" asked Felix.

"Yesterday morning." Thinking back, he wasn't sure they'd actually spoken. She was still asleep when he left to cover the county economic development committee work session, and he'd driven straight to Manhattan from there. "I stayed over in the city last night."

"Oh yeah?"

Chief Hawkins, apparently done with his phone call, appeared, closing the gate behind him. Roman felt a fat raindrop on his arm.

"You all live with your mom, right?" said Felix. "Did she notice Ashley didn't come home?"

"Let's let the poor kid get some rest," said the chief, looking at the sky. "You want a ride home, Roman?"

"My car's here."

"I was just thinking it's good to get a few things down while they're fresh," said Felix.

"We're about to get poured on. I think it can wait."

"Bella's not back," said Felix. "I'd like to stick around and—"

"You looking for overtime, Sergeant?"

"No, sir," he said. Felix kept a straight face, but his newly stiff posture betrayed his clear irritation. "How about I just tape off the other side, too—"

"I've got it under control," said Hawkins.

Felix stared at his boss as the clouds broke and the rain came down. Chief Hawkins lifted his arm to shield his face. "You're working tomorrow?" he asked Felix.

"Yes, sir."

Hawkins nodded. "We'll regroup then." He turned to Roman. "Let us know if you or your mom need anything, okay?"

"Okay."

Roman jogged through the rain to his car and sat inside, but as soon as Hawkins's and Felix's taillights were out of sight, he got back out and ran to the shelter of Bella's front porch, and then inside. He realized that at some point he had to go home, but he wasn't ready. He walked through Bella's house, looking, vaguely, for clues. For bits of Ashley. Had she drunk from any of these cups or bottles? Which sofa had she sat on? Felix told him they hadn't found her wallet or phone. Could it have fallen down toward the tracks? He made his way to the back patio and sat beneath the weathered awning as the rain came down. Rivulets poured like faucets off the sides of the house where the gutters were clogged. In the distance, cars moved across the bridge. After a while, he heard a truck's motor. Getting closer. Stopped.

"Roman?"

John came around the side gate, head bowed against the rain, with an eighteen-pack of Bud Light. When he got to the shelter of the patio, he shook his head. "Damn, it's coming down hard."

"Did my mom send you?" Roman asked.

"Yup." He was still wearing his work boots and, as usual, his pants were splattered with white paint, or maybe it was caulk. Roman couldn't tell.

"What did she say?"

John hesitated. "She said you might want some company."

"Did she tell you I told her not to bring Mason here and she did?"

"No," said John. "She was pretty upset."

"Of course she makes it about her," Roman muttered.

John found a chair, righted it, and sat down. "Do you want a beer?"

Roman didn't answer for a few moments. He didn't know for sure if Mason had seen Ashley's body lying on the stretcher. But he couldn't stop seeing it himself. What would she have looked like to her little boy? Whatever was happening inside him—rage or sorrow or terror—felt like it might explode out of his fingertips. He breathed out hard and looked at the rain.

"Yes," he said finally, "I want a beer."

John ripped open the damp cardboard and handed Roman a can. It was cold and Roman swallowed it greedily. John passed a second.

"Good thing you got the case," said Roman.

"I figured we might need it."

They each finished another can before Roman spoke.

"What did my mom tell you?"

"Not much. Just . . . you know. That they found her." He looked at Roman. "I'm so sorry, man. I know how much you loved her. This is insane. It's totally fucking insane."

Roman covered his face with his hands. It didn't feel real. But it was all that was real. It was all that would ever be real. Mason was barely four. How much would he remember of his mother? A handful of moments. Maybe a smell? Mostly he'd know her, like Roman knew his father, from pictures and stories that always ended with sadness.

"I don't know what to do."

"How could you?" said John. "Take a minute. We'll finish these beers. We can get some more if you want. Then we'll go home. Mason needs you."

"Does he?"

"Ah, come on, man. You know he does."

Roman knew no such thing. His phone rang again. Larry wasn't going to stop calling.

"What do you want, Larry?"

"Excuse me," said Larry, indignant. "Where are you? I've been waiting on copy and photos from the ceremony. And there's police activity on Hudson View. I need you to go over there."

"I'm there."

"Oh. Okay. What's going on."

"Ashley's dead."

"What? Who?"

"Ashley. My Ashley."

John grabbed the phone. "Roman can't talk right now."

Roman heard Larry bark "Hold on!" before John ended the call.

"If he fires you, you can come work for me. I'll teach you how to hang drywall."

Roman didn't respond. He opened another beer. *Police activity on Hudson View.* What else had the dispatchers said over the radio? Had he really woken up this morning in Manhattan? Was Ashley already dead when he texted her a final *sweet dreams* at 2 a.m.?

CHAPTER TEN

Roman didn't want to leave the backyard. Ashley was gone, but he felt as though staying here, where she'd last been, kept him tied to her. If he left, he was stepping into a life without her. He wasn't ready for that.

At some point, John's phone rang.

"It's your mom," he said. "I'm sure she's just worried. Okay if I pick up?"

Roman offered a barely perceptible shrug.

"Hey," said John into the phone. "He's okay. We're still at Bella's." John listened. "No, she's not back. Who knows where she is . . . I'll ask." He addressed Roman. "She wants to come over. Mason's down. I'll go home."

"No," said Roman.

His mom started talking; Roman could hear her voice but couldn't make out what she was saying.

"I know, Tara," said John. "I'm trying. I can't force him—"

"Give me a fucking minute, Mom!" shouted Roman, his voice cracking.

"I'll call you back," said John. "I will . . . I *will*."

Roman let the tears and snot run down his face. He felt like he was watching himself. A blubbering boy-man. John laid a hand on his back.

"I'm so sorry, man. I wish I could make it better. You'll get through this. Mason will get through this. We'll get through it together. You've got people who love you. We won't let you down."

Roman bent over, his head between his legs, the pain pouring out; liquid misery. John got up and brought back a wad of paper towels from the kitchen. Roman pressed them to his face. Eventually, the acute agony drained. The heavy rain had passed; just a drizzle now. Roman walked to the edge of the lawn to empty his bladder. Was this how it happened? The working bathroom was occupied and Ash had to pee. She wandered into the trees, high on whatever was in her pocket, and stumbled. Or maybe someone followed her. Or maybe she looked down and thought about her useless boyfriend and her strained relationship with her son and the fight she felt she'd never win against the sadness in her brain and wondered: *is it better down there in the dark?*

Roman's phone rang again. Larry. He zipped up and took the call inside.

"What is it, Larry?"

"Did you see my text messages?"

"No."

"I talked to Hawkins. I'm really sorry."

"Thanks."

"I'm sorry. But listen, you can't miss our meeting with Wolfe tomorrow."

Nicholas Wolfe was the lawyer for the Davenports—the family that owned their newspaper. Eighty-eight-year-old Asa Davenport's father had made the family fortune in radio and recording during the Depression, and by the 1960s the family owned more than a hundred local news stations across the country. After an early investment in Yahoo!, they started selling off the stations and buying commercial real estate—office buildings in New York, Chicago, Miami, Los Angeles.

But it wasn't until Asa's grandson, Asa III, who everyone called Trip, got paired with Mark Zuckerberg for a freshman computer science project at Harvard—and later convinced grandpa to invest in Facebook—that the family got the kind of rich that led them to do things like vacation on Rupert Murdoch's yacht, while simultaneously starting a foundation dedicated to "preserving local control of local news." The small-town newspapers they still owned got just enough funding to stay afloat, but not enough to do any actual journalism. Still, the Davenports were last year's winners of the Democracy Fund's Saviors of the Republic medal for "reviving" local reporting in "media deserts." Roman's paper, of course, covered the honor.

Every year around this time, Wolfe came to the second-floor Main Street office suite that the *Advocate* occupied to meet with Larry and Roman and Enid, the paper's part-time ad sales and subscriptions rep. It was never fun. The *Advocate* lost subscribers every year, and last year Wolfe hinted they were being evaluated.

"The family is doing a little Marie Kondo with the portfolio,"

Wolfe had said. Roman had to tell Larry who Marie Kondo was later that day.

But the reason Larry wanted Roman at the meeting so badly was because late last year, Roman had stumbled upon some less-than-flattering information about the Davenports—and nearly gotten them both fired.

It started back in December when an elderly woman named Rose O'Bryan slipped on a patch of ice on the sidewalk outside her apartment complex. It was early morning and by the time someone found her she was unconscious and had frostbite on two fingers. A week later, she died of the head injury she'd sustained.

The death likely wouldn't have made the newspaper as more than an obituary, but Roman knew Rose, and liked her. Every day, she walked the length of town, twice. *Gotta get my steps in,* she'd say. He had written a profile of her for the "Active Adamsville" column and they'd stayed friendly. Whenever she saw Mason, she managed to have a piece of candy for him.

When Covid hit, it took Rose's husband early. He'd had complications after a hip replacement in early March and was living in a rehab facility one county north when the pandemic started. By May, 60 percent of the patients were dead. Roman proposed that the newspaper keep a running memorial of residents the disease had taken, but Larry deemed it too morbid. Roman kept pushing as the numbers kept climbing, trying to convince his boss that thirty-four people in three months in a town of less than twelve thousand was huge news. "That's almost an entire school bus," he'd said. "If a school bus fell off the side of the mountain and everybody died we'd be doing follow-up for years."

But Larry said no. If it was a school bus, he argued, it would be kids. Kids are different. The slow-motion death of the elderly and less-than-prominent residents along their slice of the river—the cashiers at the grocery stores; the warehouse workers; the cooks—it didn't move Larry. He didn't want too many dead people in his family newspaper.

Roman, however, was barely a year out of NYU and eager to do something to take his mind off the misery at home. He was watching his former classmates publish reports from the front lines of the pandemic: dispatches from emergency departments and homeless camps and processing plants. Was he really going to ignore the impact of the biggest news story of his life? Hell no. He still had the microphone and the student subscription to editing software he'd gotten from his multimedia class. He started interviewing people in the town who'd been affected by Covid: widows and orphans and survivors—with the idea of cutting them into a podcast. He didn't tell Larry, figuring that once it was done, if Larry didn't want to publish it under the *Advocate* banner, he could start his own channel.

Rose was one of the first people he interviewed, and when she died in her front yard three years later, he was pissed. Landlords are responsible for keeping the walkways around their properties safe, but Rose's daughter said the owners were ducking their attorney. Roman had never followed through on the podcast, but in the wake of Rose's death he started digging. Not a single human name was listed on the one-page website for the Washington Arms Apartments. The company that had the landscaping contract gave him the number for a property manager, but that man said he dealt with the owner's representative in Delaware. And the representative's office didn't return Roman's calls.

Frustrated, Roman went to the county building inspector's office and found eleven complaints in the last eighteen months over various problems at Rose's complex, including mold, vermin, and water damage. It was, he decided, an important local story, and soon after the New Year, when Larry had to miss the final read-through because of a procedure on a mole, Roman snuck in a short article about Rose's daughter fighting to get a proper settlement. The article described the complex as "plagued with tenant complaints" and the owners as "mysterious."

Roman hoped the article might shake somebody from the LLC loose, shame them into a reasonable settlement—or at least a comment. Instead, Wolfe called Larry and reamed him out for printing the piece. Roman was in the office when the call came in, and he was pretty sure Larry went into the unisex bathroom they shared with the insurance agency down the hall to cry afterward. Because Larry had long since lost any actual journalistic curiosity, the call did exactly what it was intended to do: frighten him. Larry didn't even ask: *why do you care?*

But Roman was not Larry. He used his NYU alumni email to log into some databases and eventually figured out that Peak Properties, the LLC listed as owning Washington Arms, owned apartment complexes in seven states. And these were not luxury residences. Google Earth showed one- and two-story buildings near highways and industrial parks. Landscaping was slim to none. He spent hours scrolling through documents online and finally found a single Manhattan address: 1567 Avenue of the Americas. Headquarters of the Davenport empire. Digging after Rose, Roman had stumbled on an entire revenue stream the family was apparently trying to keep quiet: vast swaths of low-income, badly maintained housing. What would the Democracy Fund think? And what else, he wondered, were they hiding?

Instead of going to Larry, Roman messaged a classmate from NYU, who offered to put him in touch with his editor at the *Times*. Roman wrote a pitch, but months had gone by and he hadn't had the courage to send it. Now Ashley was dead, and he wondered if he'd ever care about anything again.

"I know the timing is really bad," said Larry when Roman didn't answer about the meeting. "But I think our funding is legitimately in jeopardy. I'll do all the talking. If you don't go, he might just pull the plug. He'll feel disrespected. And listen, you don't want to not have a job right now. Not have benefits for your family? Funerals cost thousands of dollars . . ."

"I'll be there," said Roman. He ended the call.

CHAPTER ELEVEN

Tara had declined Scott's offer to drive her to urgent care to get checked out after the accident. Instead, she asked him to supervise the tow company taking her car to the repair shop. Not exactly part of his job description, but he did it.

Back home, she'd managed to feed Mason dinner: pb&j with apples slices for both of them, although she ate nothing. She couldn't stop trembling. She poured wine into the first glass she saw in the cabinet: the oversized goblet with the word "Bride" written on it in now-chipping script. The glass was a gift from Ashley and a group of Tara's friends who threw a surprise engagement party for her and John in February. It was beyond tacky—bride wineglass, groom beer stein; a tiny coffin with "YOUR SEX LIFE" written on it—but they had fun. The wedding was supposed to be Labor Day weekend. Six weeks from now. Would they put it off? She couldn't imagine how she'd ever smile again, let alone celebrate.

Mason was dirty from the hike and the donut and the crying, so she ran a bath—nice and hot like he liked—and read to him while he pushed plastic boats around in the water. She'd read the book so many times that she barely needed her brain and eyes to work together as she turned the pages.

"Will we go see Mommy in the hospital tomorrow?" Mason asked as she toweled him off. She'd told him that Mommy fell and the ambulance they'd seen at Bella's took her to the hospital. It seemed to make sense to him.

"I hope so," she said.

"I bet Mommy is sad we missed the movie."

"The movie?"

"The river movie."

Ashley loved summertime movies by the river. Before the sun went down, after they'd finished their picnic and while they were waiting for the show, she would take Mason to the rocky shore to look for batnuts and throw sticks into the water. She was the only one of the three of them who could reliably send a flat stone skipping three four five times into the distance. She'd been teaching Mason.

"Mommy says I'm getting better at skipping my rocks," he said.

"I know you are, mister."

"Can we FaceTime with Mommy before bed?"

Tara's face itched with the tears she refused to let Mason see. Why hadn't she let Ashley do bedtime last night? Why had she been so fucking selfish?

"No, I'm sorry. Maybe tomorrow. She loves you so much."

Mason climbed into his bed and positioned his stuffed animals around him. Tara sang "My Favorite Things," switched on his turtle night-light, kissed his warm, smooth cheek—a cheek that she knew would feel different by this time tomorrow—and said good night.

In the kitchen, she saw that she had missed a call from Ashley's mom. She called back, but the phone went to voicemail.

Had Roman been the one who actually found Ashley's body? Jason, at least, had spared her that. The police fished him out of the water a few hours after half a dozen people called 911 to report that they'd just seen someone jump off the Bear Mountain Bridge. They weren't married, so Tara hadn't been asked to identify him. That fell to his mom and dad, who divorced soon after. There was a memorial service that Tara refused to attend. She cringed now, thinking of the scene she'd made, demanding her parents leave little Roman home with her.

"He doesn't need that!" she'd screamed at them. "He'll be confused. All those people crying and pictures of his dad. It's too much!"

"He needs to say goodbye," her mother had said, softly, trying to reason with her.

"What are you talking about! He's a fucking baby! He doesn't know what's going on."

"Lower your voice, Tara," her father said. "He absolutely does know what's going on. He knows something terrible has happened, and he's watching us. He's watching how we handle it."

"Fine! Take him!"

Not even her mom's and dad's deaths—together, in a car

accident five years later—had turned her into a decent mom. For more than a year Tara had flailed. More than flailed. She'd neglected Roman; drank too much—almost all the time—then slept through mornings and made excuses when the school called. People in town tiptoed around her. As if her bad luck—teenage pregnancy, Jason's death, and then her parents'—might be contagious. She barked away anyone who tried to help. And then, one summer afternoon, she picked Roman up from the YMCA camp drunk and drove her car into a building. She remembers looking back at her son, unharmed because he'd belted himself in, and seeing the lack of surprise on his face.

If it hadn't been for her mom's cousin taking Roman while she wound through the legal system, Tara might have lost him for good.

That was when she got her shit together. By the time Roman was in fifth grade, she was managing the best restaurant in town; she paid taxes, and they both had health insurance. She invested in the house, drank rarely, and did nothing more than an occasional hit from someone's joint after a long shift. She slept around—she needed something, after all—but kept the men from Roman, and never made any promises. She was officially a parent he could count on—but, she realized soon enough, he probably never would.

And then Ashley appeared. Tara vividly remembered the first time they met. It was a school night; Roman was old enough to come home alone, but she knew that if she left him to fend for himself for dinner, he'd probably end up eating a bag of chips. She made sure the dinner service was set at her job, then took off. At the house, she found Ashley on the front steps, a sleeping bag rolled up beside her.

"Does Roman know you're here, honey?"

Ashley shook her head.

"The door's open," said Tara.

Ashley started crying. "I can't go in," she said, hiding her head in her knees. "We have bedbugs. They're everywhere. It's like the plague. I'm like the plague."

Tara hesitated, then stroked Ashley's white-blond hair. It was corn-silk thin and extended halfway down her bony back. Was she even thirteen yet?

"You're definitely not the plague," said Tara. "You can borrow some clothes. They won't fit well but they'll fit. Take a shower. It'll be fine."

"I can't," she said. "They don't go away. Seriously. This is the second place we've had them. They're not just in the beds. They, like, travel in your clothes. In the TV even. Can I sleep on the porch? I would *die* if I gave you guys bedbugs. I'm surprised the school hasn't found out yet. I should stop going."

"Don't stop going," said Tara. Ashley's mom, Kelly Marchand, was almost fifteen years older than Tara and their lives rarely overlapped. Ashley had been in Roman's preschool class at the church in town, so she and Kelly were connected on Facebook, but they weren't friends. All Tara knew about Ashley's mom then was that Kelly was from near Rochester, worked at least part-time at the local Stewart's gas station, and posted near-daily memes about Jesus. At one point, they'd lived in an apartment across the street from the elementary school and Tara would see

Kelly on the sidewalk at all hours of the day and night, smoking cigarettes in ratty slippers, often having what looked like intense, even painful conversations on her phone. Tara wasn't in a position to judge, but she felt for Ashley.

"Come inside," Tara said.

Ashley shook her head again.

"Okay," said Tara, "we've got a tent in the shed. Will you at least let me give you clean clothes?"

Ashley agreed to that, and Roman came outside to help. Tara watched them from the kitchen window and marveled at how easy they were together, and how happy her son seemed; she didn't see his smile wane once the entire time they were setting up the tent. And Ashley changed, too. Gone were the tears and the crooked posture of shame she'd had next to Tara on the porch, replaced with what Tara could only describe as a kind of radiance. Radiance! In a middle schooler. But that was Ashley.

Ashley wouldn't let Roman sleep in the tent with her, but for the next three nights, she stayed in the yard, checking and rechecking herself and the tent for the tiny monsters. On the fourth night, her mother appeared.

"We bombed the apartment," she said. Ashley must have gotten her height from her father, because she was already taller than Kelly. "I put all my clothes, all the towels and shit in bags and took 'em to work. I promise, they're gone."

Ashley hesitated.

"It's time to come home," said Kelly. "You can't bother these people forever."

"She's no bother," Tara said.

"Ashley can stay as long as she wants, right, Mom?" Roman asked.

"It's not appropriate," said Kelly, her voice hard. "Does this boy know you like girls?"

"Mom!"

Tara looked at her son, but his expression revealed little. She wasn't entirely sure what to do. Ashley hadn't mentioned anything that sounded like abuse or neglect. Kelly was uncouth, and bedbugs sucked, but who was she to keep this woman's child from her?

"Ashley came by after—"

"Save it," said Kelly. "Ashley: now."

Ashley went.

The next couple days were quiet around the house. Finally, one morning while he was filling the cat's food bowl, Roman said, "I told Ashley about Dad. Her uncle killed himself, too. Did you know that?"

"I didn't," said Tara.

"When we were in fifth grade. He was her mom's brother. She said he was kind of like a dad to her. Her dad's, like, a deadbeat. She's not even sure where he lives. Texas, maybe."

"That sounds really hard."

"She's really easy to talk to," Roman said. "She's a good listener."

After two hours on the porch in the dark, Tara heard the rumble of John's truck. Behind him, Roman in his Accord. She stood up to greet them. She imagined Roman falling against her like Mason might do. She imagined wrapping her arms around her now-grown boy and holding him, comforting him. But when Roman saw her, he slowed. John tugged at his sleeve. On the front walk, Roman stumbled, then vomited onto the grass. They were both drunk. Maybe it was just as well. Her son was home safe; he'd sleep it off. He could sleep for days. Weeks. Whatever he needed. She'd take care of everything.

CHAPTER TWELVE

The next morning, Roman woke up to Mason.

"Hi, Daddy," said the boy.

Roman cracked open his eyelids. After he and John had driven home last night, he'd gone straight upstairs, and the pale green glow of Mason's turtle night-light beckoned from beneath the boy's door. There lay his son, covers kicked off, face slack with sleep. Roman took off his shoes and crept in beside him, laying his head on a stuffed giraffe. Now it was morning; early, and a sunny day to judge by the blue-white light coming through the window.

"Hi, mister," said Roman.

"You smell sweet."

"Sweet?" Roman propped himself on his elbow. His brain pulsed in his skull, pressing against the back of his eyes.

"Kinda like a bad banana."

"I smell like a bad banana?" It was funny, but Roman's body couldn't laugh.

Mason giggled, and Roman told himself to smile. Mason

deserved a smile. He thought: *this is what I can do for him. I can pretend.*

Roman tried to pull Mason toward him. In the birthing class they took before he was born, the instructor said that the nurses would give the baby to Ashley within seconds of the birth for "skin-to-skin." *It's not just for feeding,* she'd explained. *Touch creates endorphins. Think of it as the body's positive vibes. Comfort and happiness flood into mom and baby. It helps create a bond.* She'd been quick to say that that bond would extend to other family members, too—though she didn't specifically mention dads, perhaps because fewer than half the pregnant women in the class had a male partner with them.

The class was the first time Roman got the sense that he was, as the father, nonessential. He joked that he was the help, and while she was pregnant, when they were still just them, Ashley thought it was funny. His role was, essentially, determined by her desires. If she wanted something—a glass of water, an orgasm—he hopped to. If she needed to be left alone, he gave her space.

But the humor of the situation disappeared when coronavirus shut down the country two weeks before her due date and Roman had to take Ashley to the hospital and *leave* her there. For twelve hours, he sat alone in the car in the parking lot, waiting for a call. Tara joined him for a while, but he told her to go home. What could she do? When his phone finally rang, it got worse. The baby was breech and Ashley was bleeding, her blood pressure dangerously low. A decision had been made to do a C-section.

"If we can only save one of their lives, which should it be?" the voice on the phone asked.

"Ashley!" he shouted as he opened the car door and ran toward the emergency entrance. "I'm right outside. Can I see her?" He didn't even know this baby. The baby was little more than an idea to him. And it might kill the one person on earth he could rely on? He hadn't known, of course, that after that day he'd never fully be able to rely on her again. He ran up to the glass doors, assuming they'd open, but the motion sensors must have been switched off. He banged on the glass until a woman—at least he thought it was a woman; whoever it was was so thoroughly wrapped in protective gear it was difficult to tell—came to the door.

"My girlfriend is having a baby!" he shouted, pointing behind her. "Something's wrong! I need to see her."

"No visitors."

"But she's bleeding!"

"I'm sorry," said the person, and as she turned to walk away, Roman screamed. He'd done this to Ashley. He'd gotten her pregnant at twenty-one and now she was going to die. He'd killed her.

She didn't die; they called an hour later to say Ashley had survived and his baby boy was healthy. But when she and Mason came home a few days later, everything about their lives was changed.

"Can I have a hug?" Roman asked Mason.

"Let's read," said the boy, twisting away, reaching to get a book from the floor.

"Can I have a hug first?" Mason was so close, and that whiff of the warmth of his body almost made Roman tremble with craving for the happy hum that the endorphin flood the instructor talked about created. *Please*, he wanted to say, *just for a second?* He needed it so bad.

"Can you read to me?" Mason handed him a book about airplanes. *This is a 747. This is a glider. This is a propeller plane.*

"Quick hug first?"

Mason leaned in and allowed Roman to wrap an arm awkwardly around his shoulders and kiss his head. Roman closed his eyes and breathed deeply, squeezed hard.

"Ow!" said Mason, but he was smiling. "Daddy, did you know there are a million worms under the house?"

"A million?"

Mason nodded and put his finger on the book. "Read?"

Roman opened the book to the page marked with a musical birthday card Ashley had bought for Mason last year. It played a high-pitched electronic version of "Ain't No Mountain High Enough," but Mason had opened it so many times the battery was long dead.

"Have you ever gone on an airplane, Daddy?"

"I have."

"Mommy went on an airplane for a whole day when she went to Hawaii. When can we go to Hawaii? Mommy said there's a volcano there. And she said I can climb a coconut tree. Can we go to Hawaii, Daddy?"

"I'd love to go to Hawaii."

"Let's go!" Mason threw his arms into the air and bounced onto his knees on the bed. "Hawaii!"

"Hello?" Tara opened the bedroom door. She was clearly surprised to see Roman. "I'm sorry," she said. "I heard him up."

"It's okay," said Roman. He pressed his fingers into his eyelids. Water.

"We're going to Hawaii, Gerty!"

"Oh?"

"Mommy will show us the volcano! Boom!"

Every time Mason said "Mommy," Roman felt the blood drain from his body.

"When is Mommy coming home?"

Roman pushed himself up and climbed out of the bed. He was going to break down again.

"John's making waffles," said Tara.

"Waffles!" cheered Mason.

"Let's get you dressed," she said.

Roman stumbled out of his son's room and made it to the bathroom, knelt before the toilet and vomited; the sour taste of beer and snot pouring out of his nose as he choked trying to muffle the wails that rose inside him. How many more of these purges were in his future? He turned on the shower and stepped inside when it was hot. It was seven o'clock. The meeting with Larry and Wolfe was at nine. He wanted to lie in bed for six months; six years.

But Larry was right—if he lost his job things would get a lot worse. The roof and the bathroom downstairs were going to cost at least three grand, and they had to spend that now if they were going to salvage any income from late summer and leaf-peeping tourists in the fall. Interest rates on another home equity loan were insane, so that wasn't an option. As is, including taxes, they paid the bank nearly three thousand a month. And they paid out of pocket for health insurance because the paper only covered Roman and none of the rest of the family had the kind of job that offered benefits. And then in January, his student loans had become an issue again. All that plus utilities and food and gas and car payments and car repairs and the family needed to come up with at least eight thousand a month. Ashley's income—from yoga classes, her yoga YouTube channel, and occasional Koffee shifts—made up almost half of that, and now it was gone. Tara hadn't worked since Mason was born, and John's income was sporadic. Without Roman's four grand a month, they'd lose the house in a year.

If Wolfe pulled the plug, what then? The idea of having to look for another job was terrifying.

Downstairs, Mason was happily forking waffle into his mouth, while John and Tara moved around the kitchen, their voices strained as they tried to answer the boy's endless questions. Roman caught his mother's eye.

"Can I talk to you?" he asked.

"Want a waffle, Daddy?" asked Mason, his mouth red with jam.

"Not right now, mister," he said. Roman pushed the kitchen door open and stepped outside onto the driveway. Tara followed.

"What did you tell him?" Roman asked.

"I told him she got hurt. I said the ambulance took her to the hospital. But we need to tell him the truth."

"We will." He paused. "She had pills in her pocket."

"Pills? Like . . ."

"I don't know what, exactly. I have to go to work. Just stay with Mason. He needs you."

"He needs you, too."

"I'll call you," said Roman, opening the car door.

"Do you want coffee at least?"

"I'll get one at—" He stopped. He couldn't walk into the coffee shop. They'd all know by now. The air would go out of the room when he opened the door. They'd stare. They'd expect. "I'm good."

CHAPTER THIRTEEN

Larry called just as Roman was pulling into a parking space at the newspaper office.

"Wolfe wants us to meet at his house," said the old man, shouting into his speakerphone. "How soon can you be there?"

"Five minutes," said Roman.

Wolfe's house was less than a mile away, atop a hill that looked out over the entire town and onto the river. Mini-Monticello, his high school English teacher had called it. Redbrick, plantation columns, pristine landscaping, iron statues of lions at the driveway entrance. Tara hated it. Wolfe had the house built on a vista that had once been open to everyone in the town willing to trek up the hill. They'd clear-cut the land, carved tiers for patios and a pool and an endless expanse of kelly-green grass, mowed in neat lines every week by the landscaping company owned by the mayor's son.

The town had lots of big houses, some perhaps with even more square footage than Wolfe's, but they were mostly older, closer to the river, like Bella's, and tucked behind decades-dense hedges or groves of trees. Wolfe's, on the other hand, was built mere feet from the road and seemed to thrust its chest forward. The house had a fishbowl quality. Its floor-to-ceiling front windows were rarely covered by drapes, and especially at night, the house seemed almost like it wanted you to peer inside and see Fox News playing on the enormous television above the fireplace.

As far as Roman knew, Wolfe lived there alone.

The paved driveway was short and steep, and Larry was waiting by his forty-year-old Volvo when Roman pulled up. Larry eyed him when he got out of the car, probably trying to assess whether or not he was going to fuck this up.

"I've never been here," said Roman as they started up the walkway, lined with annuals, freshly mulched.

"Listen," said Larry, "I'm sorry about your wife."

Roman did not correct Larry. Why hadn't they gotten married? He'd never asked, but neither had she.

"All you gotta do is keep it together for thirty minutes. An hour tops. I'll get one of the high school students to cover this week. We've got some evergreen stuff. Just play nice in there, please."

Larry knocked and a moment later Nicholas Wolfe opened the front door, clad in khakis and a teal polo shirt with "Hilton Head" embroidered on the breast.

"Roman," he said, his face wrinkling with apparent concern. "I didn't expect you to be here. Come in. My God, Larry, why didn't you tell him not to come?"

"I . . ." Larry seemed genuinely stumped. "How did you . . . ?"

"Never mind," said Wolfe, ushering them into the kitchen and adjacent breakfast room. Morning light flooded in from the double-height windows. On the marble island was a spread of muffins and fruit and small plates. "What can I get you? Coffee? Something stronger? Are you hungry? I bet you haven't eaten. When my dad died, I don't think I ate for a week."

"Coffee would be great," Roman said. He sat down at one of the stools and reached for a pastry, suddenly famished.

Wolfe picked up a stainless steel coffeepot and poured, ignoring Larry, who stood behind one of the other stools, looking too nervous to sit. Roman supposed he shouldn't be surprised that the lawyer for the family who owned the newspaper and the largest number of commercial buildings in the county would have heard about Ashley's death less than eighteen hours after she was pulled up from the cliffside.

"If you can believe it, before I got the call, I'd actually gotten champagne," said Wolfe, sitting down. "I wanted this to be a bit of a celebration."

"The call?" Roman asked.

"About Ashley. Again, I'm so sorry. I'll make this quick: we're ready to commit to funding the *Advocate* for the next five years."

"That's great news," said Larry, beaming. "You won't be sorry. Right, Roman?"

Roman wasn't really listening. Who had called Wolfe about Ashley?

"The family understands that what happened with the apartment story was an honest mistake. We get it. You were trying to help raise the profile of the paper. Get those clicks, impress the boss. But we're not trying to win a Pulitzer here. This is a good, old-fashioned community newspaper. Our mission is to—"

"Celebrate the town," interrupted Roman.

Larry sucked in a breath. Wolfe smiled, though. He was good, Roman had to admit. In college, his theater friends had told him about the rule of improv: always say "Yes and" to your partner. Never let them see you flustered or unhappy; roll with it, no matter what insane idea ("I'm a cow!") they threw at you. Roman wondered what rules governed the country-club-law-school-class-ring-wearing set that Wolfe belonged to. Maybe something similar.

"Exactly," said Wolfe.

Roman could feel Larry's eyes on him.

"But now isn't the time to talk about all this," Wolfe continued. "You need to be with your family, Roman. Take the next week or two. I'm sure Larry can hold down the fort. Right, Larry?"

"Absolutely," he said, nodding vigorously.

"The Davenports asked me to send their sincere condolences," Wolfe said.

Roman doubted that, but had spent his snark for the day. He stood up. "Thanks."

Wolfe walked them to the door. "Please let me know if you need anything," he said, shaking Roman's hand. Wolfe's palm was smooth and dry, almost like he'd chalked it. *Never let them feel you sweat.*

"Thank you," said Larry. And then, humiliatingly, the old man said it again: "Thank you so much."

CHAPTER FOURTEEN

John and Tara were in the living room watching *Dino Train* with Mason when they spotted Bella coming up the walk in her oversized T-shirt, buzzed hair a faded pink.

Tara kissed Mason's head and looked at John: "I'll be right back."

John nodded. He understood: keep Mason away from Bella. Happily, the television lived up to its pejorative, and while it was on, Mason turned near-idiot. The boy might not have looked up even if Bella barged in behind him. Or if a pink elephant had, for that matter.

Tara intercepted Bella on the front steps.

"Where's Roman?" demanded Bella.

Her face was blotchy and swollen. The spritely, artistic teen she'd been in high school was buried beneath thirty extra pounds. Back then, Bella was at their house almost every day. But looking at her now, Tara didn't think she'd seen the girl in years. There'd been tension after graduation, and Tara remembered Roman and Ashley talking about Bella in hushed tones. She was in love with Ashley, but Ashley chose Roman. Bella was hurt, maybe lashed out; Tara wasn't privy to the details. Roman was living in a dorm in Manhattan and Ashley had found an apartment with Daniel and another friend. Tara didn't want to pry. Pre-pandemic, she saw Bella occasionally around town, although half the time Bella was so intoxicated she didn't seem to recognize Tara. Once, maybe a year after Mason was born, Bobby told her he'd had to ban Bella from the coffee shop because he caught her selling pills at one of the picnic tables outside.

"Selling?" Tara asked. "Are you sure?"

"It wasn't the first time. I gave her a bunch of warnings. I mean, I feel sorry for her. The Covid fucked her up, and I think she's in a lot of discomfort. She uses to feel better, and she sells to use. But not at my place."

And not at mine, thought Tara, as she faced Bella on the front porch.

"Roman's not here."

"I need to talk to him," Bella continued. "I thought Ash left. I—"

John came outside. "Everything okay here?"

"Stay with Mason," Tara directed, her anxiety rising. The way Mason found out about his mother's death was going to matter a lot. Tara had been sitting next to him on the sofa trying to figure out the best strategy for breaking the news. She'd googled "how to tell a child his mother died" and the advice came in bullet points, like a recipe: use simple words; cry with them; listen. But that wasn't what she was looking for. What she wanted was a script, and some assurance that this wouldn't destroy him. That, of course, was nowhere to be found.

John nodded and went back inside. Bella paced in front of the house, blubbering. Tara sat on the steps, motioning for Bella to sit down, calm down, talk. Splinters poked into her bare thighs. That was another thing that needed doing: repair—or at least sand and paint—the steps and porch.

"Why would he call the cops?" shouted Bella. "Why does he hate me?"

Next door, Melissa Larkin stepped outside, the twins barreling past her into the yard that separated their houses. The Larkins had moved from the city during the pandemic, buying and meticulously renovating the house that used to belong to Tara's first-grade teacher. John had done the bathrooms and there was a dispute about his tiling: they'd wanted checkerboard subway tiles but didn't specifically articulate that, so John laid it straight up and down. They refused to pay at first, and John had to decide whether $3,000 was worth getting an attorney that would cost at least half that. Eventually, Ryan Larkin suggested John redo the work: they'd pay for the tile, but not the extra labor.

John took the deal but told as many of the tradespeople he knew in the county—and he knew most of them—not to work for the Larkins. Last year, they all indulged in a little schadenfreude watching Ryan curse over the side hose spigot that froze and split, cracking some siding, because he didn't know to drain it before winter. Tara was pleasant to the couple—the twins were Mason's age and they had a jungle gym and she couldn't exactly tell her grandson he wasn't allowed to play if he was invited. But they were not, she understood, her people. And while this conversation with Bella was not one she wanted to have in front of Mason, neither did she want the Larkins, or the rest of the street, involved. She stood and put a hand on Bella's shoulder.

"Let's go out back," she said.

"I thought she went home! I swear to God! Do you think I would have *left* her there?!"

"No," said Tara. "Of course not."

Tara tried to guide Bella around the back of the house, and as she did, Roman pulled up in his car. He got out and went toward Bella.

"What did you do to her!" he screamed.

"Nothing! She went home! She said she was going home!"

Bella started bawling.

"We need to take this out back," said Tara.

"Where have you been?" Roman asked Bella, ignoring his mother.

"Why did you call the cops on me?"

"What?"

"They came to my work! If I get fired, I'm fucked, Roman."

"She'd *dead*, Bella! She was just lying there. In your yard."

"Stop yelling at me!" she wailed.

"Both of you stop it," Tara hissed. "Mason is inside."

"*Kevin* found her," continued Roman. "He was taking a piss and he—"

"Stop!" screamed Bella, cuffing her hands over her ears like a child.

Tara grabbed her son's arm. His eyes were full of rage. He jerked out of her grasp and backed up.

"God forbid we upset the neighbors. Fuck you both. Seriously, fuck you both."

He was shaking. He stumbled toward his car, dropping his keys.

"Roman," said Tara.

"Don't," he answered. He bent over, picked up the keys, and practically ran into his car.

"Roman!" shouted Tara. *He can't drive*, she thought, her heart alighting with fear. *He can't drive like this.*

Roman didn't even look at her. He turned the ignition and pressed the gas and reversed out of the driveway, bouncing over the curb.

"I'm sorry!" screamed Bella.

Roman's response was a middle finger stuck hard out the window as he raced away.

Bella crumbled to the lawn, and Tara turned to gauge who had seen what. Melissa was openly gawking by the mailbox and the twins were leaning against the pristine waist-high white picket fence the Larkins had erected between their yards. The fence that made it very clear exactly where the mowed and treated sod ended and Tara's crabgrass, dirt, and moss began.

"Where's Mason?" asked the boy, River.

"Can Mason play?" echoed Frannie.

"Not right now," said Tara.

The kids accepted that. River ran inside while Frannie climbed up the slide and slid down face-first. Melissa turned her

focus to the mailbox and what was inside. She lingered, maybe
considering whether she should say something. Tara hoped she
didn't. She was going to have to handle this woman's pity and
judgment eventually—eventually the Larkins would ask if they
could "do anything"; maybe they'd put a lasagna from BJ's on the
porch—but not this moment.

Bella's face was a mess of bloat and fluids. The poor girl had
nobody. But right now, that wasn't something Tara could afford
to focus on.

"Bella, I'm sorry but you need to go."

"It's not my fault!"

Little River came back outside, followed by his father. Had
they been watching? Of course they had.

"Everything okay out here?" Ryan Larkin asked.

"We're fine," Tara said.

Ryan turned on the hose and started to fill up a kiddie pool.
River and Frannie came running with plastic squirters. If Mason
saw them out the window, he was going to want to join in.

"I need to get back to Mason," Tara said.

"You know I'd never do anything to hurt her, right?"

"Bella, this is a really hard time—"

"For me too!"

The screen on the front door banged open.

"Gerty! Can I play in the water!"

John was behind him; he looked at Tara like *Sorry*, but what
could he do? The boy wanted to play. As far as he knew, today
was no different from any other summer Sunday.

"Yeah!" shouted River and Frannie in unison.

The smile on Mason's face—it would be gone when she told him.

"If it's okay with their daddy," she said.

"Sure," said Ryan, though Tara noticed wariness in his voice.

The kids all screamed and Mason ran around the fence and into their yard, ignoring Bella completely. Frannie handed him an extra squirter and they commenced squirting and laughing and chasing each other.

"He's gotten so big," Bella said, wiping her face. "Have you told him?"

Tara shook her head.

Across the street, the garage door opened at the Overlands'. They were a military family; Keith Overland was a bigwig at West Point. When they'd moved in, while Roman was at NYU, they'd installed a twenty-foot flagpole in the front yard. Every morning Keith or one of his three sons raised the Stars and Stripes, and every evening they brought it down, folded it, and took it inside. At least it wasn't a Trump flag; there were several of those on the block. Tara wasn't sure she'd be able to keep her mouth shut looking at that name waving its middle finger across her view every day.

One of the sons emerged from the garage, carrying a cooler. He ignored Tara and Bella as he walked to the massive recreational boat parked in the driveway. Typically, Keith and his wife waved when they happened to see each other, but Tara had never been inside her neighbors' home, or they hers.

As the boy began unhooking the boat's cover, Tara heard the rumble and clack of a car in need of repair. The sound got closer, and a low-riding coupe rolled around the corner. The car sped up and the emphatic pop of a backfire bounced off the houses on the street, startling her. The coupe raced toward them. It blew through the stop sign and jumped the curb in front of the Larkins', nearly taking out the mailbox, where Melissa still lingered. Melissa ran, the kids screamed, and the car screeched to a halt in front of Bella, half on the driveway, half on the lawn.

"What the fuck!" shouted Ryan, dropping the hose.

A young man about Roman's age who looked vaguely familiar bolted out of the driver's seat and went for Bella. He was wearing plastic shower-style slides and baggy gym shorts and a tank top. Tattoos covered his arms and legs. Bella stumbled backward and couldn't seem to stand up. The man towered over her. "You need to answer your phone!"

"I'm sorry!" she screamed, covering her head.

John came running down the front steps.

"You need to leave," he said.

The young man cocked an eyebrow. "Fuck you, old man. This is none of your business."

"I'm calling the cops," shouted Ryan from next door.

"No!" screamed Bella. "It's okay." She looked up at the tattooed man. "I didn't say anything. I swear to God."

The man grabbed Bella's shirt and started walking her toward his still-running car.

"Let go of her," said John.

"Make me," said the man.

As if on cue, from across the street came Keith Overland, handgun raised.

"Get off this street, asshole," said Keith.

The man dropped Bella's shirt and put his hands up. "I'm going." He turned to Bella: "You need to be careful."

"Now!" shouted Keith.

The man got into his car and gunned his engine, spitting soil and grass from Tara's yard behind his wheels. He screeched around the corner, the sound trailing for blocks.

Keith lowered his weapon and walked across the street.

"You all right?" he asked.

Bella was shaking and crying. She'd let herself fall to the ground again. Tara extended a hand, which she accepted, then stood.

"I think we're okay," Tara said.

"Do you know that man?" asked Keith.

"No," said Tara.

"Young lady?" he asked Bella.

"I don't think she's in any shape to be interrogated," said Tara.

"Please don't call the cops," said Bella.

Keith looked at Tara, and then at Ryan, who had come to the fence line. Melissa and the twins were huddled on their porch. Mason grabbed Tara's legs.

They all expected an explanation.

"I'm sorry," Tara said, finally. "We've—had a family emergency. If you could just give us a little time."

"I've probably got it all on my Ring camera," Keith said to Ryan.

"I'll make sure he doesn't come back," said Bella.

Keith didn't seem convinced.

Tara was going to have to deal with this.

"John, could you take Mason inside?"

"Of course," he said. "Come on, mister. Wanna find some ice cream?"

Mason seemed skeptical. He kept a hold on Tara and asked, "What's our family emergency, Gerty?"

CHAPTER FIFTEEN

Roman drove north, to the waterfront in Newburgh. He parked in the lot meant for trucks towing boats and sat in his car looking at the river. He watched the boaters and jet skiers slide their machines in or lug them out at the public launch. He watched the kids skip around the goose shit while their parents fished or smoked or talked into their phones. He watched a group of Hasidic girls get off the ferry and load into a waiting bus.

Why was Ashley at Bella's house? As far as he knew the two hadn't spoken in literally years. When she found out Ash was pregnant, Bella had told them point-blank she thought keeping the baby was a stupid idea. And things had been tense even before that. Roman knew that when Ashley first came back from Hawaii to care for her dad, while Roman was finishing his junior year at NYU, Bella was one of the people she leaned on. And maybe too much. Roman remembers Ashley calling him one night in tears about it.

"I hooked up with Bella," she'd said. "I know it was stupid. I know how she feels. I just . . . I mean, I love her, too."

"But not like she loves you."

"I know! I mean, *she* knows. And she said it was fine. I was sad and we were bored and . . ."

"Were you high?"

"She had Adderall."

"I can't tell you what to do."

"Why not!" She laughed sadly. "Sometimes I wish somebody would tell me what to do."

"If you need to get laid, I'll come up," he said.

"It's not that. She's so unhappy, Roman. You know her dad didn't call her on her birthday. Didn't even fucking text."

Roman's patience for Bella had long been thinner than Ashley's. He was missing a parent, too. And until her dad came home to die, Ashley's father had been entirely absent as well. But Bella somehow always made Ashley feel like she needed taking care of. And Ashley, who felt guilty for not loving Bella like Bella loved her, got sucked in every time.

When he thought about it that way, Roman supposed it made sense that Ashley might have kept a rekindling of her relationship with Bella a secret from him, even if that relationship had been platonic. She probably assumed he'd disapprove, and she would have been right. But if he'd known, maybe he would have paid more attention. Maybe he would have asked more questions about nights she was out with "friends"; maybe he would have asked to come along.

As the sun set, Roman started to think about the cliffside where Ashley fell. He imagined her there the night before last, sitting on the big rock that looked out onto the river. The rock they'd sat on together so many times. He imagined her looking out at the river, through the mountains nearly touching at the wind gate and beyond. Ashley loved the water. She used to say that just looking at it made her happy. And so they'd sat on that rock looking together. They'd sat on that rock and sneaked joints or beers and talked for hours. As teenagers, it had always felt like a safe place, despite being barely five feet from a dramatic hillside. Five feet from falling to your death. He imagined her there on Friday night, looking at the moon over the water, the pill she'd taken kicking in. She stands up to return to the party, trips over a root. Gone.

It was after dark when he got home. One of the police cruisers was parked along the curb and inside the house he found Felix at the kitchen table with his mom and John. Felix stood when Roman came in.

"How are you holding up?"

Roman shrugged. "I want to know what happened."

"Me, too," said Felix. "I was just telling your mom and John that I think it's worth trying to analyze the pills we found. I sent the bag to the lab. Fentanyl doesn't fuck around. I worked at the VA after my first tour, and the old guys got hit really hard when the synthetic shit started showing up in heroin. A lot of people are hopeless cases. Hard-core addicts—just a matter of time before it kills them. But now it's in everything and we're seeing more people like Ashley. They take a pill they think is Molly or Klonopin and boom. One pill."

"Is that what you think happened? The pills had fentanyl in them?"

"We're going to find out. She had some injuries, too. Maybe from the fall. But that's part of why I'm here. I want to get as much information as I can while it's fresh in everybody's minds." He looked at Roman. "Yesterday you said she used occasionally. Any idea where she got her stuff?"

"Nobody specific, that I know of. Like I said, it was usually at a party. If someone had it." He tried to think back: when was the last time they'd been at a party together? When was the last time they'd had fun? "Did you ask Bella?"

"Bella says she didn't give them to her."

"Do you believe her?"

"That's the question, isn't it? She's pretty broken up. I guess they were close."

"They used to be," said Roman. "Honestly, I didn't even know they were back in touch."

Felix looked at Tara and John. "What about you two? Did you know Ashley was hanging out with Bella?"

Both shook their heads.

"The other strange thing is that we didn't find her phone or a wallet or any kind of purse at Bella's. I suppose she could have had them on her and maybe they slid down when she fell. But I walked along the tracks and didn't see anything."

"Did you search on the cliffside?" asked John.

"Not thoroughly, no," said Felix. "It's steep enough that we need assistance, frankly, with specialized equipment."

"Okay," said Roman.

"What kind of equipment?" asked John. "That doesn't seem like it should be a problem."

Felix raised his eyebrows. "I'm working on it. Hopefully soon." He paused, though it seemed to Roman like he was considering saying more.

"I know her passcode," said Roman, weakly. "If you can find her phone it might help find . . ." What?

"Good to know," said Felix. "In the meantime, I'd like to get a sense of what she was doing yesterday before she got to Bella's. You said you were in the city. Did you talk that morning, before you left?"

"No. I didn't want to wake her."

Felix nodded. Roman started thinking back. What could he tell Felix that would matter? Did it matter that the bitterness between them had been growing? That they'd stopped being sure allies. Was it relevant that they hadn't had sex in weeks? How many weeks? Memorial Day. Roman had to cover the morning parade and wreath ceremony and when he got to the BBQ in their backyard it was already crowded: Tara's "mom" friends from the playground and their families; Bobby and his girlfriend and some of the café crew; John and a handful of his friends and their wives or girlfriends and kids. It was more people than Roman had expected and he had to park down the block.

Upstairs, he found Ashley getting out of the shower. She was smiling and he pulled her to him, bent her over the third-floor window so that if someone had looked up they might have seen their faces together. When it was over, Ash jumped back in the shower to rinse off and Roman joined her. They splashed and laughed and it was the nicest he'd felt with her in ages.

By the end of the night, they were irritated with each other.

She'd pulled him aside and asked why he was being rude to her friends. He denied being rude, though he didn't like them, didn't know them, and wanted them to leave. *They're your friends*, he'd said, stubbornly. *They could be yours, too*, she'd said. He shrugged and she rolled her eyes and they separated. Later, Roman seethed as he washed dishes and his mom put Mason to bed; Ash stayed outside, laughing with her friends. He watched her through the kitchen window. *She'll never pull her weight*, he thought. *She'll never make this family her priority.* He'd gotten used to the way the rage could pop up fast inside him. Tiny slights—a raised eyebrow, an ignored question—set his chest ablaze. He lifted a middle finger at the window and brandished it at her. She wouldn't see but he didn't care. He needed to send his anger in her direction. How could he love her some moments and hate her so many others?

No, he decided, Felix did not need to know all that.

"Listen," Roman said, "could we do this tomorrow? I've had a really shitty day."

"Say no more, man," said Felix. "You all take care of yourselves. I'll be in touch."

CHAPTER SIXTEEN

When he opened the door to the bedroom he shared with Ash, the smell and the silence hit him like an anvil. He couldn't imagine lying down in that bed without her. But it was late and he was tired, so he curled up on the old sofa in their living room and let the throw pillows stifle his sobs.

Ashley was in every scene in every dream. She was at Wolfe's house, rolling out a yoga mat in the kitchen. She was in the car in front of him driving home from the city, her arm with the hibiscus tattoo on her tricep playfully floating on the breeze out the window. She was on the swings at the park; she was behind the counter at the coffee shop, greeting him with a smile. She was on their rock. She was floating on the river with leaves in her hair, missing a sandal.

He woke up sweating the next morning. He had to pee but the idea of moving felt impossible.

The door opened, and his mom peeked in.

"You're awake," she said. "I need to talk to you. I told Mason about Ashley."

He sat up. "What? When? You didn't wait for me?"

"He was really upset after what happened with Bella yesterday. He kept asking when we were going to see her at the hospital. You were gone and I didn't know when you would be back. I had to tell him."

"You absolutely did not," he said. His voice and heart rate spiked. "You're the adult. You made a choice. You told him because you wanted to."

"I thought he needed to know."

"And you didn't think his only remaining parent should be there?"

"Roman, you were gone and I had to make a decision."

"It's all about you. You can't handle seeing him upset."

"I did what I thought was best."

Roman closed his eyes. What could he do? "What did he say?"

"Not a lot. He kept asking about the hospital. But I think he understands now."

"Where is he?"

"Downstairs."

Roman got up.

"Bobby's here."

"Why is Bobby here?"

"Because he cares about us. He offered to do a memorial service at the coffee shop."

Roman walked past his mother toward the bathroom.

"I came up because Mason is asking for you."

"I'll be down soon."

Two bulbs were out when he flicked on the light. Mason's

toys took up the tub: plastic boats and dinosaurs and a fishnet. There was toothpaste in the sink and spots of dried urine on the rim of the toilet bowl. Ashley was the one who usually cleaned the bathroom. He rinsed his hands and face. In the mirror he saw nose hairs and the glint of his copper stubble, bloodshot eyes, and wild hair. What was he going to say to Mason?

Downstairs, Tara and Bobby were at the kitchen table and Mason was on the couch, staring at the TV. Roman could hear banging around the other side of the house. Presumably John. Ashley was dead, but the roof wasn't going to fix itself. Had his mom canceled the upcoming Airbnbers?

"Hey, mister," said Roman, putting his hand on Mason's brown hair.

Mason didn't say anything at first, and Roman just kept stroking him, running a hand down his back.

"Mommy's dead, Daddy," he said finally. His eyes glued to the screen.

"I know." He tried to catch Mason's gaze. The remote was on the coffee table. Roman picked it up and hit mute.

"No," said Mason.

"I just want to talk for a second."

Mason shook his head. Roman saw that there were stains on his cheeks where the tears had run. His nose was red, his eyes puffy.

"I love you," said Roman. He hit power and the screen went black.

"No!" Mason turned to him. "No, Daddy! Gerty said I could watch TV!"

"You can," said Roman. "I just want to talk." But what did he want to say? "Mommy loved you more than anything in the whole world. I do, too. We're gonna take care of you."

Mason started to scream. "Gerty said! Gerty said I could watch TV!"

Roman tried to wrap his arms around the boy, but Mason pushed him away. Roman's chest constricted, sunken with need.

"Okay, mister, I'll turn it back on. I just want you to know I love you. And I'm so sorry. I'm always here for you. Me and Gerty will always be here. And Mommy will always be here." He put his hand on his heart. "She'll never go away if we keep loving her."

"What?"

"If we keep loving her, she'll always be here."

"She'll come back?"

"No," said Roman. *Shit.* "I mean, we'll keep her alive in our hearts."

"But Gerty said she's dead. That means she's not alive."

"I know," said Roman, seething at his mother. "Gerty's right. I mean—" He stopped. This wasn't going well. "I love you."

"Is Mommy coming back?"

"No," said Roman.

Mason started to cry. "I want to watch TV."

Roman acquiesced. For a few minutes, he sat with his boy, watching the cartoon animals and vegetables who lived beneath the sea. Mason allowed him to put his arm around him, but his son's body was stiff. What had Mason looked like when Tara told him that Ash was dead? What did he say? What more would his mother take from him if he let her?

Roman kissed the boy on his head and went into the kitchen. He couldn't bring himself to look at Tara, but he acknowledged Bobby, who stood up to embrace him.

"I don't want to overstep," said Bobby, "but when my sister died I couldn't do anything. All these people kept calling and asking about a service, and me and my mom just weren't up to it. I'll make all the arrangements. We can do it on the patio. Susan and Gary want to play a couple songs. If people want to say something they can. You don't have to do anything."

Is that what Ashley would have wanted? A memorial service at the coffee shop? With fucking Gary and Susan singing James Taylor songs while everybody cries? She'd want them in Hawaii, holding hands on the beach as the tide came in. But that wasn't going to happen. Roman was in no shape to materialize a remembrance worthy of her. Bobby and Daniel and the people in town who would gather at Koffee were the best she was going to get. Had anyone even called Ashley's mom?

"Okay," he said. "Just tell us what to do."

CHAPTER SEVENTEEN

On Wednesday, Felix came by to tell them that they were still waiting on toxicology reports for Ashley's blood, but that two of the pills in her pocket had tested positive for fentanyl.

"She probably thought they were Percocet," Felix told Roman. "That's what they were marked as."

It was just the two of them in the kitchen. Tara had taken Mason with her to the grocery store—she was using Ashley's car while they waited on an estimate for the damage to hers—and John was at a job in Westchester. A week ago, Roman had been at work, too. Probably driving somewhere he didn't particularly want to go, distracted, thinking about the weekend.

"So, that's what killed her?"

"We don't know for sure," said Felix. "People react differently to fentanyl. You can actually build up a decent tolerance. But if she wasn't used to it, a lot less could kill her than someone who was. I know you said she sometimes did drugs . . ."

"Not fentanyl. Or heroin. She didn't have a death wish." But as soon as he said it, his heart froze. Would he even have known if she'd started taking risks like that?

"There's another thing," Felix said. "We dusted the baggie for fingerprints and there was nothing. Not a single print. Not hers or anyone else's. Not even a smudge."

"What does that mean?"

"Well, I don't know for sure. It could mean nothing. But it's odd. Most dealers aren't nearly that fastidious. Fingerprints on a baggie can't prove anything other than that you touched the thing at some point, which isn't illegal." He paused for a moment. "On the other hand, if you don't want to be associated with the bag at all, I suppose it makes sense to wipe it. But if she was the one who wiped it, why put it back in her pocket?"

"I don't know," said Roman.

"Me neither," said Felix. "Anyway, it stuck out to me. I wanted to see what you thought."

Roman wiped his face with his hand. "I don't know what to think. I just want to know what happened."

"I know you do," said Felix. "And I promise I'll do everything I can to get your family some answers." He paused, and it looked to Roman like he was weighing whether or not to say what he was thinking. "Did Ashley ever suffer from depression?"

Roman had been waiting for this. If it wasn't an accidental overdose, maybe she'd meant to do it. Roman knew way more about suicide than most people; he'd gone down a rabbit hole on research and personal stories in college when he reached the age his father was when he'd jumped off a bridge to his death. Men were more likely to choose so-called "violent" means: guns or nooses or wild one-car crashes or dramatic leaps from high places. Women tended to leave the world "quietly": with a silent razor slice in the bathtub, or a handful of pills. He imagined Ashley on the rock in Bella's yard again. Not delicately placing a pill on her tongue, warmed by the beautiful view and the knowledge that a lovely, humming high was just a few minutes away. But gobbling a half-dozen Percocet, alone, at the most beautiful vista in town. The latter meant she was miserable. It meant she hated her life. Her life with him.

"Yes," said Roman, finally. "After Mason was born. And since, I guess. On and off."

Felix nodded. "I'm going to talk to as many people as I can," he said. "I want to know where she got the pills. And I want to know what she was doing that day and that night. I'm going to find you some answers, Roman. Okay? I promise."

Roman nodded.

"I heard there's going to be a service this weekend?"

"At the coffee shop," said Roman.

"I'm sure you're anxious to . . . have some closure," he said, "but unfortunately, we can't release the body until we have a firm cause of death." He paused again. "This is a little awkward, but what were you hoping to do with her body?"

"Do?"

"Cremation? Burial? I'm not sure if you're religious, but some people want an open casket . . ."

"No," said Roman. "We definitely don't want an open casket."

Felix seemed relieved. "That brings me to the next question. Would you approve an autopsy? I'll be honest: it might prolong the process. The coroner's office is short-staffed and overdoses tend to be lower priority. It might take weeks. Maybe even longer. But it could give us some answers."

Roman sat for a moment with the fact of Ashley's body. It was an object now. And he had to make decisions about it. What other people would do to it. Where it would rest.

"Are you in touch with Ashley's mom?" Felix asked.

"Not really," said Roman.

"Chief said he got ahold of her Saturday to inform her, but I haven't been able to get her on the phone since."

"I can try," said Roman, though talking to Kelly was the last thing he wanted to do. Maybe he could get Tara to make the call.

"Thanks," said Felix, standing up. "So if she's okay with it, you guys are good with an autopsy? It's the best way to be sure what happened."

Roman nodded, but he couldn't help thinking that knowing what happened might make him feel even worse than he did now.

CHAPTER EIGHTEEN

Tara made mac and cheese and hot dogs and they all sat in front of the television to eat dinner, plates on their laps. The TV had been on pretty much nonstop since they'd told Mason that Ashley wasn't coming back. A never-ending loop of *Octonauts* and *PAW Patrol* in the daytime; HGTV and *Law & Order* at night. Anything to keep any of them from having to be alone with their thoughts in the house that now felt so empty.

At nine, Mason fell asleep on the sofa watching *Cars* for the umpteenth time. Tara carried him upstairs. John and Roman tag-teamed cleaning the kitchen.

"We got some bad news about the house today," John said as he put dishes into the dishwasher. "Connor came by while you were lying down. We went to pull out the old tub, and there's rot. All through the sill above the basement. The beam holding up the first floor back there is basically pulp. I can't see the rest of what's behind the siding but it might be like that all the way across. Which means the whole exterior wall is at risk. Which means we might have to tear the whole back of the fucking house off."

Roman almost laughed. "How much is that going to cost?"

"I mean, me and Connor can do it. We have to pay him, though. And lumber, maybe some steel joists, new siding. It could be five grand. Or more. And that's on top of what it's costing to fix the roof and patch up the bathroom."

"Can we put it off?"

"Remember what happened last year over on Maple?" Roman remembered. A heavy snowfall collapsed the roof of a nearby house on Christmas Eve, killing the old man who lived inside. "That was a rotted sill."

His mother came downstairs, rubbing her eyes.

"I told him about the sill," said John.

"I already canceled the Airbnbers," she said. "So now that money is gone, too."

Too. No Airbnb income. No income from Ashley. It made him feel a little sick that that was what his mom was thinking about, but he supposed somebody had to. Roman opened the refrigerator and took out a beer.

"Felix was here," he said. "The pills she had tested positive for fentanyl."

"Fuck," said John quietly.

Tara sucked in a breath. "Did you know she was using?"

"I don't think she was 'using'—"

Tara cut him off. "Do you realize that this means she may have had that shit in her pocket when she was with Mason? You read about kids finding drugs like that all the time."

She was right. And she wasn't finished.

"I can't believe she was so fucking careless. Now look what she left. Mason is never going to be the same. He's—"

"Tar," said John.

She slammed a cabinet shut. "What stage of grief is anger? I'm in that stage right now."

"Felix said they dusted the baggie for fingerprints, but it had been wiped clean." Roman paused. No one said anything. "And we have to think about what to do with her body."

"Do you know what she wanted?" Tara asked.

"No," said Roman. "Do you?"

Tara shook her head. "They cremated her dad."

"Right," said Roman.

Ashley's dad died of stomach cancer during Roman's senior year at NYU. The diagnosis was the reason Ash had come home from Hawaii. Or at least it was the reason she gave. Steve Lillian, whose alcohol abuse and tendency to miss court hearings resulted in him losing all visitation rights to his only daughter when she was two, wrote her an email saying that the doctors had given him six months to live and that he knew he didn't deserve her sympathy but that he hoped maybe they could see each other before he died. Ash got the email, called Roman, and told him she wanted to come home—much to the chagrin of her mother. But by that time, Ash was beyond caring about what Kelly wanted. Ashley had Roman and Tara and Daniel and Bella and a dozen other people who loved her and didn't think she was going to hell for being who she was.

When she came back from Hawaii, Ash made the Grady

house her home base, but spent most days and nights at the shitty apartment complex where her dad was living out the rest of his days. Roman took the train up to visit as often as he could.

"This body is nothing but tumors," he remembers Steve saying from his perch in the La-Z-Boy, blanket over his lap. "I don't care what you do with it."

Steve's parents and grandparents and even a great-aunt were all buried in the cemetery behind Adamsville's Episcopal church, but when Ashley called, the church said the graveyard had been full for twenty-five years.

"Just burn it," Steve said. "Spread my ashes in the river. It'll be cheaper."

And it was. A plot and a marker and a casket and a burial cost nearly $10,000, and Steve had almost nothing to his name when he died. The cancer ate his body and the treatment meant selling his car and cashing in the meager 401k he'd amassed. All he'd managed to hang on to was a barely water-worthy canoe his dad had left him. Ashley took the canoe and her dad's remains out to the river between Breakneck Ridge and Storm King Mountain and she laid them in the water. After that, if she wanted to be with her dad, she'd walk down to the shore. Roman suspected that if she were here to ask, Ashley would say that she wanted them to spread her ashes in Hawaii. She'd once mentioned that when her therapist or another yoga instructor asked her to go to a peaceful place in her mind, she went to a particular black sand beach—a secluded place, she said, with palm trees bent low enough to climb on and relax for hours, as if the trunk were a hammock.

Roman looked out the front window, and there was the big river. It wasn't Hawaii, but he hoped she would understand.

"Maybe we spread her ashes in the river, too."

John nodded. "I like that."

"Do you think Mason should see her again?" asked Tara.

"What do you mean?"

"Some people think that seeing the body, like at a wake, helps a child get closure," she said. "Of course, everybody has a different opinion. Maryanne Wilco's sister died a couple years ago and her daughter was around Mason's age. She posted for advice . . ."

"You posted about this on Facebook?"

"No, I said . . ."

"Do you ever make a decision without getting fifty opinions from people you barely know?"

His mom's need for social media validation infuriated Roman. If you looked at her Facebook feed you'd think she was Mason's mom. Tara and her sweet little boy eating ice cream and taking hikes and finger painting and marching for Black lives and trans lives and abortion rights. Roman and Ashley both thought Facebook was toxic, and despite several discussions about Mason having no control over how his grandmother was using his image online, Tara couldn't seem to help herself.

"Roman—"

"What do *you* think? Is it possible to discern that?"

Tara sucked in a breath; his blow had landed.

"She's just trying to figure out what's best," said John.

"I don't think we need to crowdsource the fucking funeral," said Roman.

Tara was silent a moment, then spoke slowly. "I didn't want you to see your dad's body. I didn't want that to be what you remembered. You were younger, though. Mason will have more memories of Ashley."

Roman's heart smarted. His son was barely four; what memories would he have? A snippet here or there? An image; a fragment of a scene. Maybe a scent. It was more than he had, but would it hurt more, too?

"Ashley thought open caskets were creepy," said Roman. Plus, he thought with a shudder, she hadn't looked like herself on the cliffside. It was her hair and her face and her arms and legs, but those things didn't make her Ashley.

"I agree," said Tara. The matter was settled: no open casket. "We need to talk to her mom. I left her a voicemail and sent a couple texts. But I haven't heard anything. I want to make sure she knows about the . . . thing at the coffee shop."

What were they supposed to call it? A service? A memorial? A remembrance? A celebration of life?

"One of us should find out if her mom has an opinion," said Roman.

"I'll go," said Tara.

Roman felt a familiar mix of relief and shame. Should he be the one to talk to Kelly? Ashley was his partner, not Tara's. But it would be painful, and possibly acrimonious. And, just as she had been over and over since Mason was born, Tara was willing to step in and relieve him. *Why?* he wondered. Did she not think he was capable? *Was* he capable? How would he ever know?

CHAPTER NINETEEN

Kelly Marchand hadn't been a part of Ashley's life for years. Tara didn't even know where she lived, exactly, although she knew that she'd been with the same boyfriend—a math teacher in New Paltz named Jim Riley–since before the pandemic. Tara messaged Jim on Facebook, and Jim got back to her with their address.

She hasn't left the house since the police called, he wrote in a message. *I don't know if she wants to see anybody but she'll be here.*

When Ashley got pregnant, Kelly came to the shower and managed to make her daughter cry by telling everybody who would listen that she hoped this finally cured her daughter of being a lesbian.

Covid hit a month before Ashley's due date. None of them were allowed in the hospital with her, and once she recovered, people weren't letting groceries into their homes, let alone relatives they didn't particularly like. Kelly and Tara talked on FaceTime a few times, so Ashley's mom could see her grandson. But as

Ashley got more depressed, keeping Kelly in the loop slipped off
the priority list.

The first time Kelly met her grandson in person he was nearly
six months old. Tara and Ashley and Roman brought him to a
playground halfway between their homes, but Ashley wouldn't
let Kelly hold the baby unless she wore a mask—and Kelly hadn't
brought one.

"I have an extra in the car," Tara said.

"You know they don't actually filter anything. Plus we're outside. In the fresh air."

Tara remembered seeing that Ashley was becoming agitated.
Since Mason was born, Ashley had vacillated between terror
that he'd get Covid and terror that the virtual checkups the pe-
diatricians were performing would miss some key problem that
would afflict him forever. Ashley insisted on breast-feeding. Too
many late nights on the internet had convinced her that formula
would adversely affect Mason, and that taking antidepressants
would sully her breastmilk. It wasn't until he was nearly one that
Tara said she thought Ashley's sickness—her sadness and exhaustion and total inability to experience joy—might be worse
for Mason than cow's milk or SSRIs. It was all she needed, Tara
saw now: permission.

Ashley clutched Mason while Tara went to the car for a mask.

"You know these things are a breeding ground for disease,"
Kelly grumbled, making a big show of fumbling as she put it on.
She reached her hands out to Mason. Ashley held tight. Roman
put his hand on her shoulder.

"What?" demanded Kelly.

"Can you sanitize your hands?"

Kelly sighed dramatically. "They really have you brainwashed, don't they?"

"I've got some right here," said Roman, popping the flip-top on a travel-sized Purell.

"I can't believe you think I'd do anything to endanger my own grandson," said Kelly, allowing Roman to drop a dollop of gel into her palm. "It's ridiculous. It's insulting."

"Ashley's just being extra careful," said Roman. "Mason was born a little underweight—"

"Are we good now?" Kelly interrupted, waving her hands.

Ashley hesitated again, but relented, laying Mason's little body in her mother's arms. Tara wondered what Kelly felt, looking at her first grandchild. The first time she'd held Roman—and far too many times after—there was no bliss. There was disappointment and anger and exhaustion. But her grandson was entirely different. Her grandson felt like a miracle every minute of every day. The first time she put her lips on his skin, she was in love. Once, early on, she caught a glimpse of herself in the mirror as she gazed at him: she looked so besotted she seemed to be pleading. Wide, soft eyes, lips parted, every pore a smile. Tara watched Kelly for a similar expression as she held Mason; she watched for tears. But Kelly was stoic, or seemingly so. Tara had long found her inscrutable, with her unflattering haircuts and her "Jesus Saves" bumper sticker and her absolute disdain for her daughter's sexuality, all mixed up with a habit of living with men she wasn't married to.

"Well, he's definitely Roman's," said Kelly.

"Of course he's Roman's, Mom."

"Don't get defensive, Ashley. I just mean he looks like him, Same nose. Same eyes."

Tara could see that Ashley was on the verge of losing it.

"Same temperament, too," said Tara, trying to lighten the mood. "That first month all he did was cry. Sleep is still a bit of a struggle."

"Ashley was a good baby," said Kelly. "Slept through the night after just a week or two at home."

"Bullshit," said Roman. Tara put her hand on her son, a weak attempt at holding him back. They were all still sleep-deprived and, Ashley and Roman at least, were perpetually agitated as they dealt with Mason's colic.

Ashley started to cry. Kelly handed the baby back to Roman and took off her mask.

"Well," she said, getting up from the park bench. "That was fun."

They didn't see her much after that. Kelly refused to get vaccinated, so Ashley had to inform her that if she came to Mason's first birthday party, she'd have to mask, which Kelly refused to do. For his second birthday party, Tara relented and said it was okay if Kelly didn't wear a mask, as long as she stayed outside. Kelly showed up with Jim and a gift, but left early, offended that Mason wasn't interested in interacting with her. Every Easter and Christmas, Kelly invited them to her church, but Ashley knew what they thought of her there.

Tara's car was likely to be in the shop for at least two more weeks, so she took Ashley's to talk with Kelly. Ashley's keys were, thankfully, on the wall-mounted series of hooks beside the kitchen door. Tara guessed it made sense that she had walked to Bella's instead of driving on Friday evening; especially if she didn't plan on going anywhere else. It had been a nice night; warm, but not sticky hot. Tara opened the car door and scrunched up her nose. Tara was fastidious about maintaining her vehicle. It carried Mason, after all. The most precious cargo in her world. Every weekend, her grandson helped her vacuum the RAV4. They made a game of sucking up all the crumbs from his snacks and pulling out the various wrappers and stray Legos and superhero figurines that found their way between and beneath the seats. They dumped what they grabbed into a Tupperware and whoever gathered the most won. Tara showed him how to wipe the dashboard with a cloth and if the weather was good, she enlisted John to help them soak and soap and wash the outside.

But Ashley's car was a bit of a disaster. When she got in for the first time yesterday, there was half an iced coffee from Dunkin' still in the cupholder and the sticky residue of some sort of spilled drink on the center console. Random receipts and a plastic water bottle and a couple pens lay on the passenger side floor mat; a sweatshirt and pairs of shorts and sneakers—a whole outfit?—were tossed in the back next to Mason's car seat. She'd shivered, thinking of the pills they'd found in Ashley's pocket. Could there be pills in the car? Or worse. Needles. She imagined Mason digging his little fingers between the seats to unearth the seat belt buckle, stabbing himself, crying out. It took an hour of cleaning before she was ready to let Mason climb inside for the trip to the grocery store. How could Ashley have been so careless? And how could Tara have known so little about the girl she thought of as a daughter?

Tara rolled down the windows and headed north. In addition to the smells and sediment she wasn't used to, Ashley's car had little eccentricities: the back windshield wiper popped on at random intervals and the brakes were more sensitive than in her Toyota. After about forty minutes, Tara turned onto a private gravel road about a mile off the interstate. The little house was set back among a grove of evergreens, half-hidden by craggy, overgrown rose of Sharons and rhododendrons. A stone angel prayed at the foot of the steps and a mismatched set of wicker chairs took up much of the narrow porch. Two cars were in the driveway, and as Tara turned off the engine, she saw Jim coming around from the back, dragging a garden hose.

"Thanks for the address," she said. "She's home?"

"Yeah. She should be in the kitchen. If not, come get me."

"We're having a gathering and I wanted to make sure you both knew you were welcome."

"I appreciate that. I'm so sorry. How are the boys?"

"Not good," said Tara. "None of us are."

"Well, let us know if we can do anything. We're praying for you."

Tara resisted the urge to roll her eyes. Her parents had been atheists and she'd inherited their disdain for church people. Once, as they drove past the packed parking lot of the local

Catholic church, her mother had commented: "I bet all those people are going to be real surprised when they die and nothing happens." But the older Tara got, the more she understood that people did what they had to do to get through the days.

"Thanks," she said.

Tara knocked at the front door and tried the knob. "Kelly? Hello? It's Tara."

The house was silent and smelled faintly of cat litter and cigarettes. Tara stepped into the living room.

"Kelly?"

She found Ashley's mom in the kitchen, sitting at the table with her hands around a mug.

"Hey," said Tara. And then, because it just came out: "How are you?"

Kelly looked up. Her eyes were red and her mouth turned down.

"Sorry," said Tara, "I don't know what to say. I just wanted to come and see if you need anything. If I can do anything." No response. "Can I sit?" Kelly didn't say no, so Tara sat, and kept talking. "I left you a couple messages. We're going to have a memorial on Friday. At the coffee shop. Bobby and Daniel will make it nice."

Kelly looked at her. Was she hearing?

"She's still at the medical examiner," Tara continued, "and we need to decide what to do. With—"

"I get it," said Kelly.

Outside, Jim turned on the hose. A motorcycle roared by, and for the first time Tara thought: *what if it had been Roman?* The notion shot bile up her throat and she had to catch it with a fist against her lips. Tara had regrets with Ashley, but nothing, she imagined, like what Kelly had. Being here, asking her for input into the management of her only child's dead body, felt cruel. She and Roman should just take care of it.

"If it were up to me, I'd bury her," Kelly said quietly.

"I don't know who it's up to."

"Roman doesn't have an opinion?"

"He wanted to ask you."

"But he didn't. He sent you."

"He's watching Mason."

"Does Mason not ride in cars?"

Okay, thought Tara, she's angry. But it was Ashley's choice to keep Kelly at arm's length, not Tara's. More like Kelly's choice, really, with her beliefs and her behavior.

"Do you want me to bring him?" Tara asked. "I can do that."

Kelly looked out the window. "You're officially Mom, now, I guess."

"What?"

"I want to bury her. Okay. If you're asking what I want, that's what I want."

"Do you have a plot or—"

"No, I don't have a fucking burial plot for my twenty-five-year-old daughter," she snapped. "I don't have a plot and I don't have all kinds of money, but you asked what I want and that's what I want. I want my baby's body—" Her voice caught, and she stood up abruptly. "That's what I want." She left the kitchen.

CHAPTER TWENTY

Tara stopped for gas on the way back to Adamsville and called the Parker Funeral Home on Main Street while she was pulled over. In high school, Tara babysat for Lily and Brian Parker, whose parents were second-generation owners of the funeral home. Lily played to type. Even at nine, she wore mostly black and wrote stories about dead people. Brian, two years older, was an athlete with an easy smile. When they talked about what their parents did for a living, Tara could tell he took the work seriously, while Lily seemed mostly interested in shocking whomever she was speaking with. *My dad had to put somebody's eyeball back in at work yesterday*, the girl told her one evening as Tara poked hot dogs around a pan of boiling water for their dinner. Brian added context: *It was a car accident. A drunk driver.*

Brian answered her call and told her to come by anytime. She called John to check in.

"What are you guys doing?" she asked.

"I brought Mase with me to the hardware store and we just got back."

"Is Roman there? How's he doing?"

"He and Mason just turned on *Toy Story*. You want some company?"

"I don't know," she said. "Do you think Roman's okay by himself?"

"Tara," said John, "Roman is a grown-up."

Well, when you say it like that, thought Tara. But her grown-up son was without the love of his life, and, frankly, not used to parenting his son alone.

"Can you ask him?"

"Hold on," said John. "Roman, I'm gonna go meet your mom. You two okay for a couple hours?"

Tara couldn't hear his response, but heard John say, "Whatever you want." A pause, then John returned. "We're all good. I'll meet you at Parker."

As she drove south, Tara imagined her son and grandson on the sofa watching TV all afternoon. She'd been fastidious about keeping the boy away from screens until age two, and even now she considered the television a parenting dodge. She took care of Mason most of the time, and on the occasions when Ashley or Roman had to take over for a few hours it drove her crazy when they'd watch TV. *Play with him!* she wanted to yell. *Read to him! It's not hard.* And yet, somehow it seemed to be—for them at least.

When she arrived at the funeral home, Brian greeted her in the entry vestibule. He was barely forty but Tara could see white already in his beard. She knew he was married now, with two daughters. His wife was from Poland, and Tara sometimes chatted with her on the playground while the kids ran around.

"I'm so sorry," he said. "She was so young."

"Thanks. I just talked to her mom. It still doesn't seem real."

The words felt meaningless; cliché. What had she said to people after Jason died? Or her parents. Why didn't she remember? People must have said *I'm sorry* ten thousand times. They must have asked how she was and she must have answered in some manner, but she was finding it hard to figure out what to say now. Every time she saw someone she hadn't seen since Ashley's death she would have to confront the information anew; confront all the various reactions. Was she supposed to comfort people? It was exhausting. There were things she wanted to express, but how, and to whom?

"We're having a service at Koffee," she told him. "But I wanted to get a sense of what our options are in terms of her body."

"Of course," said Brian. "She hasn't been released yet, and they're telling me it could be a few days—maybe even longer. Do you have a plot?"

"No," she said.

"Don't feel bad. With someone as young as Ashley, no one is ever thinking about death." Brian paused. "If you think you'd like to do a burial, I know of two places with plenty of space."

"Do you have a price list?"

"Don't worry about that."

"Unfortunately," she said, instantly irritated, "I have to. We've lost an income. Two, actually, because the fucking house is falling apart."

Tara's eyes began to sting. She'd been responsible for years, and yet, here she was, weeping in a funeral home because her grandson's mother was dead and they were probably going to need a payment plan for her fucking coffin.

"I can't imagine how stressful this is," said Brian, "but don't worry about the money. You just decide what you and the family want. Someone from the community has been in touch. They want to cover the costs."

"What? Who?"

"They asked that I not say."

Tara wasn't sure how to respond. "'They'? Is it some kind of organization?" Ashley sometimes ran yoga classes at the county Boys and Girls Club, but she couldn't imagine them using donor money on a funeral for a volunteer.

"No, just someone local who wanted to make things easier." Seemingly out of nowhere, he produced a glossy brochure: *Final Rest.* He was so poised. "But for now, why don't you take a look at your choices."

"Can you tell them we're not comfortable taking money if we don't know where it's coming from?"

"I can certainly do that."

"Will you call us when you . . . get her?"

"Yes," said Brian. "We'll take care of everything."

CHAPTER TWENTY-ONE

John was waiting for her in the parking lot.

"Somebody wants to pay for the funeral expenses," she told him.

"Who?"

"Brian wouldn't tell me. Apparently, they want to remain anonymous."

"That's weird."

"I agree," said Tara. She couldn't think of anyone she or Ashley knew who had thousands of dollars to throw around on a funeral. A GoFundMe, sure—she'd even considered that—but a single benefactor?

John took off his hat and scratched his forehead with it. "Wanna get a beer?"

"What time is it?"

"I told him we'd be a couple hours. They're fine."

"Mason's watching too much TV."

"You need a break, Tara," said John. "Let Roman be with his son."

"What do you mean, 'let'? Of course I let him. I practically have to beg him."

"That's not what I meant."

"I know," she sighed, putting her hand on his chest. "You're right. Yes, I want a beer. Or three."

They took John's truck to the waterfront. It was that dead time between lunch and happy hour and they found a table by the river. Tara drank her whole first beer without saying anything. John did the same. She loved that about him. He wasn't always up in her shit, asking what she was thinking, forcing her to talk about things just to make him feel like he was important. He was easygoing, and he was the only lover she'd ever had who got her off every time. Which, in a funny way, was part of why it had been so easy to say yes when he asked her to marry him.

It had been New Year's Eve. They'd all watched the ball drop in London on TV—so Mason could celebrate without having to stay up until midnight—then Tara put the boy to bed and Roman and Ashley walked to the gazebo at the end of Main Street where the town sponsored a celebration. She and John smoked a joint in the backyard. She rarely got high anymore. Since Mason was born, her motto (with a few exceptions) had been: don't do anything you wouldn't want Mason to know about. Getting stoned was one.

"When was the last time you smoked?" John asked.

"A long time," she said. "I used to need it—or alcohol—to feel happy. Or happy enough to notice I was happy. But not since Mason."

They finished the joint and went upstairs. The stoned sex was electrifying. Afterward, they lay in bed together, sweaty and, for Tara at least, deliriously happy. *How did I get so lucky?* she remembered thinking. *I have a house full of love.* Everything was good. Mason was safe, Roman and Ashley were getting along, and she was having supremely satisfying sex with a hot man who loved her. Her parents had been a happy couple. She smiled thinking of them. They'd be proud of her. They probably wouldn't have picked John—they wouldn't have liked that he didn't have a college degree—but once they got to know him, they'd probably bug her to get married.

"Do you think you'll ever get married again?" she asked, really just thinking out loud.

"Married?" said John. "Sure. I'd get married again. I'd marry you tomorrow."

"Shut up," she said, slapping his chest.

He turned toward her and smiled. "I'm serious."

"You want to get married tomorrow?"

"I'll get married tomorrow."

"Stop!"

"Okay," he said. "It doesn't have to be tomorrow. How about June? That's the wedding month, right? Wanna get married in June?"

She laughed, but why not? And then she said it out loud. "Why not?" Why not keep what she had? Why not make it official?

"You serious?"

"Are you?"

"You know I wanna marry you. I've wanted to marry you since I was seventeen."

"I didn't know that, actually," said Tara. "You never said anything. You never even tried to hook up with me back then."

John shrugged. "I love you. I want to be with you for the rest of my life. That's easy for me to say."

Did she feel the same way? She did. So why not? Why not make a grand, optimistic leap into the future. She said yes. And it had been fun, telling Mason he would get to wear a tie and carry the rings on a little pillow; texting links to dresses and simple flower arrangements with Ashley; driving to the city to the ring-maker in Brooklyn who helped them design bands. When she was pregnant with Roman, people had asked if she and Jason were going to get married. She would have married him, but he never asked. She gave Roman her last name out of spite. And after he died, Tara hardened herself to romantic love. It was enough that she'd figured out how to love her son—and herself—properly.

Then John came back to town, and something changed in her. Maybe it was the combination of knowing him and not knowing him. Maybe it was his attention and his humor and the way he touched her, or the way he was a *grown-up* who remembered what night the trash went out and which bakery made her favorite cupcakes. Whatever it was, she felt, for the first time, like maybe she'd found what her son had at thirteen: her person. And as they planned the wedding—for September instead of June because the flights were cheaper for their planned honeymoon in Mexico—she was more and more certain that she wanted to hold on to what she had with him.

But now, before they could have the wedding, they had to have a fucking funeral.

Tara opened another beer.

"What do you think about the funeral?" she asked.

"You mean the mystery donor?"

"Yeah. Should we just let them pay?"

"I think we should ask Roman."

That made sense. She drank her beer and squinted at the boats in the harbor.

"It just goes to show," said John after a while. "Ashley had a whole life. Maybe we didn't know as much about it as we thought."

CHAPTER TWENTY-TWO

Roman woke up cold on the morning of the memorial.

"Daddy, I wet through," said Mason.

"What?"

"I peed in the bed."

Roman sat up. Indeed, they were both lying on damp sheets. He'd been sleeping with his son all week. Each night he crept into bed beside the boy and breathed deep, inhaling the tranquility that being pressed against Mason's body ignited inside him. It was the drug keeping him alive.

"Oh well," he said, "let's get changed then."

He got up and extended his hand to help Mason out of bed.

"Is Mommy really dead?"

"She is, mister."

"But we're going to see her today?"

"What do you mean?"

"At her party. She'll be there to say goodbye?"

He couldn't help it; Roman started to cry.

"No," he said. "She won't be there. I'm so sorry."

"Are you sure?"

"I'm sure. You know where you can see her, though? In your dreams. I saw her there last night."

Mason didn't like this answer.

"Dreams aren't real."

"Sure they are," he said.

Mason began crying. "I want to hug Mommy," he said. "I can't hug her in a dream."

"You can," said Roman. "She'll be there when you go to sleep and you can talk to her and—"

"No! That's not real!"

Roman wrapped his arms around his son and held him tight, as if the pressure might squeeze out the pain. "I know. I know." What else could he say? Should he tell his four-year-old that he felt like he'd lost half his own body? Should he tell him that he knew none of them would ever be the same? Should he say that they'd hurt forever and they'd all just have to live with it? What should he say? There was nothing but: "I love you. I love you forever and so does Gerty and even though she's gone, wherever she is, Mommy loves you, too."

They cried together for what seemed like a long time. Finally, Mason said, "I need a nose blow," and when they went to the bathroom for some toilet paper—the Kleenex box was empty—the boy seemed ready, for the moment at least, to move on. Roman helped him take off his wet pajamas. He pulled out the little stool for Mason to pee into the toilet and then he scooted the stool to the sink for him to rinse his hands and brush his teeth.

Tara knocked on the door to the apartment.

"You two up?" she said.

"We're up," called Roman.

"I'm making pancakes."

"I want pancakes," said Mason from the bathroom. He walked out, still naked. "Mommy won't be there to say goodbye today."

Roman closed his eyes and heard his mom sigh, then say, "I know, mister. I know. I'm so sorry."

"I wish she was."

"Me, too," said Tara.

"Me, three," called Roman. He looked at himself in the mirror and saw that, somehow, he looked the same. He felt so different. Everything had changed, but his nose and cheeks and forehead were exactly as they'd been a week ago when Ashley had found an eyelash below his left eye, pinched it into her fingers, and held it out for him to blow a wish on. What bullshit had he wished for? Why had they been together in the bathroom? What had they said or done just before? Just after? Were all those moments lost forever? Would every memory fade to nothing? And what was Ashley now but their memories? What did anyone amount to if the things they did and said were forgotten when they were gone?

While he dressed, Roman thought about whether he was going to stand up and say anything at the service. What he wanted was to skip the whole thing; or else hide in the back. Widows got to wear black veils in movies. He could handle it if no one could see his face. But people were going to expect him to be strong.

Mason needed that, probably. Mason needed his daddy not to hide. Could he do that?

He could.

They walked together, Roman and Mason and Tara and John, to the coffee shop. Bobby and Daniel and the rest of the staff had turned the café's typically threadbare back patio into what felt almost like a small church. Rows of mismatched chairs—gathered, Roman imagined, from basements and backyards around town—were lined up in front of a microphone stand, and almost every other chair had a picture of Ashley taped neatly to the back. Ashley flashing the peace sign at the river; Ashley leading a yoga class in the park; Ashley sticking her tongue out at a party; Ashley in Hawaii in a lei; Ashley and Roman; Ashley and Mason; Ashley and her dad. The images, Roman realized when he got closer, were color photos printed on copy paper. Someone—many people—had taken the time to scroll through their phones and her social media, find a color printer (the library?), then give the image to whoever was collecting them. Somebody had to get scissors; somebody had to get tape. Somebody had managed to turn their pain into this beautiful thing. This thing that, when he looked at the result, a hundred smiling Ashley faces brought him both piercing joy and hurt. Somebody had done all this while Roman had barely gotten out of bed.

"Look at all the Mommys!" said Mason, pointing. He ran up to a row and reached out to one. He put his finger on Ashley's face, petting it, almost. "I love you, Mommy."

"Did you know about this?" Tara asked.

Roman shook his head. His chin was crumbling and sobs felt like stones in his mouth. He managed to say, "I don't think I can sit here and look at all these."

"Let's go to the front," said his mom.

Tara put her hand on his back and they walked to the first row. But the stage area had more pictures, bigger ones, on easels. Mason went to the biggest, the one of Ashley holding him as a newborn. Roman knew that photo. He'd taken it because his mother insisted. Since none of them had been in the hospital, they didn't have any of the seemingly obligatory photos of Ashley in a hospital gown, beaming at her boy. So they staged something similar. *Smile*, he remembered Tara saying. Ashley raised the corners of her mouth. He captured the moment and to everyone who looked, then and now, it seemed as if Ashley was exactly what she was supposed to be after bringing her baby into the world: exhausted and elated.

What the picture didn't show was what she'd whispered to him just hours before, while Tara changed Mason: *I think we made a terrible mistake.*

They'd been so full of optimism when they found out she was pregnant. It was about a month after her father died; Ashley had been caring for him for months and Roman spent much of the late spring and early summer after he graduated from NYU helping. He'd won a fellowship at the *Los Angeles Times* but wasn't scheduled to leave for California until August. The three of them sat together in front of the television in Steve's apartment, watching old action movies: *Bloodsport* and *Die Hard* and *Red Dawn* and *First Blood*. His possessions were few, but they included VHS tapes of the movies he'd loved in his youth. Movies, he told them, he'd snuck into when he should have been in school. He told them he'd eventually talked himself into a job at the concession stand, where he could treat his friends to free popcorn and hook up with his girlfriends after hours in the upstairs booth. Steve watched those movies as he faded away, losing twenty pounds, despite what Ashley fed him, in the weeks between the Memorial Day and the Fourth of July.

They conceived Mason just a few days before Steve died. Roman stayed in the living room as she helped her dad to the bathroom and stood near while he peed, ready to catch him if he stumbled, then tucked him in. When she came back to Roman in the living room, she flipped off the TV and took off her clothes. Looking back, Roman imagined that she felt somehow pumped full of life as she watched it drain from her father. They were quiet, although they didn't need to be. Her dad's sleep was aided by morphine and even if they'd bothered him, he could scarcely get up and scold them. They slept tangled on the sofa together that night, and the night after, until the night they heard a strange sound and found him on the floor beside his bed. He wasn't breathing. Ashley called 911, and when the medics came, they bowed their heads.

Six weeks later, she showed him the two lines on the plastic test.

"I can defer the fellowship a year," said Roman.

"I don't want you to do that," said Ashley.

"I want to. I want to do this with you. We got through death together, let's do *life!*"

The loose plan was to have the baby, get adjusted, save some money by living with Tara, and go to California the next fall. And—perfect timing!—Martha McGovern, who'd written for the *Advocate* for thirty years, was moving to North Carolina to help take care of her grandkids. The job even had health insurance. Then Covid hit, and Ashley nearly died giving birth, and Tara took over—doing things like staging photos that none of them could imagine would end up blown up and displayed four years later at a memorial service Ashley's family hadn't even had the wherewithal to arrange.

CHAPTER TWENTY-THREE

They sat in the front row and waited. Tara had a bag with books for Mason and he asked Roman to read him a story about a group of sheep seeking revenge against the wolves who stole their coats.

Daniel appeared wearing a pink and white Hawaiian-style shirt and yellow overalls. He was carrying a basket of postcards, colored pens, and ribbons.

"Is it okay?" he asked. "I know it's a lot. I just . . . We couldn't choose. There were so many great pictures."

Roman nodded. It didn't feel okay, but what would?

"These are for people to write things to you. Or Ash. Or Mason. I'm gonna say they can take them home or leave them here for you."

"Okay."

Behind him, Roman could hear people coming into the back-yard, commenting on the photos, sitting down, their voices low. Was it rude not to greet people? He didn't care. He finished the sheep book and opened a graphic novel about two alligators.

At some point, Gary and Susan wiggled onto their stools and started playing a song by the Indigo Girls.

"I know this song," said Mason. "It's on my playlist. Mommy sings it to me before bed."

Roman squeezed Mason's hand and said a prayer to a god he didn't really believe in: *Please help me get through this.*

As the de facto head of their secular community, Bobby led the service, which mainly meant introducing people who had asked to speak, then nodding at Gary and Susan for a song. Roman hadn't prepared anything, but at the very end, he stood up and walked to the mic. It was his duty to stand before these people for her. He looked out onto the faces that went back not just to the coffee shop, but onto the sidewalk, onto the street. He saw that Felix and Scott had parked their cruisers and were redirecting the cars carrying whatever apparently small number of people in town weren't sitting or standing in the hot sun for Ashley. He saw his mom smiling up at him, her face bloated and red. He saw John nodding encouragement, making an almost imperceptible fist to say: *you can do it.* And he saw Mason.

"Ash was my best friend," he said finally. "She was a lot of people's best friend. I bet there are a dozen people here who would call Ash their best friend, or one of them. But the person she loved most in the world was you, Mason." Roman didn't say that she didn't love him right away. That when that picture in front of him was taken she probably would have given him up if she could have done it without shame. That didn't matter. What mattered was what had happened in the years since. Ashley's love for her son hadn't been immediate, but Roman had watched the boy change her. He'd watched her fall in love. That's how she put it. She'd said precisely those words just after he turned two. She'd whispered, smiling: *I'm in love with him, Roman. Finally.*

"Your mommy had some hard times, and she made some hard choices, but every choice she made was to help you be strong and happy."

His voice broke, because he knew that her final choice, her choice to party, sure as shit wasn't about Mason and his well-being. He looked around. A thousand eyes on him. He should have prepared something. If it had been him on that hillside, Ashley would have prepared something. Even in death, he was failing her.

Roman cleared his throat. "She loved everything about you, Mason. I hope you can hold on to that, and keep it forever. She'll always be with you. And so will I."

He went back to his chair and, as if the boy knew his father needed it, Mason climbed into Roman's lap and wrapped his arms and legs around him.

"I love you, Daddy," said the boy.

Roman bowed his head and let the tears flow.

CHAPTER TWENTY-FOUR

Roman never did come visit me in Hawaii. I understood; truly. The flight is crazy expensive, and it's a whole day of travel each way and he had school. What mattered most was that he supported me. I'd been in Adamsville two years without him—except for vacations, which went by so fast—and I was dreading another winter in the coffee shop; another winter subbing for more experienced yoga teachers. Another winter dithering over whether I wanted to get a degree. It was Roman who encouraged me to do something dramatic to break out of the funk I'd fallen into. One night I googled "free yoga retreat."

I called Roman the next day, giddy. "You help keep the place up. Cooking and laundry, cleaning, whatever. And they have yoga masters so you can add to your certification. I might even be able to teach at a studio on the island!"

He thought it was a great idea. All I had to do was get there and back. I had enough saved for a one-way ticket, with nearly $500 left over. Tara promised that if I got stranded or if the people at the retreat turned out to be sex freaks or Jesus freaks or Trumpers, she'd buy me a ticket home.

But the people at Kelai were awesome. It was mostly women and I hooked up with a girl from Michigan the third night; she was on her way home and I don't think anyone found out. After that, I decided I probably shouldn't entangle myself with people at the retreat. I was there to focus on myself, on building my practice, on experiencing the almost unbelievable beauty of this paradise you didn't even need a passport to visit. And then in February, Bryce sent me a DM saying that he'd be on the island for a shoot.

I hadn't seen him since graduation—since he went off to travel the world. We'd liked each other's posts on social media, but that was it. Why didn't I tell Roman? It's not a question I have a good answer for. I told him about everyone else—before and since. In fact, the first time I kissed Bella, I basically asked his permission. It was junior year and we'd started going to her house after school with Daniel and Matt and a rotating crew. I remember we were watching Pulp Fiction, and Bella got up and imitated Uma Thurman dancing. She had just buzzed her hair for the first time, and she was wearing a shirt that showed her belly ring, and baggy pants slung low with an enormous brass belt buckle she'd found at a thrift store. She was fully out as gay, finally. She was happy, among her friends. And she looked sexy as hell.

"I wanna kiss her," I whispered.

"Me, too," said Roman. "Is that weird?"

We giggled. Bella danced outside, and I followed her. I remember looking back at Roman; he was smiling, excited for me. I found her *lighting a cigarette—she smoked the skinny menthols—looking out over the water. I put my hand on her bare waist and pulled her to me. We intertwined our fingers and opened our mouths. I felt hungry for her. It you had tried to stop me from moving the kiss forward, from putting my hands on her breasts, from dragging her to one of the cracked plastic lawn chairs and pulling her shirt down and sucking on them, I'd have thrown you off like an animal. It felt like all I'd ever wanted. I put my hand down her pants and she came with a high-pitched sigh. Fluttering eyelashes, cheeks aflame. When we walked back into the house, we sat down, each on one side of Roman, flushed and happy. And we all laughed.*

But Bryce was a secret.

CHAPTER TWENTY-FIVE

Facing the crowd felt mildly freeing. And when Mason climbed off his lap and said he was hungry, Roman was ready to confront the people who had gathered. Specifically, he was ready to confront Bryce Lorimer, whom he'd seen near the back. But as he made his way through the crowd, Bryce seemed to have disappeared. He found Matt Biaggi on the sidewalk, vaping with Bella's cousin, Kevin.

"Did you see Bryce?" Roman asked.

Matt didn't answer immediately. He looked at Kevin.

"What?" said Roman. "I know he had a thing with Ash. I just want to talk to him."

"I think he took off," said Matt.

"How long has he been back in town?"

Matt shrugged. "He's back and forth from the city."

Roman had long suspected Ashley hooked up with Bryce in Hawaii. They were supposed to be open with each other—and she'd told him about other people—but for some reason, Bryce was an exception. Was he the only exception? Roman didn't know the details, and he might not have known at all had someone from her yoga retreat not tagged him and Ash in a group shot on the beach. Bryce Lorimer, six-foot-three and rail-thin, with sapphire-blue eyes and silky black curls, got scouted and scooped up by a modeling agency the spring of their senior year in high school. Everybody in town knew the story: he was busing tables at Captain Tom's along the river when a woman from Manhattan told him she could get him a thousand dollars for four hours' work in the city next weekend. He bit, and two months later he was gone. They saw it all on social media: the photo shoots in Miami and Milan and the Maldives. Swimming pools and movie stars. The airplanes, the alcohol, the fancy apartments overlooking cities across the globe; the greased-up abs and seemingly endless parade of beautiful faces and bodies beside him. It looked like a lot of fun. Had he just happened to be in Hawaii? Or had they been communicating and planned a trip? Roman didn't ask, and Ashley never told.

"Was he at Bella's the other night?" Roman asked.

"I didn't see him," said Matt. "But I wasn't there long."

"They found pills on her," said Roman. Matt's sunglasses hid any reaction. "They had fentanyl in them."

"Shit," said Matt.

"Any idea where she might have gotten them?"

Matt shook his head. "Maybe ask Bella."

"I'm asking you."

"I don't know, dude."

"You sure?"

"Yeah, I'm sure."

"I know she got Molly from you a couple months ago."

Matt took off his sunglasses. "Did you tell Felix that?"

"No."

"Good, because it's not true."

"That's not what Ash said."

"Well, then she was lying. I've been strictly weed and shrooms for years. I don't fuck with anything chemical. And this is exactly why. I'm really sorry, but I didn't give her anything. You're barking up the wrong tree."

"What tree should I be barking up?"

Matt put his sunglasses back on.

"Come on, man," pleaded Roman. "You were *there*."

"I didn't see any pills."

"But you know who's selling."

Matt sighed.

"What the fuck?" said Roman, suddenly buzzing with rage.

"Roman," said Kevin, putting a hand out to calm him. Roman swatted it away. People were now watching.

"You're really going to hold out on me? She's *dead*."

"I know. I'm really sorry."

"Then tell me what you know."

Matt looked at Roman with a mix of pity and mild panic.

"I'm gonna head out," he said, slipping his vape into one of the pockets on his cargo shorts. "I'm really sorry, man."

"Felix is going to find out where she got those pills," he called after Matt.

"I hope he does."

"No thanks to you, asshole!"

Matt shuffled off in his Birkenstocks, head down. Roman wanted to lunge after him, but when he turned around, he saw Mason, sitting at Tara's feet as she stood with Gary and Susan. They were all looking at him. Mason was holding a Popsicle; the cherry red covered his chin and ran down his hand. He didn't want his son to see him acting like a maniac.

"What do you want to know about Bryce?" asked Kevin, bringing Roman's attention back.

"Everything."

"He sells pills."

"Were he and Ash hooking up?"

"Yeah," said Kevin. "But Bella said it's been over for a while."

Over for a while. Could he have been more clueless?

"I thought he lived in Miami or something. How long has he been back in New York?"

Kevin shrugged. "My sense is that he's kind of always on the move. Bella says he's the guy who's, like, always at the bar or the club with whatever you need."

"Ash could have gotten the pills from him."

"Maybe, but not at Bella's. Bella doesn't like him."

"Did you see him at the party?"

"No," said Kevin. "I didn't come till late, but if he was there, he crashed. No way Bella would have invited him."

CHAPTER TWENTY-SIX

They walked home together. Mason wasn't crying anymore, but something seemed to have slipped out of the boy. Will, maybe. They crossed the street from the coffee shop and he just sat down. John picked him up and Roman walked behind, watching Mason, whose eyes were glassy, staring at the sidewalk below him, his mop of hair moving a little with each step.

Once at the house, Roman found he couldn't go inside. Not yet. They'd gone through the motions, said the public goodbyes, and now it was realer than ever. Ashley would never come home. The house would be quiet forever.

"I'll make brownies," said Tara, kneeling down to Mason as John set him on the porch chair. "Wanna help?"

"Can I watch TV?" the boy asked.

"Let's make the brownies first."

"I wanna watch TV."

Tara hesitated. "Okay, mister, that's fine."

Mason followed her into the house.

"You coming?" asked John.

"I need a minute," said Roman. "I'm gonna take a walk."

"You did good," said John.

Good? He'd gone where he was told, rambled something about loving Ashley, managed not to attack Matt. The bar was low for a young widower, he supposed. But the bar for being a dad had suddenly been raised so high he couldn't see it.

Roman walked toward the gas station. Maybe he'd get a soda. Or a forty-ounce and start drinking. Nobody would blame him. He kept his head down and his sunglasses on, avoiding eye contact with neighbors out walking dogs and accompanying kids on scooters. Nobody calls the widower rude if he doesn't wave back.

When he got to the gas station he spotted Matt inside, chatting with the clerk. He didn't want to talk to Matt. But, he realized, there was someone he did want to talk to.

A torn piece of yellow police tape was still tied to the tree beside Bella's driveway, flapping against the ground. Bella's car, a Mazda that had been her mom's, was parked beside the house. Roman knocked and knocked and after about a minute he saw movement. Bella opened the door. She was wearing gym shorts and a threadbare "I ♥ New York" T-shirt. The first thing she said was: "I didn't give her those pills."

"Okay."

"I don't care if you don't believe me. I know it's true."

"So, who did? Bryce?"

Bella looked mildly surprised. "Maybe."

"How much do you know about him?" Roman asked.

"How much do *you* know about him?"

"I know he visited her in Hawaii. And I know they were hooking up."

"She told you that?"

"No," said Roman.

Bella didn't press.

"So, what do you know about him?" he asked.

"He's a lowlife."

"Was he here that night?"

Bella hesitated.

"I'm going to find out," Roman said, raising his voice. He was angry, but he couldn't bring himself to puff up at Bella the way he had at Matt. It was strange, standing here again. He had loved this girl in the doorway. Eight years ago, she'd been beautiful to him. Her fingers always smeared with ink; the way she often covered her smile, embarrassed by the crooked teeth nobody ever bothered to fix. Bella wasn't radiant like Ash, but she was one of the only people Roman had ever met who never tried to be anything other than herself. Sometimes angry, sometimes weak, but always entirely Bella.

She and Roman and Ash formed a bond that last year in high school, each in a kind of mourning: Bella's mom dead and her dad absent; Ashley's mom fallen down a QAnon rabbit hole; and Roman, who'd just learned that his father had not, in fact, died in a car accident when he was two, but had killed himself by jumping off the very bridge they looked at from their front yard. Bella helped him figure out how to manage the feelings that came with knowing his father had decided he'd rather be dead than be his parent; or at least she tried. They'd both loved Ashley, and although there was definitely a time when Ash loved Bella, too, it didn't last. He watched Ashley pull away as Bella became more attached. Roman didn't ask Ash why she made the decision to break off her romantic involvement with Bella soon after he left for NYU. He was just happy he hadn't been the one she decided she was no longer in love with. And he couldn't really blame Bella for the mess her life seemed to have become in the years since. What would he have done if Ashley had decided that what they had was no longer worth keeping?

"Just tell me," Roman said again, quieter this time.

"Bryce was here."

"Why? Kevin said you hated him. You just said he was a lowlife."

"He is. He must have come because he knew Ash would be here. I didn't invite him, but I didn't, like, check IDs at the door."

"Did you see them together?"

Bella nodded.

"Were they using?"

"I didn't see that. I just saw them talking."

"When?"

"I don't know."

"Where?"

"Um, outside. I think." She looked uneasy.

"By the rock?"

"No. Wait. What are you asking?"

"I'm trying to figure out what happened."

"I don't know!" she screeched. "It's not my fault! I thought she left!"

"I didn't say it was your fault, Bella."

Bella blew a dramatic sigh. Then she lifted a middle finger.

"What the fuck?" said Roman.

But the finger, he realized, wasn't for him. He turned around and saw who it was for: neighbors. Since he'd walked down the steep driveway, two families had let their kids outside to get a run-around. Had they been watching Bella's house? He knew both families vaguely. Remembering people was part of his job, and he sometimes created little rhymes to help. Across the street and one over was Tech Guy Alex Dufry and his wife, Tan Anne; next to them was Old Tom Morris, the former vice principal at the high school, whose grandkids spent much of the summer in town, and who had spoken at every single school board meeting since Covid, freed after retirement to crusade against masks and critical race theory and anything that might smell of rainbow. Tom and Larry had a long-running feud as well, stemming from the fact that Larry had limited letters to the editor to 250 words back in 2015. How long would it take before Tom or Anne or Alex texted somebody—who would then text somebody else— that the borderline-unstable Gen Zer whose shitty little house was bringing down their property values is arguing on her front step with the local reporter whose girlfriend OD'd in the yard last week?

"Can I come in?"

CHAPTER TWENTY-SEVEN

The house was somewhat tidier than it had been the day he found Ash, but it still smelled faintly of urine and stale beer and mold.

"I'm sorry about coming to your house like that the other day," said Bella as soon as they were inside.

"It's okay," he said.

"I was really upset. I mean, I know you guys are, too. I just . . . Will you tell your mom I'm sorry?"

"Yeah," said Roman.

"And I know it's, like, the least of your worries right now, but having the cops here was really bad for me. Those assholes across the street have already filed two complaints against me. They've been here nine months."

Roman knew about the complaints because he'd rejected them both for the paper's police blotter. *Police were called to a house on Hudson View Street when a woman complained her neighbor was failing to properly secure her garbage, drawing racoons. Patrol reminded neighbor to cover her cans.* And: *Police were called to a house on Hudson View Street when a woman complained about marijuana smell coming from her neighbor's yard. Patrol reminded the woman that marijuana is legal.*

"Did your mom tell you about what happened after you took off?" asked Bella.

"She said some dude came screeching up. Do you know who it was? My mom and John didn't recognize him."

Bella didn't answer.

"Was it Bryce? Come on, I'll find out. I think our neighbor got the license plate."

"Fine. Yes."

"Why lie for him? Mom said he threatened you."

"I know! He's freaking out. A girl he sold to a couple months ago OD'd at a lake house in the Catskills. It was a different county, so I don't know if the cops here know about it, but obviously he wants to stay off the radar."

"So, he crashes his car onto our lawn and screams at you?"

"Right. I mean, he was probably high. Clearly, he wasn't thinking straight."

"Are you?"

"Are *you?*"

"No," said Roman, sighing. "I'm all fucked up."

Bella almost smiled. "Who isn't?"

"I have questions."

"Me, too," said Bella. "I really thought she'd left that night."

"What was going on with her? I didn't even know you two were hanging out."

Bella sat down.

"I saw her out in Newburgh a few months ago. March,

maybe? She asked how I was doing. I said I'd finished a comic book. I showed her some on my phone and she said you'd gone to school with someone in publishing. She was, like, I'll ask him about it."

Roman squinted. Ash had asked him—though she hadn't said it was about Bella—and he'd gotten angry at her. He remembered feeling attacked, like she was rubbing it in his face that he was a lowly small-town reporter while his sophomore-year roommate had become the youngest editor at his publishing house to hit one million sales. *Thrilled to announce that . . .* the post on LinkedIn read. Leon Palumbo plucked a graphic novel about a trans superhero out of the slush pile and now Disney was producing the first in a franchise— and Leon was an executive producer. Ash told him he was being ridiculous, but he couldn't let it go. He allowed her innocent question to ignite a cascade of shame. And when she asked why he was so upset, his sense of betrayal ballooned—how could she not know him?! They kept at it, digging at each other, until he left the room, walking away while she sobbed into her pillow.

Bella went on.

"Nothing came of it, but we started texting. She was supportive. She seemed happy."

"Was Bryce around?"

"Yeah," said Bella. "I didn't pretend to like him, but it wasn't really my business."

"But they broke up? Do you know why? Or when?"

"Maybe a month ago? Maybe two? I'm not sure. And I don't

know if there was a big reason. She probably just got tired of him. Or maybe he got tired of her."

"Did they use together a lot?"

"Every time I saw him he was high. I saw her do a couple lines here and there. And I know she'd sometimes take Molly."

"Do you know where she was getting it?"

"Bryce, I assumed."

"Felix said the baggie in her pocket was wiped clean."

"You talked to Felix?" Bella's leg started bouncing. "Did he say anything about me?"

"Just that you said you didn't give her the drugs."

"I didn't."

"Then don't worry about it."

"Easy for you to say. They *grilled* me. Felix came to my fucking job the day after. I didn't even know she was . . ." Bella couldn't say the word, apparently.

"Where were you that night? I stayed at your house till, like, midnight."

"I worked all day and had an early shift," she said. "There's a girl at work I'm kind of seeing. I went to her place and stayed over."

"And what, your phone ran out of juice? Nobody had a charger? We texted you about a million times."

"I was fucked up, okay? What do you want me to say? I went to work, I went to a friend's, I got high, and I fell asleep. I woke up and went back to work and fucking Felix shows up like I'm a fucking criminal." She sniffed. "The neighbors are *loving* this, by the way. You know, they're trying to run me out of town."

"Your mom left you this house, Bella. You own it."

"For now."

"What are you talking about?"

"Forget it."

Roman closed his eyes. He'd come here to talk about Ashley, who was *dead*, and somehow the conversation seemed to be veering toward a Bella pity-fest.

"Fine. What else did you tell Felix?" Roman asked.

"Just that Ash got here early that night, like around eight. I saw her drinking but that was it."

"Who was she hanging out with?"

"I don't know. Me, at first. Then Bryce. I didn't keep track."

"Do you remember the last time you saw her?"

"I think maybe nine? Or ten? I crashed late, like two or three. I just figured she left."

"Without saying goodbye?"

"I guess."

"Did you see Bryce after that?"

"I don't remember the timing. It's all kind of a blur."

"I want to talk to Bryce. Do you know where he lives?"

Bella snorted. "Ash said he was living with his grandma."

"Where's she?"

"Washington Arms. By the middle school."

Bella promised that if she remembered anything else about that night—anyone weird who was there—she'd text him. As he walked up her driveway, he encountered one of the town's three mail carriers. Paul Burrows was, Roman knew, two years past the official retirement age, but he'd held on to his route because he had a sick wife and, he said, he liked the exercise. Every day, Paul pushed his three-wheeled cart through Bella's neighborhood, his back bent but his pace steady. His white hair was long, often wild, sometimes tied in a ponytail.

"How you doing?" he said when he saw Roman.

"I've been better," said Roman. "How about you?"

"I'm real sorry about Ashley," he said. "I came to the service. It was a nice one."

"Thanks," said Roman. He hadn't noticed Paul. Who else hadn't he noticed?

"I know you and your mom'll take good care of that little boy," said Paul. "I know there's a lot of love in your house."

Roman wanted to ask how he knew, but decided to just smile and say, "Thanks."

Paul dug into his bag and brought out Bella's mail.

"How's she doing?" he said, nodding toward Bella's.

Roman shrugged.

"Must have been really scary, what happened," said Paul, referring, he assumed, to Ashley's death. Roman didn't mention that Bella had completely missed it. That she'd left her former friend and lover on a hillside while she got high with someone else. "That poor girl's been through the wringer."

Again, Roman decided to just smile and nod. "I'll take these to her," Roman said.

"Thanks," said Paul. "It's the hills that do me on this block."

"I hear you."

"Take good care," said Paul. "It's good to see you."

"You too, Paul," said Roman.

He walked back toward Bella's door to bring her the mail. It was a thin pile, just three pieces of paper, and two were junk mailers—one for a window company, one for lawn maintenance. The only personal piece looked official, almost like a paycheck. But it wasn't from Walmart. It was from something called WinGate, LLC, with an address in Albany. He pulled out his phone and took a picture of the envelope.

"I brought your mail," said Roman when Bella answered the door.

"Thanks," said Bella. "He's early today. I try to go up and greet him when I can. Dude needs to just retire. He's gonna have a fucking heart attack on one of these driveways someday."

"What's WinGate, LLC?" Roman asked.

"What?"

Roman pointed to the letter in her hand.

"None of your business," she said. And shut the door.

CHAPTER TWENTY-EIGHT

Roman looked up WinGate while walking to where Bryce's grandma lived, but didn't find much. The address, according to Google Earth, was an office building near the state capitol. Maybe something to do with her dad's airline pension. Or her mom's estate.

The Washington Arms complex was made up of three two-story buildings, each with a separate mailbox vestibule. Roman figured there was a fifty-fifty chance Bryce's grandma had the same last name as him, but he checked the name cards on the boxes in all three, and none were marked "Lorimer." His mom had described the car Bryce rode up in as a blue two-door, with a spoiler and a pinstripe; nothing like that was in the parking lot. He needed a better plan. His best bet, he decided, was online, so he went back home, marched upstairs to their apartment, and dug Ashley's laptop out of her bag.

The laptop was Ashley's lifeline during Covid. When Mason was about nine months old and she was physically healed from the emergency caesarean, the therapist they'd insisted she start seeing—virtually, of course—told her she needed to reconnect with yoga, and other people. But there were still no vaccines. More than half a million people were dead and there was no end in sight. People were starting to talk about "variants." So one afternoon Ash set her laptop on the coffee table and recorded herself talking through a yoga session. A simple series of sun salutations. She logged on to YouTube, created an account called Yoga for Joy, and uploaded the fifteen-minute video. She did the same thing the next day. And the next. By Easter, she had more than a thousand followers. She changed the settings that summer, allowing for access to extra content—Yoga for Moms; Yoga for Pregnancy; Yoga for Anxiety—for a monthly $10 subscription fee. By Halloween, more than $30,000 had flowed into her PayPal account. By Valentine's Day, it was nearly double. A real job, in the living room.

But by then, Ash was restless. With Mason and the depression and Covid, she'd been inside for nearly two years. Roman and John got out of the house for work, but Tara forbid any nonessential indoor activities for anyone until Mason could be vaccinated. There were lots of angry discussions, but it always came down to the same thing: Mason's health was the most important thing. If you disputed that, were you even fit to care for him? But when Mason's vaccination dates came and went, Tara's arguments changed. She'd been reading more about long Covid, about blood vessels and lung complications for males under four years old.

"It doesn't prevent infection," Tara argued. "I still think we need to do everything we can to keep him from getting it."

Privately, Roman and Ash agreed that they were going to break his mom's rules. For a little while, it was fun, sneaking around behind Tara's back again. When she asked, they assured her the bar or restaurant or venue they were headed to had a backyard and enough room to socially distance. Did she believe them? If she didn't, she never said. Neither worried about their activities being revealed online, since they rarely posted on social media if it wasn't work-related. Both disdained Tara's near-daily "Look at me" Facebook posts. "Look at me with my grandson on the trail!" "Look at me working out!" "Look at me masking in the library!" "Look at me in the community garden!" "Look at me remembering to get my mammogram!" When Ash did her yoga videos, she said "you." "Give yourself a warm smile for showing up to practice today." "You made it. Follow your body today." "We'll end seated or lying down today. It's your choice."

But the thrill of emerging from lockdown together faded quickly. They had an argument about paying for drinks one night and the magic vanished. Before Mason, they rarely argued. Before Mason, they gave each other the benefit of the doubt. But since they'd become parents, tiny slights became attacks; tone enraged. Most days Roman managed to feel aggrieved by something at home, and he sensed the same from her.

Late in the summer of 2022, Ashley started teaching yoga in person again. She didn't ask permission, she just came home one day and told them that she'd be teaching Saturday mornings at a studio in town—the studio her high school mentor Chris Aldrich owned.

"Why?" Tara demanded. "You make enough money with the YouTube channel."

"It's not about money," said Ashley. "I need to be out in the world. It's not healthy for my whole life to revolve around this house."

"What about Mason?"

"What about Mason?"

"Did you even think about him? Did you even think about the risk you're adding to his life?"

Roman remembers seeing rage flash in Ashley's eyes. He knew she probably wanted to scream, *Of course I thought about Mason! He's my son!* But he also knew that she was working hard to manage her feelings and their expression. Her mother had been a screamer. Ashley used to say she'd rather get grounded for a month than endure one of Kelly's adult-sized tantrums, and she'd promised herself she wouldn't subject Mason to that. So when Tara questioned whether she'd thought about her son, she stepped away rather than risk slipping into the fury Roman could tell she felt.

That night in bed, Ash asked him what he thought it meant that she'd rather teach yoga than take care of Mason.

"I could take over," she said. "Tara could get a job."

"That's true," he said.

"But I don't want to."

"I know," he said. "I don't either."

"I love him. I love him more than I've ever loved anything. But . . ."

"You don't have to convince me," Roman filled in when she

trailed off. He knew that neither of them wanted to say the words: it's boring. Caring for a toddler is boring and tedious and annoying and exhausting. It's thankless. It's uncreative. It had gotten a little better since Mason started talking, but those first two years, just carrying him or following him around, having to entertain him, stimulate him, remember a thousand tiny stupid but somehow important things that he needed or needed to stay away from. For hours and hours and hours. Stack the blocks and bang the spoons and read this shitty book again and again and again. Somehow, Tara genuinely loved it. She was good at it. They didn't. They weren't.

It should have—could have—been a happy situation. It takes a village, right? All the articles said the nuclear family was toxic and isolating and created an unnecessary burden on the biological parents, especially the mother. But not in their house. In their house there were three generations! In their house, they shared the burdens: Roman's work provided a steady paycheck. John's income was often in cash, and they never had to call a plumber or a carpenter or a mechanic or even a landscaper. Ashley cooked and cleaned and shopped and her income was growing; just before she died, it had surpassed Roman's. And Tara took care of Mason.

Not even a week after the yoga class argument, Tara started coughing. The swab confirmed Covid and it spread to everyone in the house. Tara and John were the sickest: two days of fever and lingering exhaustion that limited John's ability to work for several weeks, but nobody needed to be hospitalized, and Mason's only symptom was a two-day cough. The seal was broken.

Ashley added more live yoga classes to her schedule, and each morning she opened her laptop and recorded a session for the people online. Roman didn't have her phone, so he couldn't get her texts, but maybe there was some clue in her computer.

He plugged in the machine, which had run its battery down in the week since she'd died, and it booted up to the lock screen. Username: ashblonde98. He typed the password she'd used for years: alohaSunshine! Incorrect. He tried it again. Incorrect. He tried her Instagram. Also incorrect. Ashley had changed her passwords.

CHAPTER TWENTY-NINE

Roman set the laptop on the floor and curled up on the sofa, but his brain wouldn't let him sleep. After a while, he sat up and started making self-flagellating attempts at new passwords: *brycelorimer* and *ilovebryce*. Incorrect. And now he was locked out. He pulled out his phone. He'd avoided all social apps and most text messages since finding Ashley, and his notifications were in the hundreds. He ignored them, and opened Instagram, clicked into her account, which was almost entirely yoga. Videos and stills and occasionally a text "inspiration." Ashley's last post was that Friday morning, day seven of an ongoing series called Breathe, which focused on opening up the body to allow for deeper breathing. The play arrow covered her face. He pressed it.

"Good morning," said Ash, greeting her class with a warm smile. "Welcome to Day 7—lucky 7—of Breathe. Let's get started." A little music and the video ended. The tease for free on Instagram, click the link in her bio to go to her YouTube page. He clicked another post, and another. "Good morning," she said, over and over. "Welcome." "Aloha." His heart swelled in his chest; swelled and smarted like a blister; like it had been stung by a wasp. He wanted to scream at the screen, but instead he clicked on her YouTube channel and let her talk him through a yoga class. And then another. After an hour his eyes started to burn. He clicked back to Instagram. Should he start reading all the comments? Check if Bryce was liking her posts? He zoomed in, looking at her eyes. Was she high? Did she have a problem he didn't know about?

Downstairs, Mason and John were watching TV.

"Where's Mom?" Roman asked.

"She went to the store."

Roman put his hand on Mason's head. "How you doing?"

"Okay," said Mason quietly, not moving his eyes from the screen.

John got up. "You need anything, mister?"

"No."

"Me and John are gonna talk for a minute," said Roman. "Maybe we can watch something together after?"

No response.

In the kitchen, Roman told John what he'd learned about Bryce.

"Did you know?" asked Roman.

"About him and Ash? No. But listen, I want to be honest, I do know Bryce a little."

"Really?"

John exhaled. He was nervous. "Look, you know, sometimes I like to party. I mean, way less often since I've been with your mom. Couple, three times a year. At the most. But right after my divorce, it was more. I was messed up. I was pissed. I'd take a bump and, you know, have some fun. Forget for a couple hours."

"I don't care." John's face fell. *Shit. That sounded rude.* "I mean, it's fine. You don't have to explain yourself to me."

"Right," said John, "but it's not something your mom likes. I don't want her to think—"

"My mom gives you shit about drugs? Are you kidding me?"

"She doesn't give me shit, Roman." John's tone irritated him; he was talking to him like he was a child. "It's just not something I want her to think I'm big into. When I moved in she was clear she didn't want that stuff around Mason."

"You're not using *in front* of him."

"Roman, we're off track here. This isn't about your mom."

"You think she's a saint. You weren't around when I was young. She has *no* leg to stand on about being fucked up around kids."

"I know she's not a saint. Nobody is. And I know she made a lot of mistakes. But again, that's not what we're talking about. You asked about Bryce. So I told you something I know, which is that that's his scene. Drugs. I still see the guys I used to party with and some of them buy from him now. If he and Ashley were hanging out, that's probably where she got the drugs. All I'm saying is that I'd rather you not mention to your mom that I still indulge occasionally."

"Right, sorry. Understood."

"Thanks."

"Bryce came to the memorial but ducked out," said Roman. "Bella says he's been crashing with his grandma at the Washington Arms, but I don't know her name."

"Have you checked his social media?"

"No," said Roman. *Duh.* His brain really wasn't working very well. "That's a good idea."

Roman unlocked his phone. At some point, possibly in college, he'd followed Bryce, but he never liked his posts so the algorithm had stopped serving them much. He searched "Bryce" on Instagram and up popped the verified account: *BryFliesHigh.* Roman scrolled. The account was a mix of stills and video. The first several pinned posts were glamor shots: Bryce on a runway; Bryce by an infinity pool with some pristine body of water in the background; Bryce brooding in an unbuttoned shirt. They were all more than two years old. The more recent were less spectacularly attractive, but still staged. Lots of images of alcohol; portraits in low light, neon smearing behind. The captions were an accounting of where he was and who he was with, and while his official account location was New York City, the check-ins were mostly along the Hudson River: Haverstraw and Peekskill and Newburgh and Beacon and Kingston and Poughkeepsie. Bryce got around. Was Ashley really into this? Tuesday night parties and sloppy selfies?

Bryce's last post was from the night Ash died, a whole week ago. At six p.m. he'd posted a selfie flashing a peace sign in front of a poster advertising "Sunday Spun-Day" at a bar in Newburgh: "Two for one shots and my boy @CougarBrasi on the turntables every Sunday until Labor Day!"

"Tomorrow's Sunday," said John.

"Let's do it."

CHAPTER THIRTY

The next afternoon, Roman and John drove to the waterfront for Sunday Spun-Day. They paid the $10 cover and got their drink tickets and split up, scanning for Bryce's curly black mop. The Roadhouse was a BBQ restaurant on the waterfront with ten thousand square feet of picnic tables. There were three bars; two had a threesome of elevated televisions going. Roman saw the Mets; he saw the Cubs; he saw European motorcycle racing and bass fishing. It was two-deep at the bars, but the tables were sparsely populated. A few families out for brunch. Roman spotted a boy Mason's age running around the empty tables with a girl who appeared to be a little older. Tara and Ash didn't let Mason do that. It was one of the things they agreed on: the boy needed manners, and a restaurant wasn't a playground.

The kids were outnumbered by the people there to party in the summer sun. It was a mixed-race and, nominally, mixed-age group. Twenty- and thirtysomethings flirting, enjoying a few hours away from kids, if they had them. And there were people his mom and John's age, working on second belly rolls and second—or third—spouses. Ash loved a boozy brunch before she had Mason. Even when she was pregnant, she'd tag along, order a mocktail, and rub her belly and laugh at the girls stumbling on heels to the bathroom. The DJ was set up in a corner, headphones huge over his ears, dancing with himself. A banner hung across the front of the turntable with a QR code and a URL and the words "Hire DJ Cougar Brasi For Your Next Event" printed in faux wild-style graffiti. John and Roman each walked the space several times, checked the bathrooms, the alley behind the kitchen, the promenade outside the gates. They took turns walking all the way to the docks and back. But Bryce was nowhere. And none of the people they asked had seen him.

They drove home at sundown, when the DJ packed it in. Both were over the limit, but it was a stretch of five miles they'd driven literally thousands of times. They knew most of the cops likely to pull them over, and, two days after Ashley's memorial, it seemed likely that even the chief might give them a pass.

Tara was putting Mason to sleep when they stumbled through the kitchen door. Roman went to the bathroom for Excedrin and John went to the fridge for two cold beers. When Tara came downstairs, they told her they'd struck out looking for Bryce.

"Maybe switch to coffee," she said, pulling a tin of grounds from the cabinet. "Felix is on his way."

Ten minutes later, Felix knocked at the kitchen door. Tara offered him coffee and he declined but took a glass of water while Roman explained where they'd been all day.

"If Bryce gave her the drugs that killed her, I want him to tell me to my face," he said.

"I can understand that," said Felix, "but that's why I'm here. We got the toxicology report back. Ashley didn't have drugs in her system. No Percocet, no fentanyl. And her blood alcohol was only slightly elevated."

"So, she didn't OD," said Roman.

"No," said Felix.

"Then what happened?"

"I don't know. She did have a pretty significant wound on her head." He put his hand on the back of his own skull and patted it. "About here. We won't know if it was enough to actually kill her until after the autopsy."

"What's the holdup?" asked Roman.

"The ME's office is short-staffed," said Felix. "They're working through a backlog. And, frankly, while it looked like an OD, it wasn't a priority."

"But this will bump it up, right?" John said.

"Maybe," said Felix. "But it's not going to tell us everything. Did she die because she hit her head? Maybe. But why did she hit her head? On what? There's been rain so it's unlikely we would be able to find blood on the cliffside, though we can look. But even that . . . Did she trip and fall? Was she being careless? Was she pushed? Was the push an accident? Like, was she over there just messing around with someone and . . . something happened?"

Roman didn't know what to say. Neither, it seemed, did Tara nor John.

"I will make sure the ME knows we need this done, but," he paused, "you may need to exert some pressure yourself."

"On who?" asked Roman.

Felix sighed.

"We get calls for bodies in town once or twice a month. Often it's a senior. Someone who died at home. And these days there are more overdoses. So, we go, we take a look around. Look for what might have happened that could explain how this person ended up there. We start creating a story. Is there a needle nearby? Or pills or powder? That tells a certain story. Does the person live alone? Does it seem like there was some struggle? That kind of thing. We look for medication. Are there pills for heart disease? Or antidepressants? More pieces of a story. We take pictures. We call the family.

"Usually, when I get to a scene, I get a sense if something's wrong." He rubbed his forearm with his hand. "Goose bumps. It looks like one thing, but feels like another. Best I can describe it."

He paused. "When I saw Ashley on that hill, I got goose bumps. I don't know why, but it didn't seem right."

"What didn't seem right?" asked Tara.

"I wish I could say exactly," said Felix. "Maybe it's because I didn't really know her. Not like Chief and Scott did. They saw a house where they knew people used drugs. They get there and there's clearly been a party. Did you know they'd gotten a noise complaint that night?"

"No," said Roman.

"A neighbor called and Scott rolled by, but apparently things had quieted down." Felix looked at Roman. "It probably won't surprise you to learn that I got more than one message about your visit to Bella's yesterday."

"Mine? Why?"

"The neighbors really don't like her."

"Fucking assholes," said John. "His partner is dead and they're spying on him?"

"More like spying on Bella," said Felix. "But the point is that Chief and Scott are thinking one thing: drug party, drug overdose. They find drugs in her pocket. They know she's had mental health struggles . . ."

"Who hasn't?" said Roman. "She didn't, like, hurl herself off the hillside. She was healthy. She was . . ." He paused. Was he going to try to convince Felix she was happy? "She wouldn't leave Mason."

"That's not what I'm saying," said Felix. "I'm saying these are the things they saw when they got there. They know her history, and it includes drugs. They know about your dad . . ."

"Again, totally irrelevant," said Roman. "That was twenty years ago. And he wasn't *her* dad."

"I know. I'm not arguing with you. Look, we did the right things when we found her. We bagged her hands. We took pictures. But we didn't treat it like a crime scene, not really. She could have fallen ten minutes before you found her or ten hours. We didn't do a body temp. And we didn't do a thorough search of the hillside. We still haven't. Her phone and wallet are missing. So is the one shoe. But even if we find them now, it's not the same as if we'd found them that evening."

The kitchen fell silent.

"You said crime scene," Tara said. "Do you think someone killed her? Like, on purpose?"

"I think it's possible. Right now, I don't have a good answer for why she ended up down that hill. I think we have to look into it."

"So, why are you here instead of the chief?" asked Roman.

Felix shifted in his seat. "He's out of town. At a conference."

"Does he know about all this?"

"He knows that Ashley's tox came back clean. I talked to him a couple hours ago."

"And? What does he think?"

Felix sighed. "I don't know."

"What about Scott?" asked John.

"He's still pretty stuck on the OD."

"But she was clean," Roman said.

"Labs *can* make mistakes."

"He thinks it's a mistake?"

"He does."

"But you don't," said John.

"I don't," said Felix. "But I'm the new guy. Technically, I out-rank Scott, but the chief sets the agenda. Which is part of why I'm here. If you want this looked into, you need to think about applying a little bit of pressure."

"When does the chief get back?" asked Tara.

"Day after tomorrow."

"What are you going to do in the meantime?" asked Roman.

"With your permission, I'd like to ask a judge for a warrant to get her cell phone data. Even without the phone itself, we should be able to see whatever is backed up to the cloud. And maybe get some clarity on her movements that night."

"Do it," said Roman.

"Great," he said. "I'd also like to start conducting some interviews."

"Good," said Roman.

"And I'd like to start with each of you."

CHAPTER THIRTY-ONE

Roman understood, as he walked to the police station the next morning, that if the police thought someone had killed Ashley, he would be the first suspect. He planned to tell Felix what he knew about Bryce, but he also knew he had to tell the truth: that the night she died, he was in Manhattan with a woman he'd been infatuated with since college.

Roman didn't tell Ash about Emily when he first met the redhead from Connecticut. Hooking up with other people was expected; it was part of what he and Ash had since almost the beginning. *We're ethical sluts!* They were so young and sex was new and fun and no one they dabbled with ever seemed to undermine how they felt about each other. Until Emily. Somehow he knew, even back then, that if Ashley asked him questions about Emily he wouldn't be able to play like it was no big deal. For six months during his junior year—from the moment she was assigned to edit his feature story on the food pantry for students, to the day he told her he loved her and she left for law school in North Carolina anyway—it was a very big deal. But once it was over and she was gone, it made no sense to confess. It was over. She was gone.

And then, four months ago, Emily came back. According to her social accounts, she'd been in the city almost a year, working as a lawyer at a firm in midtown. The kind of place where women still wore panty hose to the office. He knew this particular detail because Emily had posted about it. Posted her legs in the panty hose, in fact. She worked fifteen-hour days and lived in a studio apartment on the Upper East Side and, on the first day of March, after five years, she sent him a text.

> Are you ever in the city?

He wasn't much, but. They met at the bar where they'd had their first kiss—her choice. He got there before her and downed a beer, shredding the paper label as he realized that if she wanted to take him home, he would go. He'd told Ash he was going to the city at the request of one of his former professors. *She wants me to talk about my career.* It was a lie. He graduated with kids who were at *The New York Times*; he was nobody to his alma mater. But Ashley didn't know that. Or if she did, she didn't say.

"Your hair is longer," Emily said after she sat down, hanging her soft leather briefcase on the hook beneath the bar, adjusting her blue skirt. Roman swept the bits of wrapper—his anxiety made visible—into a hand and stuffed them in his pants pocket. Had he agonized over what he'd wear? Yes. He'd gained ten pounds since they'd last seen each other. But he chose a pair of pants he knew fit well and hoped that if they got to where she'd actually see his body it would be dark and he would distract her from the extra weight with all the tricks he'd learned with Ashley since college.

"Yeah," he said, tucking a strand behind his ear. He almost said, *Ash likes it long*, because that was, in fact, why he hadn't cut it in a year. But he caught himself. He wasn't certain he wanted to complicate his life by bringing Emily back into it, but he wasn't certain he didn't, either. Mentioning Ashley seemed a sure way to shut that door before Emily even put her hand on the handle.

"I like it," she said. She ordered a glass of wine and he motioned for another beer. "I can't believe it's been five years. You look the same."

"You, too," he said. "Except for the outfit."

"Occupational hazard," she said. "I don't put on a bra all weekend to make up for it."

He smiled. That was flirting, wasn't it?

"So, what's up?" he asked. "What made you reach out?"

Roman thought he knew the answer—social media indicated she was no longer with the boyfriend from law school—but he wanted to see what she would say.

"Oh, I don't know," she said, stroking the stem of her wineglass. "Just curious, I guess. You're very mysterious online."

"Mysterious?"

"You don't post. I didn't even know you had a kid until, like, a month ago."

"Yeah," said Roman, "you know me. I've never been big on social."

"Do you even have a Twitter? Or sorry, X."

Roman nodded. "But I don't really post."

"But you're reporting, right? All the journalists I know are still hanging on."

"Facebook is bigger where I am," he said, "I mean, for connecting with sources and stuff."

"You're back upstate?"

"Hudson Valley."

"Right. Do you like it? Everybody talks about hyper-local now."

What should he say? "It's a lot of work," he said. "But I get to write about things people really care about. And I can freelance, so that's cool." Could she tell it was total bullshit? Did she care?

"Cool," she said. "Did you ever meet my brother? Will?"

"No."

"He's older than me. He's at *The Atlantic*. He got an MBA and now he does their business and tech coverage. If you ever want a connection there."

"Thanks," he said.

Emily finished her wine.

"I followed your wife. On Instagram."

"Ash? We're not married."

"Oh, sorry. Girlfriend."

"Why?"

"I guess I was stalking you a little."

"Stalking me?"

Emily shrugged. "You know, just being nostalgic, I guess. What could have been. Are you guys still . . ." Emily seemed to want him to finish the sentence for her. Are you still in an open relationship? Can we hook up? But he needed her to say it. If she said it, he wasn't the one asking; he was only responding. "Do you still see other people?"

They made out fiercely in a vestibule on Eighth Street in the late winter cold. Tongues and hands and heavy breathing. She didn't invite him back to her place, and he'd caught the last train home electric with the residue of her. His dick so hard he had to jerk off in the bathroom at Grand Central. Like a freak. But the excitement, the rush, the *need* she created in him was so intoxicating, so deeply pleasurable, he knew he'd go back for more. And he did. For almost five months he'd gone into the city every chance he got so he and Emily could fuck like rabbits: rabbits without a child to raise together; rabbits who didn't share a bathroom; rabbits who'd never once had a discussion about the garbage or the groceries or pre-K or their life in the town they couldn't seem to leave.

Last Friday night, when Ashley thought he was staying at a friend's after a birthday party—when she might have been dead already—Emily floated the idea of Roman moving to the city.

"You're obviously not happy up there," she said. "You could stay here for the rest of the summer. Look for a place. See how you like it."

What tortured him now, and what he did not tell Felix, was that he considered it. He looked at her and a truth flashed through his mind: parents leave their kids all the time. Dads leave, moms leave. Ashley's dad never lived with them. John didn't live with his kids. Bella's dad was gone. Tara and Ash managed basically everything about Mason. His son was four years old and Roman still didn't have a car seat in his car. He'd never accompanied Mason to the pediatrician. Shit, if you'd asked him what size shoe the boy wore he'd have to guess. Roman looked at Emily and imagined what it would be like to be free; to live like all his college friends in Brooklyn and Queens: going to bars and seeing shows and sleeping through weekends and taking a different woman home to a single bed in a shared apartment every night.

It was the idea of the apartment that disrupted the fantasy. He'd never be able to afford a place he could bring Mason to, and in that moment he understood that the part of him that was tethered to his son and his son's mother was the best part of him. He'd neglected it, but it was stronger than anything else in his life. It was the only thing that mattered.

Roman stood up abruptly, startling Emily.

"I have to go." He looked around for his clothes. What time was it? He knocked into the coffee table, winced, bent down for his pants and boxers.

"What are you doing?"

"I have a family."

"I know," said Emily. "What did I say? You don't have to move. I was just offering. I was just—"

"I don't love you," he said. "This was stupid."

"Roman. Wait—"

"I'm sorry," he said, pulling on his shirt. "I have to go."

It was midnight. His car was parked six blocks south. All he wanted was to be home, but what would he say when he slid into bed in the middle of the night? It was nearly impossible for him to lie to Ashley's face. He texted a couple people and an hour later he was in Koreatown pounding shots and watching one of his former roommates and his colleagues at some green energy start-up sing progressively more embarrassing karaoke. When a guy got up to sing "Bad Romance," Roman started to cry.

Things went downhill from there. He vomited on a girl's purse and shoved the guy who gave him shit about it. His old roommate, Rico, took him outside and as they walked, Roman clutched Rico openly, blubbering and babbling that he was a loser who didn't deserve anyone's love. That he was worse than his own father and maybe he should kill himself, too. Another friend might have called Ash, but Rico didn't. Instead, he ordered an Uber and offered Roman a place to crash. But Roman declined.

He walked uptown. At three in the morning traffic was light and he made his way through crosswalk after crosswalk. He took a wild, splashing piss beside one of the temporary dining structures erected along First Avenue during the pandemic and somehow managed to locate his car. He collapsed in the backseat. The alcohol rendered him unconscious, and then soon after sunup woke him with a blazing headache. He opened his eyes and watched the men and women scurrying along the sidewalks; always somewhere to go, even early on a Saturday. Electric bicycles zoomed and buses honked and brakes squealed and trucks reversed. He needed to get back to Ashley and Mason and tell them that he loved them. He wasn't happy, but that wasn't their fault. On the drive home, while Ashley lay dead against a tree, he felt as sorry for himself as he ever had. Why couldn't he be what he was supposed to be? Why was his life so fucking small?

It disgusted him, thinking about it all now. Laying it out for Felix. Now that his life—his son's life—was truly, irreparably diminished. Without Ash they were a tiny fraction of what they'd been. He was a pathetic cliché in every possible way—except maybe one: he did not kill his son's mother. But he'd probably have to prove that.

"I'd like to talk to Emily," said Felix. "And Rico."

Roman gave him their contacts. Emily had texted since, but he'd ignored her—just like he'd ignored pretty much every other communication that had come his way since he'd found Ashley.

"Did you see anyone you know after you left your friends?"

"No," said Roman, his stomach churning. All those hours passed out in his own car; no alibi in sight.

"What do you think happened?" he asked Felix after he'd spilled his stupid secret. "Do you really think somebody killed her?"

"I think it's possible."

Roman thought about Ashley on their rock that night. Did someone sneak up and startle her? It wouldn't have taken any strength, really, if she'd been surprised. The drop-off is steep; all she'd need was a shove.

A story began to form in Roman's mind: Bryce Lorimer comes back to town. Shows Ash the excitement she was craving in her life with a depressed, cheating spouse and the child whose birth had nearly killed her and who now basically thought of his grandmother as his mom. But it's too much drama. She breaks it off. Bryce won't accept it. He tries to get her back; she rebuffs him; he kills her. He'd literally watched this story on *Investigation Discovery*. More than once. It was so fucking seedy. And now it was his life.

CHAPTER THIRTY-TWO

Tara told Felix what she hadn't yet told Roman: she knew Ashley had been seeing Bryce.

"She told you?" Felix asked.

"Just a few days before she died, Mason and I came home and she was sitting in the front seat of her car, crying," said Tara. "I told Mason to go inside and I asked her what was going on. She said she'd broken it off, but that he wouldn't stop bothering her. She said she'd made a big mistake hooking up with him. That he was more into drugs than she realized. I got the sense she felt stupid. Like she should have known better."

"Was she afraid of him?"

"She didn't say that, but now that I think about it, she probably wouldn't have wanted me to know if she was."

"Why not?"

"Because she knew I'd worry for Mason. If some tweaked-out drug dealer is after his mother, he's in danger." She told Felix about Bryce coming to their house the other day, threatening Bella.

"What did he say, specifically?" Felix asked.

"I don't remember exactly. Something about Bella not answering her phone, I think. Have you talked to her?"

"I have," said Felix. Tara waited for him to say more, but he didn't.

"Ash asked me not to tell Roman about Bryce," she continued. "She was really adamant about that. Which was kind of weird."

"Why?"

"Because they have an 'open' relationship. They always have."

"Open?"

"They're supposed to be able to hook up with other people. As long as they're honest about it. It's been like that since high school. Have you ever heard of the book *The Ethical Slut*?"

"I'm sorry to say I have."

Felix smiled in a way that reminded her of a thought she'd had before: the new town cop was hot. He was her age. He was single; divorced, she'd heard. But she was committed to John, and it would never be more than a romp; she wasn't going to actually date a cop. Still, when he leaned back slightly, shaking his head at the idea of an open relationship—with an expression that made her think he might have tried it—she shifted in her seat, unable to suppress a smile. Fucking chemistry.

"If you can believe it, one of them found that book in the library."

"The school library?"

Tara laughed. "No. Apparently it was tucked in nonfiction at the local branch."

"That doesn't usually work for very long," he said.

"So I hear," she said. "But as far as I knew it was still the deal."

"Was Roman seeing anyone?"

She took a breath. "Did you ask him that?"

"I did."

"I suspected he was," Tara said. "John and I both did. But I didn't want to pry. Did he say who it was? Or for how long?"

"Someone he knew from college. But he says he broke it off the night Ashley died."

"The night she died?" Tara thought back. Right; he had been in the city.

"He said she asked him to move in and he realized he'd made a big mistake. He told her he didn't love her and left. Slept in his car."

"Did Roman know about Bryce?"

"He says he didn't," said Felix. "He says it wasn't until he saw Bryce at the service that he remembered suspecting that him and Ashley hooked up a few years ago. When she was in Hawaii."

"That I didn't know."

"Why do you think they didn't tell each other?"

"I don't know," she said. "They've got a lot more to lose now, with Mason."

"Right."

"Ashley went through a really tough time after having Mason," said Tara. "He was born during Covid and she almost died during the delivery. She was alone in the hospital and it really fucked her up. At first, she was healing—physically, I mean. And then . . . she just stayed in bed. For like, months, we had to take care of her. None of us could count on her for anything. It was hard. And Roman got impatient. He struggled, too, I think, but he got up and went to work and did what he had to do. They had a big fight and she promised to do more, but then we found out she was using Adderall. And then they had another fight because she said she was only taking the Adderall because we told her she had to do more and she didn't have any energy without it.

"Finally, she got things sorted out with a therapist. Got on an antidepressant that worked. Things got better, but it was always there. Not far from the surface. If Roman found out she was with a guy like Bryce, who was into drugs, he'd be pissed."

"What do you know about Bryce?"

"Not much," said Tara. "He was in Ash and Roman's class in school but he wasn't part of their group. I have a vague memory of them talking about him going off to model after graduation. But I hadn't heard his name again until that night I found her crying. Me and John looked him up on social media, so we could get a sense of what we were dealing with. I'm a little bit of a worrier, especially about Mason. But he seemed kind of like a poser. You know?"

"What about when he came to your house? How did he seem then?"

"Angry. Desperate."

"But you didn't call us about it."

"I didn't," she said. "It was the day after Ash died. Right after, we had to tell Mason. It just . . . it didn't happen. I'm surprised one of the neighbors didn't call."

"Oh, they did."

"Keith?"

"And the Larkins."

Tara rolled her eyes. "Did Keith tell you he pulled a gun on Bryce?"

Felix raised his eyebrow. "He did not."

"They're so fucking concerned, but neither family has said a word since Ash died. No card. No fucking casserole."

"I'm sorry." Felix paused. "How is Mason doing?"

"Not great," she said. "Lots of TV."

"I can't imagine what it's like to lose your mom at that age."

"I know," Tara whispered. She looked at the ceiling in a futile attempt to roll back the tears that were coming. "I'm scared for him. I'm so scared he'll never get over it."

"Ashley had a yoga channel online, right?" asked Felix, mercifully, perhaps, trying to steer her back to mundane details. "So did she take care of Mason most of the time?"

"No," said Tara, sniffing, wiping her nose with the back of her hand. "I mean, sometimes, yeah. But I'm sort of his primary caregiver. Like I said, she was really sick after he was born. She just wasn't equipped to do all the stuff you need to do to care for a baby. Neither was Roman, frankly. Larry kept him working. So I stepped in."

"It must have been tough."

"Not really," said Tara. "I'd done it before. I'd been managing the Boathouse before lockdown, but that was closed all spring, and we couldn't have Airbnbers, so I literally had nothing else to do."

Felix took all this in. "Was it ever a source of stress?"

"What do you mean?"

"Well, things with caretaking can be tricky. Kids play favorites."

Tara shifted in her seat. "We did our best."

"You two ever butt heads?"

"Me and Ashley?"

Felix nodded.

"Sometimes. She wasn't as cautious about Covid as I was. People thought I was crazy for masking so long, but it's not like we were living in a bubble. We went all kinds of places. We just didn't take risks we didn't need to. We still don't. When the numbers go up, we mask in crowded spaces."

"When you say 'we,'" he asked, "you're referring to you and Mason?"

"When I'm with him, yeah. Which is most of the time." Was he implying something? "It's not a big deal. Everybody is obsessed with getting back to normal, but normal changed. I know two people my age who can barely walk up a flight of stairs because of long Covid. And there's just no way to know what having it multiple times does long-term to kids."

"You don't have to convince me," said Felix.

Tara took a breath. "Right."

"What else did you argue about?"

"I didn't kill Ashley, Felix."

"I'm not saying you did. I'm trying to figure out what was going on in her life. Who she trusted. What she worried about. If she was feeling stressed or unhappy, that matters. You've already told me she sought some kinds of comfort outside the family. Something she maybe regretted."

"I'm not responsible for that."

"No one is saying you are." He waited. "You said she'd gone through depression. Did she ever attempt suicide?"

"No," she said. It was the truth, as far as she knew.

"Is there anything else I should know? Anything else going on with her? Anything that seemed strange or off?"

"What seems off is this Bryce guy. Roman and John tried to find him and couldn't. He hasn't posted on social media in like a week. It seems like he's somebody you should talk to."

"Oh, I will," said Felix.

CHAPTER THIRTY-THREE

Tara left the police station and called John.

"Felix wants to talk to you next," she said. "Is Roman still there?"

"Yeah, but I think he's asleep."

"Okay," she said. "I'll be home in five."

John met her on the front porch.

"We read a little and tried a puzzle, but Mase just wants to watch TV."

"I guess it's gonna take time," she said.

"How'd it go?"

"Roman was seeing somebody. In the city."

"So we were right. Did Ashley know?"

"Felix said Roman didn't think so."

"What else did Felix say?"

"Not much. I told him I knew about Ashley and Bryce, though."

"You knew? For how long?"

"Not long. And she said it was over. She didn't want me to

tell anyone, but maybe I should have. I think she was afraid of him."

"Shit. What did Felix say?"

"He said he'd talk to him."

"If he can find him."

Tara sighed. "I'm going to try to get Mason outside for a while."

"After I talk to Felix I need to go up to New Paltz and finish that deck job. They've been texting me nonstop. It shouldn't take too long. I can pick up dinner if you want."

"I'll text you."

John kissed her on the head and gave her a tight hug. He felt solid, and she was thankful for that.

Inside, Mason was watching *Toy Story 2*.

"Hey, mister," she said, leaning over the sofa to kiss his cheek. "Let's go to the playground. We can get some ice cream."

No answer. She looked around for the remote. It was on his belly. Just like his daddy. Just like John. A tiny little man. She reached for it, but he held on.

"I don't want to go."

"I know," she said. It was impossible to talk to him with the television on. He literally could not take his eyes from the screen. "Can we just pause it, please?"

Mason didn't respond. He gripped the remote.

"We can finish watching when we get home."

"No."

Tara went to the other side of the room and turned the TV off on the monitor.

"No!" screamed Mason. "I said no!"

"Come on, baby," said Tara, "I know it's hard—"

"I want to watch TV! I don't want to go to the playground!" Mason threw the remote across the room. It hit the corner of the TV and broke apart, batteries tumbling to the ground.

Mason looked at Tara, eyes wide in terror. Two weeks ago, such an outburst would have resulted in an immediate time-out, multiple talking-tos, and definitely no ice cream. But Tara just went to Mason on the couch and wrapped her arms around him. He began to sob.

"I'm sorry, Gerty," he wailed.

"It's okay, mister. It's okay. I know it was an accident."

"I don't want to go to the playground," he said, through tears.

"I know," she said. "But it's a beautiful day and we can't stay inside watching TV forever. Mommy wouldn't like that." As soon as she said it, it felt wrong. Was this what she was going to do? Use Ashley's memory to manipulate him?

"Mommy's dead. She doesn't care."

"Oh, mister, she does care. She'll always care." What did that even mean? She was just saying words. "We'll get ice cream. Double scoop."

"I don't want ice cream."

"You don't want ice cream?" She tried to say it in a goofy voice. She tried to smile at him.

"My tummy hurts."

"Oh baby." She put her hand on his belly and rubbed lightly.

"It hurts when I think about Mommy. It hurts all the time."

"Take a walk with me. Please? A short walk. You can scoot. Please?"

Mason didn't move from the one-sided embrace, but relented. "Okay."

She looked at him, cracking a real smile. "Okay?"

He nodded. Tara stood up and held out her hand. "I love you."

"I love you, too."

Mason followed her to the back door where the shoes were. He put on his Crocs and she put on her Vans. He followed her out the door.

"Do you want to scoot?" she asked.

He shrugged, but when she offered it, he gripped the handles. She put on his helmet; gray and white and red with a shark fin on the top and teeth painted across the front. She started down the driveway and he followed, slowly. At the corner, Tara stopped and turned back. Mason was scooting, and weeping. When he reached her, she knelt down, dug in her bag for something to wipe his face.

"Do you need a nose blow?"

He shook his head and wiped his nose on his arm.

"You are a very brave boy," said Tara. "What you are feeling is very, very hard."

"I don't want to cry at the playground, Gerty," he whispered.

"Oh baby," she said, rubbing his arm, "anytime you need to cry, you cry. Anytime you need to yell, you yell. Wherever we are. You tell me what you feel and I'll help you feel it, okay? We'll cry and yell together."

"I cry whenever I think about Mommy."

"Me, too," she said. She squeezed his hands. His fingernails needed a trim. Ashley had always taken care of that. At the hospital, they showed her how to cut his fingernails and toe-nails with a pair of blunt-tipped scissors, and it was a corner of Mason's care she held on to. *Time for your mani-pedi!* she'd an-nounce, and Mason would giggle and sit on the toilet lid. Ash sat on his little step stool and they chatted as she cut and filed. He was ticklish, and he'd squeal when she did his baby toes. After-ward, she moved the stool and handed him the vacuum, guiding him as he sucked up all the little clippings.

Someone was going to have to do that now. Probably her. Roman would worry about accidentally snipping Mason's skin. Her son was more fearful now than he had been as a child. Despite the twin tragedies of his father's and grandparents' sud-den deaths, Roman, as a boy, was a kid who teachers described as a leader; someone the other kids looked up to; someone who listened more than he spoke, but who took responsibilities in the classroom. In sixth grade, his peers elected him student body president. Where had that confident child gone?

"Maybe the playground will make you feel better," Tara said. "Maybe you'll hop on the seesaw and you'll forget—"

"I don't want to forget Mommy!"

"I didn't mean forget *Mommy*, baby." And she hadn't. "I meant, just think about something else for a few minutes."

"That's hard."

"I know. Can we try?"

Mason nodded. She stood up and started walking, and he scooted slowly behind her.

CHAPTER THIRTY-FOUR

There were half a dozen people on the playground when they arrived. Tara waved when she saw Ingrid, whose daughter, Olive, was a little older than Mason. Ingrid waved back. She was holding her one-year-old, Gavin. Ingrid was a therapist and she and her husband had moved up from the city during the pandemic. They lived in a big house on the mountain.

Tara liked her; Ingrid loved to talk—about everything. A week after they'd met, she knew Ingrid had had two abortions (one at eighteen, one at twenty-five), that her stepmom hadn't spoken to her since her dad died five years ago, and that she smoked weed and occasionally did mushrooms. Ingrid also complained constantly about her husband, whose tech job had gone remote during lockdown and was high up enough in the company to keep working from home even now. According to Ingrid, he never changed a diaper, watched too much TV, was gaining weight, had lost his interest in travel, and rarely initiated sex.

Ingrid's stories were always amusing, and they made Tara feel good about her own domestic situation. John wasn't even Mason's dad, but if she needed a hand with the boy, he was always willing. And he looked good. He took care of his body and at almost fifty he was even sexier than he'd been at seventeen. Life hadn't been entirely kind to him—he'd struggled with drugs and alcohol; he'd lost his wife and, for the most part, his kids—but he carried his failures with poise. He read books about mindfulness and he was preternaturally adept at looking on the bright side. She'd seen him crack, of course; she'd seen him cry when his kids didn't call on Father's Day. But the next day she saw him sending them a goofy text, reaching out in spite of it.

Olive was on the monkey bars. She was tall for her age and could swing from rung to rung. Mason had been trying for weeks to match her, but couldn't quite make his fingers grip the next bar without a little help. When Olive saw him, she called, "Mason! Look what I can do!"

Mason dropped his scooter and ran. Tara almost wept with relief.

"She can skip a rung now," said Ingrid, hobbling toward Tara while holding on to baby Gavin's arms as he marched his chubby bowlegs across the rubber play surface. "She's very proud of herself."

"She should be," said Tara.

"How are you?" Ingrid asked, lowering her voice.

"We're doing our best," she said. "Roman's a wreck. He basically sleeps all day."

"I'm so sorry."

"Thanks." She pointed to the monkey bars, where Olive

was trying to lift Mason to the first rung. "This is good for him."

They stood in silence for a minute. Ingrid let Gavin plop down and scoot off while they watched the kids. Tara felt Ingrid look at her.

"My cousin OD'd the first summer of Covid," said Ingrid. "Fucking fentanyl is in everything."

Tara watched Mason. "Yeah," she said. "They don't actually think it was an overdose."

"Oh? Sorry. Me and my big mouth."

"It's okay. I guess that's what everybody thinks?"

"I mean, I don't know *everybody*, but that was what I heard. They found her on the hillside, right? Over on Hudson View?"

Tara nodded. "At her friend Bella's. There'd been a party. Felix thinks . . ." What did Felix think? What did she think? Did Ashley really just trip and fall, totally sober? And if not, what? Somebody pushed her? Why?

"Gerty!" called Mason, running over with Olive. "Can we get a cookie at Koffee?" His face was flushed, his eyes brighter than they'd been since she'd told him that Mommy was gone. She'd do anything to keep his eyes like that.

"Fine by me," said Tara.

"Me too," said Ingrid.

Olive and Mason cheered. Ingrid put Gavin in his stroller and Mason pushed off on his scooter, with Olive running behind. When they got to the coffee shop, they set their bags on a picnic table outside and Tara offered to go in for everyone. Through the glass door she saw Daniel and Bobby at the counter, along with a new girl she didn't recognize. The girl was blond, like Ashley, but not as tall, and not nearly as striking. Not the kind of girl who people stared at, who customers fell in love with.

Daniel came around the counter as soon as he saw her. He pushed through the people in line to wrap his arms around her.

"How are you?" he asked, eyes welling with tears. Daniel was another of the crew of high school misfits who'd made Tara's place their landing pad. She never tried to hang out with them, but she was there for a talk, or a snack, when they needed it. Daniel came out in middle school and although his parents were supportive, many of his peers were vicious, just as they'd been to Bella, and eventually Ashley and Roman. The fact that, at the time, Roman seemed to resent her for opening her home to his friends was something Tara simply endured. Her boy was close; he was safe. After what she'd put him through, that was more than enough.

"We're surviving," she said.

"Felix called me this morning," said Daniel. "He was really cryptic."

"Yeah," she said, looking at Bobby, who was showing the new girl how to tamp down the espresso for a shot. "We found out some stuff last night that . . . changes things."

Daniel's eyes went wide. "Oh my God, what?"

Tara looked back at Mason, who was sitting, helmet still on his head, listening to Ingrid read a library book.

"Honestly, we probably shouldn't talk about it here."

"Oh right, right. I'm sorry. I still can't believe it. I keep wanting to call her. I actually texted her. I know it's crazy. I feel crazy."

"I think we all do. Talk to Felix, okay?"

"Of course. Can I give Mase a cookie?"

"They both want a cookie. And let me have two chocolate milks, too. Me and Ingrid are going to have iced coffees."

Daniel hugged her again. "I love you, Mama T. You know I'm here for you. You know I want to babysit again."

Tara smiled. "I know. I think Mason would love that. Just . . . not quite yet."

Daniel went behind the counter and took two cookies from the jar and the milks from the refrigerator. Bobby smiled at her.

"She's also having two iced coffees," said Daniel.

"Two iced coffees," said the new girl, pressing a button on the register.

"She doesn't pay," said Bobby. "This is Tara. Out there with the helmet is Mason. They're family."

Tara put five dollars in the tip jar and carried the kids' cookies outside, then returned to add milk to the iced coffees. When she came back, Ingrid was talking to a woman in yoga pants and a midriff-baring T-shirt that said "Feminist" on it in sparkly letters. Her neon sneakers looked like they'd come out of the box that morning. She was probably Roman's age, maybe twenty-five. And there wasn't an ounce of fat on her. Her dark hair was braided and twisted atop her head in a style that looked like she'd paid someone a good bit of money to create.

"Tara, this is Kiera," said Ingrid.

"Hi," said Tara, handing Mason and Olive their cookies and chocolate milk.

Kiera smiled thinly.

"Tara is Ashley's mother-in-law," Ingrid said. "Did you ever meet Mason?"

"No. Sorry, I've got to run." She turned around and trotted her bubble ass across the street to a black Tesla.

"Was it something I said?" asked Tara.

"Gerty, can you do the wrapping for me?" Mason held up his chocolate milk and she tore off the straw, unwrapped it, and popped it through the tiny foil-covered opening.

"I can do mine myself," said Olive.

"You don't need to brag, Olive," said Ingrid. "Mason is younger than you."

"I'm four," said Mason.

"I'm five!"

The kids attended to their cookies and milk and Tara sat down, sipped her iced coffee.

"I thought Kiera was friends with Ashley," said Ingrid. "I've seen them together a couple times."

"Oh yeah? Well, I don't know all her friends."

"She's Nick Wolfe's daughter. Actually, stepdaughter."

That was news.

"Really? The lawyer?" A spark of recognition. "Oh, she's the girl that went to boarding school! She got kicked out here. I think she was a year ahead of Roman. She got caught doing coke in the bathroom."

"Ooh, I didn't know that," said Ingrid.

"I heard she went off to Switzerland or something."

"That seems right. She's got that 'I'm sort of European' vibe."

"I wonder how long she's been back in town," Tara said. She paused. "Huh."

"What?"

"Roman works for Nick Wolfe. If Ash was friends with his daughter, I feel like I should know that."

CHAPTER THIRTY-FIVE

Kiera came to one of my classes at Gold's Gym right after Valentine's Day. She commented on my hibiscus tattoo and it turned out she'd been at the surf retreat the year after I left. We walked out to our cars together. I remember it was afternoon, but dark. I hate that time of year: spring still ages away, whatever warmth you can squeeze out of the holidays long gone. The Gold's was in a strip mall with an empty former Kmart, a nail salon, a tax prep service, and a Mexican restaurant. We decided to go for drinks.

Her life was way more interesting than mine. She told me she'd grown up mostly in Manhattan and was staying here in her grandma's house.

"She died last year. I'm supervising for my mom while they fix it up to sell." I asked where and she was vague, but I had no reason to think she was lying.

Kiera told me she was working in fashion PR in London when the pandemic hit, so she stayed in her flat, she said, making TikTok videos from her closet.

I did not tell her what I'd done during lockdown: struggling to breast-feed and sleeping all day isn't that fun to talk about. Anyway, that was over now. I showed her my YouTube channel and she subscribed for a whole year right there at the bar. I remember thinking: I'm a different person. I'm fun again!

And the truth was, I felt fun. I'd been texting with Bryce for a couple weeks. He'd gotten in touch to say he'd be in town after the New Year. He said he was taking pictures now, and had a shoot for some travel site at a B and B in Rhinebeck. He was going to spend the week at his grandma's. He was lying about the shoot, but I didn't learn that until later. The idea of grabbing onto his energy, the thrill of sex with someone who wasn't Roman, but who I had history with—it was intoxicating. Those days with Bryce in Hawaii, doing mushrooms and surfing and fucking outside in the warm tropical air, they'd grown in my mind since. They'd become the place I went to when I needed to find some joy, some reminder that my life had been—could be?—more than my partner and my son and the crumbling house and the people who came and went and said namaste in my yoga classes. My restlessness, my nostalgia, made me stupid, and I interpreted the small-town coincidence of Bryce walking into that Mexican restaurant thirty minutes after Kiera and I sat down as a sign: a new adventure has begun!

Kiera didn't seem to like Bryce, but she tolerated him when we'd end up in the same place. She knew about Roman and Mason, but when I talked about them—which wasn't often—she rarely seemed interested. Until, one night, she did.

We were at a bar in Newburgh when a local news story flashed on the TV: a five-year-old was dead after her eleven-year-old cousin found her dad's loaded handgun, and dropped it.

"Oh my God, did you see that?" I asked, pointing to the TV. "It's so fucked up. Roman's working on a story about it. People say they keep guns for self-defense, but did you know that if you have a gun in your house you're more likely to get killed by it than anyone else? You or your family, I mean. I would never have thought that."

Kiera went quiet. She put her hands over her face.

"Are you okay?"

She milked it; I swear to God I saw real tears. "I'm sorry," she said, making a show of trying to contain her emotion. "I used to babysit for her."

"Are you serious? Oh honey!" I wrapped my arms around her. It did not occur to me in that moment, or for a while afterward, that a woman who drove a Tesla probably didn't need babysitting cash. Or that she'd supposedly only been in town a few months.

"It's okay. I'm okay. But her family. They're like . . . Can you imagine?"

"I can't," I said. "I honestly think I'd kill myself if that happened to Mason." Saying his name aloud in the context of getting shot chilled me. I suddenly felt superstitious: I shouldn't even be talking about this. Who knows how tragedy enters the universe.

"I'm worried about her mom," continued Kiera. "Honestly if she sees her baby's name on TV again, or in the paper . . . I'm worried, seriously. Like, what's the point?"

"I think, with stories like this, Roman sees it as sort of a public service, you know. Making sure people know about the dangers—"

"Please," she said, cutting me off. "I'm sorry to dump on your boyfriend, but does he really want to push this family over the edge? Leave them alone, you know?"

That night, I relayed the conversation to Roman.

"If it was Mason, would you want his name in the paper over and over?"

Roman cringed. He didn't make any promises, but neither did he write another article about the subject.

CHAPTER THIRTY-SIX

Roman spent most of the day after talking to Felix asleep. He woke up for dinner, then volunteered to put Mason to bed. They brushed teeth and Roman read the book about the creepy carrots. He switched off the light.

"Mommy always sings to me."

"I don't know very many songs."

"What song do you know?"

"I know . . ." Roman looked at the ceiling, thinking, and found a memory: singing around the campfire at the sleepaway camp he went to in middle school. The song was "Leaving on a Jet Plane." He could remember the chorus, but how did it start? He began humming and it came to him.

"Well, my bags are packed and I'm ready to go . . ." His voice was quiet, but singing the words—when was the last time he'd sung?—was almost soothing. He remembered that the friendships he made those two summers at camp had changed him; helped him find the confidence that, despite appearances, had long eluded him. No one there knew what had happened to his dad, or his mom. He kept singing, and suddenly he was crying.

"Are you okay, Daddy?" asked Mason.

"I'm okay, mister," he said. "I'm just a little sad. Is it okay if I cry?"

Mason nodded and said seriously: "Sometimes it's the best thing."

Roman held Mason until the tiny twitches of his body told him the boy was asleep. He got up carefully, not wanting to wake him, then went downstairs. Tara and John were at the kitchen table.

"Did you know Nicholas Wolfe's daughter was back in town?" asked his mom.

"No," said Roman, confused for a moment. Wolfe had a daughter? "Wait, you mean stepdaughter? The one who went to Switzerland?"

Tara nodded. "She's back, and apparently she and Ash were friends. Ingrid says she told her they met when Kiera took one of Ashley's classes at Gold's."

Roman rubbed his eyes. Why would Ashley keep that a secret?

"How long has she been back?"

"I don't know," said Tara. "I wouldn't have recognized her. And she ran off when Ingrid introduced us."

"What's her story?" asked John.

"I remember her mom," said Tara. "She was my age, I think. Not that she told anybody her age. She'd come to the restaurant sometimes and sit at the bar. She always seemed out of place.

She'd bring a magazine and have two or three drinks without talking to anyone. But this was, like, maybe ten years ago? I only saw them together a couple times, her and Wolfe. I'm sure they had a place in the city, too. I don't think they were married long. The main thing I remember are the renovations they did on that property. They blew out the side for a whole new wing, and did a stone driveway and turned the pool into an infinity pool and added a guest house.

"They weren't supposed to do that," she continued. "That's why I remember. They didn't get the right permits, and it was a big drama. Everybody was pissed. I think somebody on the planning board got fired. Or maybe the town lawyer? Or both? Anyway, they weren't interested in making friends."

"Better to ask forgiveness than permission," said John.

"If you're an asshole," said Roman.

John laughed. "And we know he is."

"Was Kiera your year?" Tara asked Roman.

"I think she was above me?" He had a vague memory of the third baseman trying—failing?—to hook up with her. He remembered thinking she was pretty, but that a lot of girls, including Ash, were sexier. Kiera seemed cold and closed off. Her hair shone and her clothes were, well, boarding-school polished instead of public-school struggle. A single memory emerged: she'd been at a party that got broken up by town police. Milo Hoffer's parents were out of town and he'd managed to get a keg of beer. Roman remembered being in the bathroom and hearing people squealing and running, yelling, "Cops!" He raced into the hall, looking for Ashley. Was she already outside?

To his right, people were streaming out the sliding glass door to the deck and the yard beyond that had a cut-through to the town park. But there was Kiera in the living room, sitting on the arm of a sofa, scrolling on her phone. She looked at him, then back at her phone. He remembered thinking she was nuts, but it made perfect sense. She knew that even if they caught her, her stepdad, attorney to the family that owned half the county, would get her out of trouble. She was probably just at the party because she was bored, or maybe on a dare. Why debase herself further by fleeing with a bunch of dumb, drunk kids?

"Nick Wolfe isn't local either," Tara said. "He must have bought the house when he started working for the Davenports." She looked at John. "Do you remember? It was after we graduated, but not long after."

John shook his head. "I was in Jersey then."

"Right," said Tara.

"So, Kiera moved here when her mom married Wolfe, then left for boarding school in Switzerland after she got expelled. But like you said, that was ten years ago. What's she been doing since? And why is she taking yoga classes at Gold's Gym?"

"That's what I was gonna ask," said John. "I mean, I'm not much into yoga, but Gold's isn't where I picture Nick Wolfe's kid."

"Totally," said Tara. "If you have money you go to a studio. Or get someone to come to you."

"Have you looked for her on social media?" Roman asked.

"No," said his mom. They all pulled out their phones.

"Do we even know her last name?" asked Roman.

"I can text Ingrid," said Tara.

"No," said Roman. "Let me think."

Bella hadn't said exactly when Ash started hooking up with Bryce, but it seemed possible she might have met Kiera through him. Roman opened Instagram and scrolled through Bryce's feed again, this time clicking into the posts with multiple photos, looking specifically for Ashley. He found her buried in two posts: one in March, one in April. She wasn't tagged and she wasn't prominent in either. In one, it was just her arm and the side of her torso, but he could tell it was her by the tattoo—the little lines and stars of the Aries constellation she'd gotten for Mason—and the way she stood and held her drink. In the second, Bryce was taking a selfie and Ash and another girl were in the background, laughing.

"Is this her?" Roman asked, handing the phone to his mom.

Tara nodded.

"So, Kiera knows Bryce," said John.

Roman clicked into the likes. Ash had liked the post, and so did sixty-six other people. He scrolled through, looking at the profile pics and usernames. Eventually, he found nybritgirl98. He clicked and it was Kiera, but the last image was more than six months old, and she'd listed her location as Manhattan. He kept scrolling. For what looked like years, she'd posted multiple times a day—mostly selfies—but in February, the account went quiet. Roman wanted to know why.

CHAPTER THIRTY-SEVEN

The next morning, Roman woke to his phone ringing. It was Larry. He silenced it, then saw he'd missed seven calls from his boss. He lay in his son's bed—Mason must have gotten up without waking him—and tried to focus his mind on the questions he wanted to ask Kiera and Wolfe. The phone rang again—Larry again. He picked up.

"Is your house on fire?" Roman asked, instead of saying hello.

"What?" Larry barked. He was originally from Queens, and his accent was most pronounced when he was agitated.

"You've called me like fifty times."

"I need to talk to you."

"I'm not working this week."

"What?" He truly sounded like a movie character.

"Wolfe said I could take a couple weeks."

"What?"

"I'm not going to argue with you, Larry. I'm hanging up now."

"Wait! I can't cover all this shit myself. Can you at least get the blotter? And the planning board is supposed to approve—"

"No," said Roman. "I need another week. Or two." At least.

"Two weeks! I didn't even take that off when my *wife* died. You weren't even married to this girl, were you?"

Roman was glad Larry wasn't standing in front of him. He hung up and dropped the phone, feeling the rage rise inside, roaring through his chest. The force felt like it might shatter his teeth. When Mason was little, he and Ash would talk about how the boy's tantrums—when he just started shrieking and hurling himself around—were more honest than the way most adults expressed anger.

"It's the same feeling," he remembered Ashley remarking. "When I get really frustrated, at you or him or my mom, it's like a storm that kicks up right in my heart and radiates out, like where I can feel it everywhere. In my stomach, in my legs, in my mouth. But at some point I must have figured out I can't actually flail around and scream like Mase does. Not in front of people, anyway. I still scream, sometimes. Into a pillow, or in my car. If I don't, I feel like I might actually explode. The screaming is the only way to let it out."

Roman knew that about Ash. He'd heard the muffled screams. But he didn't do the same thing. He had never let the pain of his grandparents disappearing from the world in a hail of twisted steel and fire get past his chin. Same with his dad. Did he think of his father choosing death over dealing with a son every time he saw that bridge? Did he imagine himself following Jason down into the water? Yes. But he swallowed hard. That's what grown-ups did.

Downstairs, Mason and John were putting on their shoes.

"Hi, Daddy," said Mason. "We're going to Home Depot and then we're going fishing!"

"That sounds fun," said Roman.

"I thought I should price some new siding," said John. "And I have to pick up some two-by-fours. Figure we can stop at the creek on the way back and see if anything's biting."

"Do you want to come?" asked Mason.

Tara cut in, saving Roman from having to make an excuse.

"No, mister. Daddy is coming with me."

"Where are you going, Gerty?"

"You two just have fun," said Tara. "We'll see you soon."

Mason gave Roman and Tara hugs, and he and John took off.

"What's the plan, Mom?"

"I want to talk to Kiera. I was thinking we drive up to Nick Wolfe's house and see if we can get some answers."

"You think she's staying with him?"

"We'll see."

They took Roman's car, cutting through their neighborhood and past the Catholic church whose bells rang on the hour; past the kids playing on the faded plastic slides at the elementary school. Past the dance studio and the hair salon and the dry cleaner. Past Koffee, past the pizza parlor, past the local GOP headquarters. Off Main Street, they turned in to a residential neighborhood and drove up the hill. The houses got farther and farther apart up here, the driveways longer, the front doors rarely visible. At the very top was Wolfe's house. On a clear day, you could see the faint purple haze of the Catskills seventy miles north from his yard. Tara pulled in, following the circular driveway and stopping right at the front door.

Wolfe must have seen them from inside—or had cameras—because he opened the door before they even knocked.

"I don't think I've ever had the pleasure of meeting your mother," he said, smiling at Tara.

"I can't imagine why you would have," said Roman.

"You have worked for us for several years, Roman."

"Have you introduced me to your mom? Or, say, your step-daughter?"

Wolfe kept the smile, and pivoted. "I'm sorry," he said, now addressing Tara. "I'm still a small-town boy at heart. Nicholas Wolfe. Nice to meet you. Why don't you both come in."

"You're from a small town?" asked Tara. "But not here."

"No," he said, ushering them into the air-conditioning. "I'm from the West Coast. Oregon."

"What brought you out here?" His mom smiled, but not in a flirtatious way. Roman wondered if Wolfe could tell the difference. Narcissists, his mom and Ash used to say, always thought you were flirting with them.

"College," said Wolfe. He led them through the double-height entry and into the gleaming kitchen.

"He hasn't told you he went to Harvard yet?" asked a female voice coming down the stairs. "*And* Harvard Law. That's usually, like, the first five minutes."

"Hello, Kiera," said Wolfe, still smiling, though maybe a speck less broadly. "My stepdaughter has a fixation with college. She didn't go."

"It's stupid to go into debt for a traditional education," she said.

Wolfe laughed. "Harder to pull off the pauper routine when you're standing in your mansion, Kiera."

Kiera shrugged. "It's true, though. College is dumb."

She came into the kitchen and leaned against the massive island. Diamond studs sparkled in her ears, and her perfectly worn vintage-style T-shirt had the Shep Fairey image of Barack Obama above the word "Hope." Roman hated her on sight. The only reason he could imagine Ash being friends with her was ironically. Or, he supposed, out of desperation.

"Are you guys here about Ashley?" she asked, not quite looking at either of them. "I'm really sorry about what happened."

"Are you?" asked Roman. He felt his mom give him a look. *More flies with honey*, he imagined her saying. "So, you were friends?"

Kiera didn't answer immediately. She looked at Wolfe—for permission? Roman couldn't tell what the man's face was telling her in response, if anything at all.

"I'm surprised she didn't tell you," said Kiera.

"Would you like something to drink?" asked Wolfe. "We have iced tea, lemonade, cold beer."

"Water would be great," said Tara.

"Sure. Roman?"

"Sure."

The house felt changed slightly from the week before, though Roman couldn't pinpoint why. There was tension between Wolfe and Kiera; they seemed to be watching each other, as if for clues.

Wolfe plucked three glasses from one of the cabinets and set them on the spotless white countertop. Then he pulled a glass water pitcher, an ice bucket—complete with stainless steel tongs attached to the side—and a small ceramic container from the refrigerator. He dropped ice cubes one by one into the glasses, poured the water, then took the lid off the ceramic container.

"Lemon?" he asked.

Roman almost laughed. "You have precut lemons?"

"I try to be prepared for guests."

"It's not like *he's* slicing the lemons," said Kiera. "The house-keeper does that."

"She has a name, Kiera," said Wolfe.

"I know that."

Wolfe set the glasses on the island bar. Tara sat down. Roman continued to stand.

"What can we do for you?" asked Wolfe.

"Did you offer to pay for Ashley's funeral?" asked Tara.

It was a smart first question, because they were pretty sure of the answer. They could learn something if he lied.

"I did," said Wolfe. "But that was straight from the family. As soon as they heard, they wanted to cover the costs."

"It's a family company, after all," said Kiera.

"Exactly."

It was amusing watching Kiera troll Wolfe. She might think even less of him than Roman did—which was interesting, given that she likely knew him better.

"How did you meet Ash?" asked Roman.

Kiera pulled a stool out at the far end of the island and sat down, tucking her long, bare legs beneath her. "Yoga."

"You don't seem like a Gold's Gym girl," said Tara.

"I heard she was good."

"From who?" asked Roman.

"I don't know," said Kiera, looking at her stepdad. "Around."

"And then, what, you guys started hanging out?"

"Yeah."

"With Bryce Lorimer."

Kiera looked at Wolfe again. "He was her friend, not mine. Anyway, I hadn't seen her in, like, weeks."

"Why?"

"She dumped me when she found out who I was."

"Who you were?"

"That Nicholas is my stepdad. She thought I manipulated her."

"Manipulated? How?" And then it clicked. "The gun story."

A few months before, Ashley had told him about her friend who knew the family of the girl accidentally shot and killed by her cousin. *They're devastated,* Ash had said, or something like that. They'd talked about the story at home, in low voices, because Mason was the same age as the girl who died. It was around Valentine's Day, if Roman remembered correctly, and Larry was bothering him to write an article about a press release he'd gotten from the county sheriff warning there might be fentanyl in packets of heart candy. He'd refused, showing Larry half a dozen articles debunking the "drugs in candy" myth, and arguing that the real danger to kids in town was the guns their parents had in bedside drawers and closet shoeboxes. Larry wouldn't give him space for a gun story, and ended up running the fentanyl press release verbatim in the paper.

When he saw it in print, Roman had thought, as he'd thought constantly for the four years since he'd been at the *Advocate*, that he needed to get the hell out of this job. The *Los Angeles Times* fellowship was no longer an option. And even if they hadn't moved on to more recent graduates, the notion of moving across the country with a small child was at least as daunting as the notion of moving with an infant. He reached out to an editor at the Albany *Times Union*, but they were laying off reporters, not hiring them. He'd done some stringing for *The New York Times* the year before when they needed a reporter to do legwork on suburban school board fights over masks and vaccines, but he hadn't even gotten a byline—just an "additional reporting by" credit—and the editor he worked with was now gone. What he needed to do was be proactive; look for stories he could anchor and report near Adamsville, but sell nationally. Which is what he initially thought he'd do with the poor little girl's gun death.

He did some digging, talked to experts and some parents in Ohio who'd started a campaign to raise awareness after their eight-year-old accidentally shot himself with their handgun. The plan was to wait at least a month or two before trying for an interview with the local family. While he was waiting, Ashley brought it up.

"Are you still going to try to interview the Donners?" she asked one evening out of the blue.

He remembered now: he'd thought she was digging at him. He'd thought she was asking about it because she was disappointed or annoyed that, once again, he'd talked a big game about working in a story he could sell to a more prominent news outlet, and the feature never materialized. So he was short with her.

"I've been busy," he said. "Is that a problem?"

"No." He recognized immediately that he'd hurt her. But he didn't care. Tit for tat. "I wasn't trying to say you *should*. I was trying to say the opposite, actually."

"Why?"

"There's a girl at yoga who babysat for them. She said they're totally devastated. Like, not doing well at all. I told her you were thinking about a story on in-home gun deaths and she said she didn't think they could handle talking to a reporter."

"Why were you talking about my story to some girl at yoga?"

"Why are you getting mad?"

"I'm not mad."

"Okay. Fine."

They fought over such stupid things. Negativity spilled into benign conversations, staining them. They'd stopped being able to ask each other for favors. A request to order wet wipes or a reminder about renewing the triple-A membership became an accusation of neglect. He felt wounded by her almost daily, and the wounds stayed open; they itched and burned in his chest as he tried to fall asleep at night.

"Anyway," Ash had said, her voice now strained, her face turned away from him, "all I wanted to say was that, from what she said, it's probably not a good time. And it might not ever be."

He believed her. He dropped the story. And he was glad to be off the hook. He'd dreaded the idea of sitting in the family's living room with his phone recorder on, asking them about the moment their lives exploded. Witnessing their tears and anger. You got ahead in journalism by writing stories like these. But he was out of practice. Most of his work was: go here (the high school football game; the library's semiannual "Read to a Dog" event; the elementary school Halloween parade), take notes, take a picture, write two hundred words. A couple casual conversations and move on. He moved on.

"You were the friend who babysat for them?" Roman asked Kiera.

"I mean, I don't babysit."

"What are you talking about?" asked Tara.

Roman looked at Kiera. "You made it up?"

Kiera didn't answer; her eyes were on her stepdad. Roman could tell the conversation had taken a turn Wolfe wasn't expecting.

"Did Ash get mad because she found out you made it up?" Roman pressed. How would she have found out?

"Obviously Kiera can't know what was going on in Ashley's head," said Wolfe.

"Why would you lie?"

Again, Kiera looked at Wolfe, who answered for her. "Kiera doesn't usually need a reason to make up a story. She's very creative. Have you seen her TikTok?"

CHAPTER THIRTY-EIGHT

Roman was trembling when he and his mom stepped out of the frigid, sterile air inside Wolfe's mansion and into the sticky July heat. His fingers felt tingly and small; he had goose bumps all over his body. For a moment, they just stood on the front steps, both stunned by the sun and the way Wolfe and Kiera had turned into robots when he started asking what happened to her friendship with Ash.

His mom took his hand. "You okay?"

"Your hand is cold," he said.

She squeezed.

"What do we do now?" Roman asked.

"We get out of here. I'll drive."

They climbed into the car.

"Look," said his mom, turning her phone to him. John had texted a picture of Mason in Home Depot, sitting on one of the low carts next to half a dozen two-by-fours. He wasn't exactly smiling, but he had his hand raised to the camera.

"He's such a good kid," said Roman.

"The best."

Tara started the car.

"Do you think he'll be okay?" he asked.

His mom didn't hesitate. "I know he will."

"How could you possibly know that?"

"He'll have a hole in him, but everybody has some kind of hole. Look at you—you're doing okay." Roman thought that was debatable, but didn't contradict her. "And he's got it way better than you did."

Tara's eyes were hidden by sunglasses. Roman supposed he shouldn't be surprised that she could admit his childhood had been shitty. It wasn't something they talked about, but it was, nevertheless, agreed upon.

"He's got people who love him more than anything," she said. "Capable people. He'll be okay. He's strong."

She nodded, like she was cementing what she'd said. Affirming it to herself. The sun showed every line on her face, and for the first time he saw clearly how many there were. Across her forehead, along the sides of her nose and mouth. And there were little spots, too. Freckles he hadn't noticed before. She'd put on makeup for the meeting, but the makeup couldn't hide the fact that the skin on her face looked more delicate than he remembered. Roman wondered what was happening inside her. Did she really think Mason would be okay? Or was she just, as Ash might say, manifesting?

They drove down the hill in silence, back toward their part of town. Halfway down Main Street, Tara tensed.

"That's Bryce's car," she said, pointing to the low-riding coupe that was turning left.

"Follow him," said Roman.

They didn't have to follow far; half a mile later, Bryce pulled into Washington Arms.

Tara pulled to the curb outside the complex and they watched as Bryce parked in a visitor space. His trunk popped open and Bryce stepped out, pulled a duffel bag from inside, then started walking toward the entry.

"I want to talk to him," said Roman.

"Let's go."

They hopped out of the car and followed as Bryce walked through the courtyard to a door in one of the buildings bordering the creek. Number 117. He used a key to get inside. Half a minute later, they knocked. Tara saw the movement at the keyhole, a pause, and then he opened the door.

"You following me?"

Bryce was wearing a skimpy tank top and cargo shorts sagging below his boxers. A dainty gold chain hung around his neck. Tattoos climbed up his arms. He smelled like it had been a while since he showered. His modeling days, Roman suspected, were behind him. Maybe long behind him.

"I have questions," said Roman.

"Join the club. I just got done talking to the fucking cops."

"Why were you at Bella's party?"

Bryce almost smiled. "Straight to it, yeah? Okay, Mr. Reporter Man. You got a recorder in your pocket?"

"Maybe."

Bryce shrugged. "I didn't do anything. I got nothing to hide."

"Can we come in?"

"I don't know anything," he said, turning his back to them. They followed him into the living room. The apartment smelled like coffee and stale potpourri. There was a matching sofa and love seat with a pink and red rose print, a glass coffee table covered in a lace cloth, and a crucifix and family photos on the faux fireplace mantel.

"Why were you at the party? Bella said you and Ash broke up."

Bryce raised an eyebrow. "We didn't 'break up.' It was never that big a deal."

"So why were you there? What did you guys talk about?"

"I was there because it was a party. What did we talk about? Honestly, I'm not sure you want to know."

"Why not?"

Bryce paused. He scratched his neck. His right leg was bouncing with nervous energy. He leaned forward. "Because we talked about her plans. Ashley was going to leave your ass."

Roman's body went hot, his armpits slick with fear-sweat.

Bryce continued. "A girl she knows from Hawaii has her own studio in Virginia Beach. She promised Ash a job. I think she might have found her an apartment, too."

"You're lying," said Roman weakly.

Bryce rolled his eyes. "Okay, bro."

"Did you tell Felix this?" asked Tara.

"Yup," said Bryce. "He was pretty interested, too."

Roman tried to focus. "Bella didn't say anything about Ash moving."

"If Bella's trying to pretend she and Ash were BFFs, she's fucking lying. They had a falling-out. Ash thought me and Bella were bad influences. She was trying to get her life straight. She was making plans, and me and Bella weren't a part of them." He looked at Roman. "I don't think any of us were."

CHAPTER THIRTY-NINE

When I met Kiera, I was teaching at Gold's on Monday nights—the night Roman almost always had some municipal meeting to cover. In March, I rescheduled that class to a different day, but told Roman and Tara that Gold's had asked me to teach twice that evening. If I left an hour early to "warm up" or "run an errand," then decided to get a drink with a fellow teacher or student, or lift some weights at the gym, I wouldn't raise any eyebrows as long as I was home by midnight. Everybody was asleep by then, anyway.

With that settled, I told Tara I wanted to make Monday a "Mommy and me" day with Mason. I'd get up with him, make breakfast, play or read, and then we'd find something to do. It was still cold, and while Tara doesn't mind staying outdoors all day in the winter, I like to be cozy. And Mason likes treats. So we combined our desires and endeavored to test the hot chocolate and blueberry muffins at every café within a thirty-minute drive. Every Monday, we'd hit the library for a handful of new books, then look at a map and pick a new spot. I bought a notebook to record our findings and Mason wrote his name on the cover.

On our first outing, we discussed a ranking system: one to five stars for muffins, one to five stars for the hot chocolate.

"This one gets extra stars for whipped cream," Mason said, dipping his finger in the fluffy white.

I opened the notebook and wrote the name of the café on the top of the first blank sheet: "Liberty Coffee and Tea." I drew a line down the middle and wrote "Cocoa" on one side and "Muffin" on the other, then handed him the pen.

"You make the stars," I said.

Mason wiped his hand on his napkin and pressed the tip of the pen to the paper.

"One, two, three, four, five," he said as he drew the stars beneath "Cocoa."

"What's your verdict on the muffin?" I asked.

"Two stars."

"Only two? Let me try."

"There's no crumble on the top," he said.

"Ah," I said. "That's important."

"It's the best part," he said.

"You're the best part, mister," I said. "I love you."

"I love you, too, Mommy." It was nothing, but it was everything: with no more than an idea, a little enthusiasm, and a few dollars, I'd created something with Mason that was exclusively ours. We were building a bond. And I was building an identity I'd never felt I deserved: mom.

Achieving that identity gave me the boost I needed to explore others. After bringing Mason home in the afternoon, I showered and got ready for "work." At the beginning, I allowed myself to think of it *as a kind of work. Work rebuilding my life; work having some fucking fun. And Monday, it turned out, was a good choice. I didn't run into a single other mom from town all spring; Monday was for real partyers. After the night at the Mexican restaurant, Bryce proposed a dive bar just north of the waterfront. I texted Kiera the address and she texted back:*

> looks kinda sketch-how about this place?

She sent a link to a wine bar across the river.
I texted back:

> next time!

Bryce was there before either of us, and when I walked in, he was laughing with the bartender, who I recognized as having been a couple years ahead of me in school.

"Did you play volleyball?" I asked the woman. She was sexy, with elaborate braids piled in a twist atop her head and shoulder-grazing earrings. A little roll of skin shimmied between her jeans and her top.

"I did," she said. "Good memory."

"I told you she was cool," said Bryce, wrapping his arm around my waist. I felt freer than I had in years. I smiled at the bartender and pressed my body into Bryce's. Our texts had gotten increasingly explicit, and I remember feeling in that moment that I needed—truly needed—the particular chemical reaction that I imagined an orgasm with him would elicit. I kissed him and he put his hand on my tit. The bartender laughed.

Kiera showed up and ordered a vodka soda.

"So," said Bryce, "you guys met at yoga?"

Kiera nodded.

"Ash is very flexible," said Bryce.

I laughed. I was horny and I didn't care that he was basically an idiot.

Kiera did not laugh. She rolled her eyes. After one drink, she took off.

"Is she always like that?" Bryce asked me.

"Maybe she just doesn't like you."

"Maybe she's jealous."

"I don't think you're her type," I said.

"No, but maybe you are."

I didn't think so, but I was done thinking about Kiera that night. We had two drinks, then Bryce took me to an apartment around the corner and we went at it on the couch in front of a wall of windows facing the river. I could see the moon. I could see the lights of the train coming up from the city. The apartment, Bryce told me, belonged to a photographer friend who was traveling. It was on the top floor of a renovated row house: exposed brick and raw beams across the ceiling, large-format art, cement countertops, subway tile in the bathroom. We stood on the back deck and he gave me a bump before I drove home. Honestly, I felt happier than I had in . . . too long.

The next Monday, after a six-star cocoa (chocolate shavings!) and a five-star muffin in Fishkill, I met Kiera at the wine bar she suggested. She apologized for how she'd reacted to Bryce.

"If you like him, I'll try to like him," she said.

"We're old friends," I said. "It's just something fun. Something to take my mind off everything."

"Are things bad at home?"

"I mean, not terrible. Mason's awesome. It's just . . ." I wasn't sure how to describe it. "Roman's pretty depressed. I think he feels kind of useless. His job sucks. He's so much smarter than the shit they have him do. You know he won a fellowship for investigative reporting? We were supposed to go to L.A. before I got pregnant. And then Covid happened."

Kiera was quiet for a few seconds. "I shouldn't have said anything about that family I babysat for."

"No," I said, "it's okay. I mean, that's a perfect example. Just because I told him what you said didn't mean he had to drop the whole idea. You had a point about that family, but there are other people he could interview. It's almost like he looks for an excuse to do the minimum. And not just at work. I know he loves Mason, but he's so uninvolved. Roman used to play baseball. He was really good. But his mom is the one who taught Mason how to throw a ball. And her fiancé, John, takes him fishing. Roman's either at work or asleep. His life has gotten so small. It's like he's shrinking."

"I'm really sorry," said Kiera.

"What's frustrating is that he'll get all excited about an idea, and it seems like he's coming out of it for a few days. He'll spend hours online looking at databases and public records, and then some little thing will happen and he'll spend like a month being angry about it."

"I feel like I'd be a good reporter," said Kiera. "I'm nosy!"

I laughed.

"Like, finding out people's secrets and shit. That would be cool."

"When he started, he was all about that. Truth to power, he'd say. He was passionate about the good journalism can do. You know, especially after Trump won. And like I said, sometimes he gets on little kicks. You know how they just legalized pot? And casinos?"

"I know about the pot," said Kiera.

"A little while ago New York legalized gambling, too. Or they changed the law somehow. Anyway, just a couple weeks ago, he was talking about how it's important to follow who gets chosen to run the pot shops and build the casinos. Like, are they super-powerful, rich people who basically pay off whoever makes the decision? Or do they give everybody a fair chance?"

"Interesting," said Kiera.

"But he totally dropped that, too."

"Do you think he'd be happier doing something else?"

"Yes," I said. "I've even sent him job listings. There was a reporter job in Syracuse that paid more than what he makes now. Like fifty percent more. But he always comes up with some excuse. Or he just ignores me."

"That sucks. He's lucky to have you."

I raised an eyebrow. "He doesn't know where I am right now," I said. "He doesn't know about Bryce."

Kiera smiled. "Well, I didn't say you were perfect."

The next Monday, I made plans with Bryce. I got to the bar

early and flirted with the bartender, whose name was Diane. We *exchanged numbers. Bryce and I went back to the photographer's* *apartment and this time he had Molly and before I knew it, it was* *midnight. I pulled on my jeans and when I found my phone I saw* *Roman and Tara had been calling and texting:*

> where r u?

> u ok?

I ran down the stairs to my car and called when I got inside. I *told them I'd locked my keys and my phone in the car and didn't* *notice until after class. I said I had to find someone to call AAA and* *I couldn't remember my account number and it took forever. They* *bought it.*

Roman was grumpy when I got home and turned away from me *in bed. But I moved closer, slid a hand down his shorts, and went* *down on him. He came fast and silent and whispered with a little* *laugh: okay, I forgive you. When he moved to take care of me, I* *knew it was possible he'd smell something different, but it felt so good* *I put it out of my mind. Could what I was doing without him bring* *us closer? I almost told him then, as we lay there together in our bed.* *The bed that had been his grandparents'. I almost said,* Hey, remember how being with other people used to be kind of hot? What if we tried that again? *But I was frightened in a way that I hadn't* *been before Mason. Now, if the arrangement everybody already dis-* *dained exploded, it would mean the explosion of our family. It would mean paperwork and custody agreements and frankly I wasn't sure I'd come out that well. History of mental illness; history of drug use; makes her living mostly on YouTube; sexual relationships with men and women.*

So I didn't tell him. Not about Bryce and not about Kiera. I knew he wouldn't understand. He'd changed since we'd had Mason; I suppose we both had.

The next Monday, the photographer had a party at his apartment and Bryce and I did Molly again. Diane was there and we made out. More than made out. I felt as bold as I had at sixteen. I took her hand and locked the bedroom door behind us. Being with a woman again was exhilarating. I'd dreamt of it so often since having Mason. My fantasy had been to be with another mother. A woman who understood the pain that could engulf the places on our body we'd always associated with pleasure. A woman who understood the misery of being so needed. Maybe even understood what it felt like to fail at something that was supposed to be innate. I wanted to soothe her, and I wanted her to soothe me. In that bedroom I discovered Diane was a mom, too. She had a scar below her belly button, just like mine.

How long were we in that room? It felt like months and only a moment. She told me she'd had her son at eighteen, and that he lived with her ex's mom. I was stupid, she told me as we lay together, slippery and quiet, the party raging on the other side of the door. She told me she'd signed away custody, thinking she'd get him back when she got her shit together, got a steady job. But her ex ended up in prison.

And his mom moved to Maryland to be with her sisters. I get to hug him twice a year if I'm lucky. I asked her if she'd thought about moving and she said she had. But. But he seems happy. What if I disrupt things? He's almost in middle school now. That's a tough time.

Hearing her talk, it was so clear what a weak excuse that was. Clear to me, anyway. And I realized that she sounded exactly like me when I gave myself reason to let Tara continue being Mason's primary caregiver. What if I disrupt things? What if he's better off with someone else as his mom?

The more I thought about Diane, the more I realized I was a coward. Tara wasn't some magic person. I could be just as good a mom as she was. Better. Because he came from my body and every day he was more and more like me. Creative and sensitive in ways Tara was not. All I had to do was take control.

CHAPTER FORTY

As they drove home from Bryce's, Tara wished she could turn back time and tell Roman about the night she found the texts about Virginia Beach on Ashley's phone. It was months ago; April or May. She'd been in the kitchen, wiping down the counters, about to start the dishwasher and join John upstairs when she heard Ashley pull in and clip one of the garbage cans. Tara went to the front door and watched. With the car still running, Ashley got out and went to right the can, but tripped and stumbled forward. Tara opened the front door.

"You okay?" she called.

Ashley, still on the ground, looked up with an expression of surprise.

"Oh!" She giggled awkwardly and picked herself up. It was a warm night and her shorts were short, making her long legs look gangly, tangled on the grass. She was shoeless.

"Did you drive like that?" Tara asked quietly, walking down the front steps. The car was still running, headlights still on.

"Barefoot?"

"Intoxicated."

Ashley's smile disappeared. "I was just at . . ." She paused. "Sorry. It was dumb."

Tara turned off the car and took Ashley's purse and sandals from the passenger seat. The sandals, strappy pink flats with a tiny gold star-shaped charm hanging off the buckle, were dirty, like she'd walked through mud.

"Where were you?" Tara asked. She put out her hand to help Ashley to her feet. Tara had been here herself, many times, and yet she found she had almost no sympathy. Ashley knew better. Had she ever driven like this with Mason in the back? She didn't smell drunk; were drugs now a problem? What did she have on her? One of the moms at the playground told a story just a couple weeks ago about her friend in Westchester whose teenager took a single pill at a party and died in his bed a couple hours later. Fentanyl was in everything. Everybody was so excited about edibles, but they terrified Tara. Mason would see one of those gummies or lozenges and stick it right into his mouth. What if Ashley had pills? In her mind, Tara saw a pill falling out of Ashley's purse, tumbling down the stairs, Mason picking it up, thinking it was a little candy—her heart stopped. She gasped. That could not happen.

"Where were you?" Tara asked again, more forcefully this time.

Ashley noticed the change in tone. She stood up and took the purse and sandals from Tara.

"Nowhere," she said.

"What happened to your shoes?"

"Jesus," she said. "I'm fine. I was just at Fir Point."

Fir Point was a tiny beach tucked off an access road on the far end of town. It was shady; not a spot for sunbathing or swimming, but a nice spot to have a moment alone by the water, or get laid, or get high.

"Do you have anything on you?" Tara asked.

"On me?"

Ashley pulled out her phone, then dropped it.

"Drugs. Mason could think it was candy and—"

"No," said Ashley, kneeling to pick up her phone. She stuffed it in her purse. "I'm going inside."

"Wait," said Tara.

"I'm going inside," Ashley repeated, more loudly. A light turned on next door.

Were they making a scene? The Larkins hadn't lived in town twenty years ago when Tara was coming home fucked up and screaming at her parents on the front lawn. Not for the first time, Tara wished she'd sold the house when her parents died and bought something out of town, with land. All these people always up in her shit. Some days, when things were going well, it could feel friendly, the waves and the casual knowledge everyone in town had about each other. But nights like this, and the people around her now—there was nothing neighborly about it. She was being watched. The whole family was being watched. Their house that was perpetually under minor repair; their house with the cracked concrete front walk and the threadbare landscaping and the dented mailbox. Their house that no longer fit.

Inside, Ashley dropped her purse on the kitchen table, righted a water glass from the dish rack, and filled it at the sink.

"I'm going up," she said, walking slowly, carrying her shoes but forgetting her purse—which Tara went for as soon as she heard the door close upstairs. Ashley's phone was unlocked. What was she looking for? She opened the text messages. Black heart emoji from "BL"; below that *ok* from Roman; below that a Zillow link sent by "JC" for an apartment: *2 bedroom, 1 bath, blocks from the water! Virginia Beach's best new neighborhood!* She clicked into the thread and saw another link, this one to a yoga studio and the message:

> so excited! you're going to love it here!

The door upstairs opened. Tara jumped, almost dropping the phone. She put it back in Ashley's purse and rushed to the refrigerator, acting like she was looking for something. Ashley didn't say a word, just took her purse and went back upstairs. Tara shut the refrigerator, her heart uncomfortably big in her chest. She tried to remain calm. Virginia Beach. They'd argued about Virginia Beach just after Mason turned two. Ashley wanted to do a yoga retreat there but there was another Covid variant and Tara disapproved.

"Is it really necessary?" she'd asked. "You're expanding our risk a lot, staying with people overnight and doing indoor classes."

"I'll ask my friend Jen and her roommate to test."

"I do not want Mason to get Covid, Ash. We don't know . . ."

"I know!" Ashley had hissed. They didn't talk about it again, but Ashley didn't go to the retreat, and they all got Covid a couple months later. Was "JC" her friend Jen?

John was in bed watching a movie when she came in. He'd had his noise-canceling headphones on—probably hadn't heard a thing. Mason and Roman had apparently slept through it, too.

She sat down on the bed, and John took his headphones off.

"Hey," he said, "you done for the night?"

She nodded.

He sat up, smiling. "I have a surprise for you." John reached over to the bedside table and pulled out a small box. "I got the rings. Look how cool they turned out."

She looked, and they did look cool. But she couldn't focus on anything except her fear.

"Ashley is thinking about moving." She told him about the car outside, and the texts.

"Are you sure it wasn't, like, a retreat or something. Didn't she talk about that?"

"I don't think that was it."

She felt frozen on the bed. John put his hand on her back, rubbed gently up and down.

"You might be overreacting," he said. "Could you just ask her? Just, lay it out like: I happened to see this text come in. She might appreciate the honesty, you know?"

"If she wanted to talk about it, she would have," Tara said. She was sitting straight up, all of her senses alert. "She could take Mason from me."

"Hey," said John, in a firm voice, "don't go down a rabbit

hole. It's probably nothing. She's not going anywhere. This is her home. Everybody fantasizes about getting away sometimes, right? You're telling me you've never looked at Zillow in, like, Florida or up in the mountains? Just to see?"

"No," said Tara. "I'm happy here."

John kept rubbing her back.

"She could take him, John. She's his mom. She can do almost anything she wants. She and Roman aren't even married."

"He's not going to let her take him."

"He might. They're not exactly bonded. And what if there is a girl he's seeing in the city? Maybe he's working on a new life, too."

"I don't think he'd just let her go. I think he'd fight for her. I think he'd figure out a way to make her stay."

"How? Why do you think that?"

"Because he loves her. And she loves him."

"I'm not so sure."

"Why would they be together still if they didn't love each other?"

"Come on," Tara said, irritated. "People stay together for all kinds of reasons. Kids, money, inertia. Depression does that, keeps you stuck."

"But she's been better," said John.

"Better than catatonic, yeah, but neither of them realize how good they have it. An intact family. A healthy family. They both want everything besides what they've got."

She was talking fast, her mind spinning out scenarios: *Roman's got some girl in the city and Ashley's getting high on weeknights with God knows who. Maybe they* are *done.*

But she wasn't.

And now, looking at her son sitting in the passenger seat of his own car, his face so drawn with sadness it looked like the skin might slip off, she realized that he might have fought for Ashley. If only he'd known. If only she hadn't allowed herself to be convinced that what was happening wasn't happening; if only she hadn't said what she said. Would Ashley have needed to find solace with Bryce and Bella and Kiera if Tara had tried to understand her as an adult as hard as she'd tried when she was an adolescent? What had Tara pushed her into? Why was she on that fucking cliffside?

CHAPTER FORTY-ONE

It took Tara several days to confront me.

"Look," she said one evening after Mason was asleep. "That night you came home, on the lawn, you left your phone on the table and I happened to see a text with a Zillow listing."

"You happened to see?" I asked.

"You left it out. I was pretty upset seeing you like that. I thought maybe . . . I don't know. But that's not the point."

"Maybe that's not the point to you."

"Why are you looking at apartments in Virginia Beach?"

"I'm not." Maybe I shouldn't have lied. But if I'd told her the truth she'd have freaked out.

"You can't take Mason away," she said. "This is his home."

Her words hung in the air. Both of us perhaps surprised that they'd come out of her mouth. But what did I expect? That's she'd just let him go? Be glad to have her empty nest back?

"Well, I can take him," I said, "but—"

"I won't let you," she interrupted. "I swear to God, I will go to court and I'll tell them to drug-test you."

"Tara!"

"He's mine, too," she said. She was sweating as she spoke, trembling slightly. I'd never seen her this worked up. "Whatever is going on with you, I can help. Whatever you need. But you cannot take Mason."

I wanted so badly to scream at her: *I'm his mother, I can do whatever I want!* But I didn't. *Virginia Beach was still just a fantasy. I needed more time.*

"You're overreacting," I said slowly. "My friend Jen lives in Virginia Beach and she's moving and she's been sending me listings to get my opinion."

"She texted something about you working at her studio."

I did my best to remain calm.

"She's been trying to get me to move there for years. She's just lonely. Did you tell Roman?"

"No," she said. "Honestly, I didn't know what to think after the other night—"

"I know it was a mistake. It was a onetime, stupid thing. Please don't make it bigger than that. Please give me a little bit of a break. I'm doing my best, Tara. I really am. I know you want me to do more and be more and I'm trying. I was just out late with some friends from the gym and I . . . let loose."

Could Tara tell I was mostly full of shit? Getting high and driving was the opposite of doing my best.

"I love Mason," I said slowly. "I love him and I know I've let him down in a lot of ways. I fucked up the other night. I know I broke your trust. But please, let me try to win it back."

Tara didn't answer immediately, but she started to cry.

"Can I hug you?" she asked, finally. "I love you, Ash. I'm sorry. I shouldn't have said that about the drug test."

"It's okay," I said.

But it wasn't.

CHAPTER FORTY-TWO

Roman was silent as they rode home, and his mom seemed to know enough not to talk about what Bryce had told them. At least not yet. It was probably true. It even made sense. Ash was better; the trauma of nearly dying in childbirth and then being locked inside during the pandemic was behind her. She took an antidepressant that helped steady her mood; she had success as a yoga instructor. And she'd talked about moving—never as far away as Virginia, but she'd floated places like Asbury Park, even out on the Rockaways in Queens—places by the ocean. Roman would pretend to be interested, then change the subject. She'd send him listings—a two-bedroom for just a hundred dollars more than their share of the house now—but other than the occasional thumbs-up emoji, he'd ignored her.

The idea of moving felt utterly impossible to him. As much as he resented that his mother had waited until she had a grand-child to learn to parent, he couldn't imagine taking Mason away from Tara. The truth was, Mason was the child he was—a strong, easygoing, thoughtful, intelligent kid—because of all the love Tara had lavished on him. It certainly wasn't because of anything he'd done, and Ash had been half-zombie the first year of the boy's life. What would happen to Mason if they took him away? Could they even handle parenting without Gerty? Were they really going to put him in some grubby day care center while they worked their shitty jobs, when he could be hiking and reading and playing with a woman who loved him more than she loved herself? Why would they make that choice? Their job was to give Mason the best possible chance. It was selfish to even think about taking him away.

Or was it? After all, Ashley wasn't proposing Hawaii. But he hadn't even considered moving. And somehow it never occurred to him that one day she'd make the move on her own. Without him, if necessary. Who knows—maybe her Emily was in Virginia Beach.

When they got back to the house, Mason and John were on the front porch blowing bubbles.

"Look, Daddy!" shouted the boy. He was smiling as he tried to catch a bubble with his mouth. "Look! Watch what John taught me! I can catch a bubble with my mouth!"

Mason tried, and failed, to catch a bubble in his mouth—but no matter; what he'd caught was a moment of joy. The first Roman had witnessed from any of them since Ashley's death.

"I see," Roman responded. Instead of nodding and walking up to bed—which he could do, which he wanted to do; as Larry had said, he was not needed—Roman knelt down on the grass. *Be here and witness the boy's delight*, he told himself. *See if you can make it last, even for a few more seconds.*

"Let me try," said Roman. John blew another round of bubbles from the porch and Roman opened and closed his mouth dramatically, like a fish. He stretched his neck and bobbed his chin like a chicken. Mason laughed. Roman felt it in his heart.

Tara knelt down next to him and opened her arms to Mason. "How ya doing, mister?"

"John says we can't eat *too* many bubbles or we'll get a tummy ache."

"That's very true," Tara said.

"Don't eat too many bubbles, Daddy. You might get a tummy ache."

"You got it, mister."

"And if you get a tummy ache you might get a spicy poop!"

"Ew," said Tara. She stood up. His mom hated bathroom humor.

"Sorry," called John. "We read the poop book."

"Daddy, will you read me the poop book?"

Roman smiled. The poop book had been a running joke since one of John's friends gave it to Mason for his last birthday. Tara wouldn't read it, which meant it wasn't in heavy rotation, but she'd never actually gotten rid of it. Every once in a while, it would pop up on the top of one of the shifting book and toy and sock piles the boy left around the house, and Mason would run to every family member asking someone to read it to him. He'd wave it around and everyone would tease Tara: *Come on, Gerty! Let's read the poop book! Poop poop poop!* She'd cover her ears and Ashley and Roman would laugh at how legitimately annoyed she got over something so ridiculous.

Roman looked at Mason now, standing in the sun, and realized that Ashley was never going to see this perfect boy again; she was never going to laugh her giggly, goofy laugh again. His eyes began to sting. He let the tears come.

"Daddy, you're crying," said Mason. His son put his arms around him. "I love you, Daddy."

"I love you, mister."

"Are you crying because of Mommy?"

"Yes," said Roman. Letting his son's body comfort him. "But don't worry about me."

"Who wants a pb&j?" asked his mom from the porch.

"I do!" shouted Mason. "Come on, Daddy. Let's go read the poop book!"

Roman followed his son up the stairs and they sat on the sofa in the living room while his mother made sandwiches and John unloaded what he'd gotten at Home Depot. Roman read all the different words for poop that the publisher deemed age-appropriate.

"Roman," Tara called from the kitchen, "would you go tell John the sandwiches are ready?"

"I'll go!" shouted Mason. He jumped off the sofa and ran to the back door, letting it slam behind him.

"He's going to break that fucking door," said Tara. "I swear to God I will lose it if we have to fix something else."

"Are you okay?" asked Roman, joining her in the kitchen.

"Are you?"

"No."

"Do you really think she was going to leave?" she asked.

"I don't know," said Roman.

John and Mason came back and they all ate sandwiches for dinner, then sat on the porch with Popsicles while Mason ran after fireflies with a glass jar. After a while, Tara announced it was bedtime.

"Can Daddy put me to bed?"

"I think you could use a bath," said Tara.

"Pleeeeeeease," begged Mason. "Daddy can give me a bath."

Tara looked at him. He was three beers in and ready for bed himself. Had he ever actually bathed his son?

"Sure," said Roman.

"Yay! We get to read the poop book again!"

John laughed.

"Poop book! Poop book!"

"Okay, Mason," said Tara. "Let's calm down. Give me a hug. I love you, mister."

"I love you, too. And I love poop!"

Tara forced a smile.

"You boys," she said. "What am I going to do with all you boys?"

Roman saw that his mom was weeping.

"We'll be good, won't we, Mase," he said.

"Poop!"

Roman put a hand on his mom's shoulder.

"It's okay," she said, wiping her face. "If poop makes you happy, you can have all the poop you want."

Mason squealed and let go a string of "Poop poopity poop poopers."

"Let's go," said Roman. "Poor Gerty needs a break from all this poop."

"All this poop!" roared Mason.

For a moment, a fraction of a moment, Roman turned his head, thinking he'd catch Ashley's smile and they'd share a look like: *isn't this creature we made the most amazing thing in the universe?* But, of course, she wasn't there. He raised his head to the sky and moved his lips: *I love you. I'll take care of him.*

CHAPTER FORTY-THREE

The only person Roman could think of who might know Ashley's friend in Virginia was her mentor, Chris Aldrich. Chris ran a yoga studio out of what had once been a barn on her property. She was in her fifties and married to the high school science teacher. They'd moved up from the city when Chris was pregnant with their twins, back in the late 1990s. When her boys started at the elementary school, she created an after-school yoga club for the kids there. Neither of Chris's sons were particularly interested in yoga, but Ashley took to it even in second grade.

Chris was Ashley's first surrogate mom—before she met Roman and Tara—and she eventually helped her get the hours for a certification to teach. Each September, right before school started, Chris hosted a free yoga weekend. Anyone who could fit in her studio or out on the lawn could take a class. Roman had taken a photo and written a couple hundred words on the event every year since he'd started at the paper. Chris usually gave him a quote like: "Back to school can be stressful! Yoga can help everybody find a little balance."

Roman was pretty sure Chris had been at the memorial, and the morning after Bryce told them about Virginia Beach, he called her.

"How are you?" asked Chris. "I've been thinking about you and your mom and Mason."

"Thanks," he said. "We're still in shock, I think. But we're surviving."

"I suppose that's all you can do right now. Rick and I are up in Maine for most of the rest of the summer, but is there anything we can do?"

"I'm looking for a friend of Ash's. She owns a yoga studio, I think, down in Virginia Beach."

"Sure," said Chris. "Jennifer Creswell. Ashley knew her from Hawaii. She's actually been texting me. She said she reached out to you but didn't hear back."

"Shit," said Roman. He'd ignored a lot of messages since Ashley died. It was almost all the same: *so sorry, man.* And: *thinking of you.* A couple: *let me know if you need anything.*

"She understands, of course. I'd been wanting to reach out, too, but I didn't want to bother you. I've been getting messages from Ashley's YouTube followers, and some of her Hawaii friends. They couldn't attend the service—which was beautiful, by the way—but they want to do something to honor her. What would you think about my hosting a memorial online? You don't have to do anything. I can manage it all. Basically, it would just allow people who loved her, who connected with her, to come together and share memories, that kind of thing."

"Okay," said Roman.

"Yeah? I didn't want to do anything without making sure it wouldn't make you uncomfortable. But, like I said, a lot of people have reached out."

"I think it's a good idea. I think she'd like that."

"I do, too," said Chris. Roman could tell she'd started to cry. "I'm so upset, Roman. I can't imagine what you're feeling. She was so *young*. I knew she struggled, of course, I just didn't know about . . . Drugs these days. They're so much more dangerous. One stupid mix-up . . ."

"It wasn't drugs, Chris. She was at a party, but she didn't have any drugs in her system."

"Oh! I'm sorry. I thought . . . Well, now that I think about it, I'm not sure why I thought that. All the posts on Facebook have been vague."

"We're still not sure what happened."

"Oh my goodness, Roman. I'm just so sorry. And you know, when I saw her a few weeks ago, she seemed *happy*."

Roman's heart throbbed. She was happy because she was leaving.

"Did she ever talk to you about moving?"

"Moving?"

"A guy she knows said she was thinking about moving down to Virginia Beach. That her friend there was going to give her a job teaching."

"She didn't say anything about that to me," said Chris. "I do know she was hoping to do some traveling, try to get to a retreat this year. She hadn't done anything like that since Mason, and the pandemic. I know your mom was quite strict about Covid, and Ashley was trying to balance that with her own needs."

"Yeah," said Roman. "Well, thanks for taking the time to chat."

"Anything you need, Roman. We'll be back in town next month. And I'll be in touch about the online service."

Roman ended the call, opened his message app, and searched the name Chris had given him: "Jennifer Creswell." A text popped up from the day before the memorial at Koffee:

Hi Roman, my name is Jennifer Creswell. I'm a friend of Ashley's from Hawaii. I don't really know what to say except that I'm so sorry for your family's loss. Ashley was one of the most vibrant, kind women I have ever met. She was a true light in the world. Please know that you and your son are in my thoughts. I am here to support you in any way I can. Peace be with you.

Roman dialed Jennifer and she picked up after the second ring.

"This is Jen."

"Hi, Jen, this is Roman. Ashley Lillian's . . . partner." He was pacing the living room in the upstairs apartment. Outside, he heard a group of kids roll by on skateboards.

"Roman! I'm so happy to hear from you. How are you? Ugh, that's a stupid question. If *I'm* a mess you must be . . ." She sighed heavily. "Sorry, Ashley was just such an amazing person."

"I know," said Roman. "Thanks. So, you guys met in Hawaii?"

"Yeah. I was super-excited when she called about moving."

"She was going to come work for you?"

"That was the idea," said Jen.

"Do you remember when she first got in touch?"

"About moving? Not exactly. A couple months ago maybe? She asked me about neighborhoods. I think she'd been looking online and wanted some local insight."

"She wasn't going to live with you?"

"No," said Jen. "I'm sorry. I'm confused. You guys didn't talk about this?"

"No," he said. "I had no idea she was planning on moving."

"Oh."

Neither of them seemed sure what to say next.

"There were some things going on with her," said Roman. "I'm trying to figure it out. I know this is awkward to ask, and I don't need details, but did you guys have anything romantic going on?"

"Me and Ashley? No. We were just good friends."

"Did she say anything about Mason? Like, did she ask about schools?"

"She didn't ask about schools, specifically," said Jen.

"Did she say when she was going to start?"

"At first, she was thinking next year, maybe in the spring. But after she got the inheritance she said maybe sooner. She found a rental agent who'd let her put more cash down in lieu of income qualifications."

"The inheritance?"

"She said her aunt died and left her some money."

Ashley didn't have an aunt. Her mom was an only child and her dad was one of three boys.

"Right," said Roman.

"Is that not true?"

"She doesn't have an aunt."

"Oh."

"Do you happen to know the name of the real estate agent she was working with?"

"I don't," she said. "I'm sorry."

Roman said he understood and ended the call, his fingers trembling. She'd been planning a getaway. Secretly building a whole life without him. When would she have come to him? She wouldn't just take Mason without a conversation, would she? Or would she have thought they'd already talked about it. She'd asked over and over about moving and he'd ignored her. Maybe she had her answer. Would he have come home one day a week from now, a month from now, six months from now, to a U-Haul and a shrug? He covered his face with a cushion from the sofa and screamed at her. *Fuck you!* Knowing, of course, the person he should be—was—screaming at was himself.

Roman emptied himself into the cushion and when he was done, he considered the substance of what Jen had said. Why would Ashley make up a story about an inheritance? If she'd offered to pay a bunch of cash up front she must have had—or anticipated she was going to have—more money than he knew about. And then it occurred to him: that, at least, he was something he could find out about her without her phone. He was a cosigner on her bank account.

CHAPTER FORTY-FOUR

The bank was easy. He knew the teller, Lisa Marrone, because she'd been a year behind him and Ash in high school. The manager, Greg Pisco, had been his T-ball coach. Both were sympathetic; both, he gathered, were under the impression Ashley had OD'd. Greg spent a little time at his keyboard, then handed Roman a debit card to swipe through a reader on his desk.

"Just key in a PIN and you'll be all set," he said.

Roman entered the PIN he'd been using since he was sixteen: 0909, Ashley's birthday.

"Do you want to transfer the funds?" asked Greg.

"How much is there?"

Greg turned his computer screen around. "A little under twenty thousand dollars."

"Twenty thousand?" He could see the numbers, but they didn't make sense. Neither of them ever had more than a couple grand at the absolute most in their bank accounts by the end of the month. Ashley made steady money from subscribers, plus the classes she taught in town, and the occasional shift at Koffee. But she bought most of their groceries, and every month she transferred money to their joint account, which he combined with his salary and transferred to his mom to pay the bank. Some months, he put 10 percent into a savings account. But after almost four years of saving, they had barely $3,000 between them. Had she really been holding on to six times that much without telling him?

"She made a couple big deposits recently. Both nine thousand."

"Recently?" Roman felt like a moron, repeating everything Greg said. But repeating it helped him internalize it. "Do you have a copy of the checks?"

"Looks like they were both cash deposits. Lisa was probably here."

Greg called Lisa over, and she didn't even have to look at the screen.

"Oh yeah, she came in with cash. She said she'd sold her dad's old muscle car and his fishing boat on Facebook Marketplace."

More lies. Her father left nothing but medical debt and furniture not even the Goodwill wanted.

"Right," he said, getting up. "Of course. I'm sorry. My brain's not working quite right."

"I can only imagine," said Greg. "We're here for you. Just let us know if there's anything we can help with."

"I have online access now, right?"

"Yes," said Greg. "Just use that PIN to log in and it'll prompt you to create a new password."

As soon as he got home, Roman did just that. The first deposit dropped on June 30, the second a week later. The only thing he could think to do was call Felix.

"Can you talk?" asked Roman.

"Sure, what's up?"

"I talked to Bryce."

"Okay."

"He told you Ashley was thinking about leaving?"

"Roman, I'm sure you understand, but I can't talk about what other people—"

"Okay, fine. Listen, I went to the bank today and found out that Ash deposited almost twenty thousand dollars in the past month. Two separate deposits, both cash. And she lied about where the money came from. She told the teller she'd sold her dad's car, but he didn't have a car to sell. And she told her friend in Virginia Beach that she'd recently come into money because of an inheritance from her aunt. But that's not true either."

There was a pause. "Interesting."

"There has to be some clue about the money in her phone."

"Maybe," said Felix. "I submitted the warrant request yesterday and I'm hoping the judge will sign off today."

"Good," said Roman.

"Do you have any idea where she might have gotten that much cash? If there's nothing in the phone, it's going to be all but impossible to trace."

"You talked to Bryce, right? More than one person has told me he deals."

"What are you suggesting?"

"I don't know. Maybe he's connected somehow? It's hard for

me to imagine her getting involved in that shit. But I didn't have any idea she was hooking up with him, or planning to leave, so what the fuck do I know." Roman paused. "And there's another possibility. You know Nicholas Wolfe, right?"

"I do."

"I just found out that Ashley was friends with his daughter."

"I don't think I knew he had a daughter. She lives here in town?"

"She's technically his stepdaughter. Her name's Kiera. I think Wolfe and her mom were only married a few years. I didn't have any idea she was back, but my mom ran into her yesterday and found out she'd been friends with Ashley."

"Okay."

"But here's the thing: Kiera lied to her. She didn't tell Ash she was Wolfe's daughter."

"How do you know that?"

"She told us. My mom and I went up to Wolfe's yesterday."

"Did Kiera tell you why she lied?"

"No," said Roman. "She was cagey. They both were. And Wolfe admitted that the Davenports, the family that owns the newspaper, offered to pay for Ashley's burial."

"Did that strike you as odd?"

"Sort of," said Roman. "Wolfe said they were just trying to be helpful. Like, because I work for them. But I don't think many bosses offer to bury their employees' family members."

"I agree. That strikes me as unusual."

"Something weird is going on."

"What are you thinking?"

"I'm not sure," said Roman, and he wasn't. "But Kiera and Bryce know each other. Did Bryce tell you that?"

"No," said Felix, "but this is the first I'm hearing about this Kiera."

"Bryce has access to drugs. He could have planted them on Ashley. And we know he was at the party."

"Why would he do that?"

"I don't know," said Roman. "Maybe the money came from Wolfe. Maybe he has a drug problem. Or Kiera does. Or somebody in the family and he's trying to cover it up."

"Why pay Ashley, then? Why not Bryce?"

"Maybe he was paying Bryce, too."

Felix was silent for a moment. "This is a lot of maybes, Roman. But I appreciate you calling. I'm going to look into all of this."

"Will you talk to Kiera? And Wolfe?"

"I'd like to look at Ashley's phone first," said Felix.

"Yeah, but that could take a while. You talked to Bryce. You talked to Bella. You talked to me and John and my mom. Why not them?"

"As of this moment," Felix said slowly, "there's no direct connection between Ashley and Nicholas Wolfe."

"There's one between her and Kiera. They were friends. There are, like, pictures of them together online. With Bryce."

"I understand."

"So? What? Are you afraid of him?"

"Roman," said Felix. "I'm going to ask you again to trust me to do my job. Speaking of which, I talked to Emily and Rico. They both corroborated your story about being in the city. I'm gonna pull your E-ZPass data just to make sure, but it looks like your alibi is going to hold up."

Roman wasn't sure what to say. "Good."

"I want to find out what happened, Roman," said Felix. "I appreciate your honesty. Your whole family. I know this is a nightmare. Chief is back tomorrow and I'll lay all this out for him. The missing phone and wallet, the missing shoe. The tox report and the lack of fingerprints on the drugs. Now this mysterious money. Hopefully, he'll see what we do."

"What if he doesn't?"

"You let me worry about that."

CHAPTER FORTY-FIVE

After his call with Felix, Roman felt like he'd drunk six shots of espresso. He went downstairs looking for his mom. Her car was in the driveway, but she and Mason weren't in the yard. Could they have gone for a walk? He looked at the time: 2 p.m. Mason's nap time. Roman crept back upstairs and gently pushed open the door of his mom's bedroom. There they were, asleep, together. The boy was sprawled, mouth open, one arm crooked above his head, blanket twisted up his legs. Tara was on her side in the fetal position, her hands tucked by her face. His mother looked tiny in the bed, even next to a four-year-old.

Mason sighed in his sleep. Tara lay motionless, and an ugly thought arose in Roman: his mother had made herself small for Mason. She'd shrunk to fit his son's needs in a way she'd never done for him. She was enormous in his childhood; loud and drunk and wild before the accident that sent her to jail, then performatively "good" after she cleaned up. She was just thirty-three when he started high school, younger than most of his teachers.

She was back in school herself, getting an associate's at the community college and managing a restaurant, but she volunteered every time the high school asked for a parent—until Roman finally told her to back off.

It was tenth grade, sometime in the spring, and his shitty day started right after first period, when Ash pulled away as he tried to kiss her.

"What's wrong?" he asked.

"Nothing."

"Tell me, please?"

Ashley looked at him with hard eyes. "Sometimes I think your mom gets me better than you do."

Then, after practice, Frankie Morris smacked him with a towel and asked if his mom was going to be at the game.

"I heard she likes athletes," he said, licking his lip. "Think I've got a chance of getting her to rub my bat?"

Roman got in a single punch before half the team tackled him. Nobody told the coaches and all the way home on the late bus, Roman seethed. When he arrived and saw Bella and Ashley and Tara all together in his driveway, painting an opening day banner for his team—his mom, as usual, in a shirt cut just low enough to expose cleavage, a shirt that screamed "open for business"—he lost it.

"I'm not sure who you think you're fooling with this perfect-mom shit. Everybody knows who you really are. Do me a favor—do us all a favor—and give it a rest. Go out. Have some fun. I get it. You didn't know how to use birth control and now you're trying to make up for nearly killing me. Fine. Thanks. But I don't need you to pretend to be mom of the year anymore. I need you to fucking disappear."

His mother's face went white.

"Don't be an asshole, Roman," said Bella.

"What is wrong with you?" said Ash.

"It's okay," said Tara weakly. She hadn't moved. Her fingertips were covered in paint, her toned arms limp beside her.

"The fuck it is," said Bella. "He can't talk to you like that."

"Go home, Bella," Roman said, and marched inside.

The next day, he apologized to Ashley, telling her about what Frankie had said. He promised to apologize to Tara, too, but he never did. And his tantrum worked. Tara backed off. She still came to his games, but bowed out as team mom, passing off the Gatorade runs and sign-up sheets and T-shirt printing to another woman. Junior year, the team went to state championships and lost the final game. When Tara came to rouse him for school on the Monday after, she found him weeping.

"That was going to be my ace," he said, in an uncharacteristic display of emotion. "Pitcher for the state championship team. At the most there would be forty-nine other kids with that on their application. Now I've got nothing. Do you know how many kids apply to NYU every year? Like a hundred thousand. You have to be *special.*"

"You are special, baby," said his mom.

Roman laughed and wiped his nose. His mom was so clueless.

"Special on paper, Mom. I need to be special on paper if I want to get out of this fucking town."

She didn't have much to say to that. What did he expect? That she would be happy he was desperate to escape her? That she would help? Looking back, of course, she *had* helped. She'd stayed out of his way when he wanted, and the next fall, when he found the thing that would make him look special on paper—when *Atlantic* magazine called and said that the essay he'd secretly written about her was the winner of their national competition and they wanted to publish it—she didn't stand in his way.

"My Teenage Mom," he was sure, got him into NYU. The editor's note announcing his win called the essay "brave": it "asks hard questions about what makes a family, and whether we can ever truly make up for our past mistakes." NPR called and invited them both to be interviewed on *All Things Considered*. Tara said she would do it, though she clearly didn't want to. Roman told the producer his mom would rather not and the producer said that was fine. He took the train to the city alone and an intern guided him into a tiny studio with a microphone and enormous headphones. The host was elsewhere; everything was conducted remotely.

"We invited your mom to come on the program, too," said the host in her clear voice.

"Yeah," he said. "She's proud of me, but it's painful, you know."

"Absolutely," said the host. He felt like he could hear her nodding. Had he done the wrong thing, using his mom's mistakes to give himself a ladder out? When Larry asked if he could interview him about the winning essay for the *Advocate*, teenage Roman declined. When the essay was selected to run in the *Best*

American Essays of 2016 anthology, Roman didn't even tell his mom. To this day, he didn't own a copy of the magazine or the book.

Roman was about to wake Tara when his phone rang again. The caller ID read: "Virginia Beach."

He went into the hall and answered. "This is Roman," he said.

"Roman! I'm glad I finally caught you. This is Denise Witt from the Associated Press."

"The Associated Press?"

"Yes. We do have to close our search soon, but we'd really like to set up an interview if you're still interested."

"I'm sorry," said Roman, walking down the stairs. "Interested in what?"

"The mid-Atlantic feature writing position? I know it's been a while since you applied; things don't move very quickly here. Did you get my other message?"

"I'm sorry, I guess I didn't. Um, my partner—my son's mom—just died and things have been a little crazy."

"Oh my God, I'm so sorry. I had no idea."

Roman wasn't sure what to say. Fortunately, Denise continued. "We were really excited when we saw your application. We're looking for someone who can grow with us. And we really want a *writer*. A couple of your clips—especially that essay from the *Atlantic*—were really impressive. I know you've been doing local news awhile. Which is great. Your pitch for the investigation into the Davenports' low-income properties—that was beautifully done. Honestly, we'd like to work with you on that

even if you don't take the position; I can assign it now. Unfortunately, the position isn't remote. You don't have to be in the office
all week, but we want someone in Virginia or Maryland—that's
the area where we have low coverage. You did indicate you'd be
willing to relocate . . . Is that still possible?"

"Um, I think so," said Roman. "Could you give me, like, a day
or two? We're still settling things. But I'm interested."

"Absolutely. Can we set up an interview for first thing next
week?"

"Sounds good."

"Great. I'll send a Zoom link. Do I have the best email? Roman
at Roman Grady dot com?"

He hadn't used that email address in years; it was one he'd
created when he had to make himself a website as part of his
major in college.

"Use my Gmail instead," Roman said, and gave her the address.

"This is great," said Denise. "See you soon. And I'm really
sorry to hear about your partner."

His partner. Ashley must have found the job listing and sent
the application through the email he never used. Unlike her, he'd
never changed his passwords. He went back upstairs to his computer and looked into the old account. Mostly it was spam, but
then, four weeks ago, he found a message to Denise dot Witt at
ap dot com in the sent mail:

Ms. Witt,
My name is Roman Grady and I write to apply for the

*Senior Feature Writer position based in Virginia. Since
graduating from NYU, I've been honing my skills—from
source-building to breaking news to FOIA and audio
production—at a small newspaper in the Hudson Valley,
but I am ready to move on and would like to bring my experience and passion to the AP. I've attached my resume and
links to clips, as well as a pitch for an investigative feature:
in a nutshell, I've discovered that the billionaire Davenport
family is in the slumlord business—and may soon face a
rash of lawsuits from tenants, including one from the family of an elderly woman who died after negligence at her
apartment complex. I've interviewed the family and they are
willing to cooperate with the story.*

*I've been reporting this piece in my off-time and think it
might be a fit for the AP—especially since two of the complexes are in the Richmond area. This is the kind of story I'd
like to dig into as a Senior Feature Writer.*

Thank you for your time. I look forward to hearing from you.

It was a damn good application letter. She'd used some of
the language from his unsent pitch to *The New York Times*, and
she'd updated his resume. It wasn't all that surprising that she
could do such a thing—she'd always been smarter than him, just
not interested in academic subjects; she paid close attention, and
she was a great mimic—but that she would. That she hadn't just
looked at apartments and found herself a job—she'd found him
one, too. She wanted him to come with her. She wanted a different

life, but she still wanted him. And she knew she'd have to make it happen herself. She'd have to do all the work and present it to him with a big gold bow: *I have a new life all ready for us. All you have to do is say yes.*

Say yes, and leave your mom.

What would he have done? Did it matter now?

Roman stepped toward the bed and touched his mom's arm. She opened her eyes.

"Mom," he whispered, "I just got off the phone with Felix. I need to talk to you."

CHAPTER FORTY-SIX

In April, Bella was at Diane's bar with a group of people I didn't know. She didn't look good. I knew she'd had Covid early, and spent time on a ventilator. Now she was overweight in a lumpy, unbalanced sort of way and her hair was a faded pink that read neglect, not novelty. But she was laughing, and the sound—a kind of honk and sniffle unique to her—propelled me back to the days when we were in love. It hadn't lasted long. I cared about her; I wanted to make her laugh and I wanted to hear her tell her wacky stories and I absolutely loved her body. But hers wasn't the approval I sought; I didn't turn to her for comfort.

Still, my teenage feelings for Bella were real and sharp and they forced me to confront truths about myself and the people around me that were complicated and painful. Loving Bella openly and loving Roman at the same time exposed us all to everything from ridicule to disgust. Roman was offended at how people—my mom, for example, and too many of our friends—reacted. Bella was defiant. I was, perhaps stupidly, shocked. It brought us all closer for a while, as the people who accepted our little triangle—Tara, Daniel, Bobby, Chris—became our chosen family, and the others our sworn enemies.

But strife doesn't always bring strength, and when Roman left for college and Bella wanted more from me than I was willing to give, things began to fall apart. She didn't reach out when my dad died. And when I saw her in the bar that night, I realized that she'd never met my son.

But all that dropped away when I heard her laugh. And the way her face lit up when I approached her—it felt like magic. We hugged and she left her friends to come sit with me. I introduced her to Diane, who she already knew, and we talked and talked. I showed her pictures of Mason and she showed me some drawings she'd been doing. It wasn't a deep conversation, but it was a beginning. Bryce showed up and I basically ignored him. After maybe an hour, he got pissy.

"Can I talk to you alone?" he asked.

I agreed and slid off the barstool, telling Bella I'd be back.

"You wanna head over?" Bryce asked, nodding in the direction of the photographer's loft.

"I think I'm gonna stay," I said. "I haven't talked to Bella in ages."

"You gonna start fucking her now, too?"

"What's your problem?"

"I heard about you and Diane."

"And?"

"And, you're being kind of a bitch."

Bella heard that. She turned on her barstool and said, loudly: "Did you just call her a bitch?"

"Stay out of it," said Bryce.

"Not if you're calling her a bitch."

Now Diane and the people Bella had been with were all listening. An argument at a bar was something that might get around. I'd seen some guys the week before who were friends with John. There were eyes everywhere.

"I'll call you later," I said to Bryce.

He looked like he was going to say something, but for whatever reason, decided against it. He stomped out of the bar like a child.

I went back to Bella, but the mood was altered. I promised to text, and I kept the promise. We met up a couple times, though if Bryce showed up, she'd bail. And then, right after Memorial Day weekend, as I was pushing my cart through the automatic doors of Walmart, I saw her standing outside in her blue employee polo—talking to Kiera. They didn't see me at first. I stood for a few moments and watched. They were arguing. I walked their way, and Kiera looked up.

"Hey," I said, smiling. "I didn't know you guys knew each other?"

Both of them looked extremely uncomfortable.

"Oh," said Kiera, attempting nonchalance, "you know, small town."

"I gotta go back on shift," said Bella, dropping her cigarette, smashing it with her shoe.

"I'm late, too," said Kiera. "Bye, ladies!"

I texted Bella from my car but she didn't text back. The next day, I went to her house. At first, she tried to get me to buy the same thing Kiera had: they were just acquaintances, they'd met at a bar and Kiera happened to be shopping while Bella was on shift and they went outside for a cigarette.

But Bella has always been an epically bad liar. She didn't look me in the eyes once when she told her little story, and her leg was bouncing up and down like it was plugged in.

"Bella," I said, "what's going on? Why are you making shit up?"

Bella wrapped her arms around her chest and started rocking.

"You know who she is, right?"

"Who? Kiera?"

Bella nodded.

"What do you mean?"

"She's Nicholas Wolfe's stepdaughter."

"Nicholas Wolfe the lawyer? The one with the big house?" I knew him—well, not knew him—because he used to come into the coffee shop when I worked more regularly before Covid, before Mason. Wolfe was one of the half-dozen local middle-aged men who thought their relative physical fitness and snappy clothing made them attractive to women half their age. I was always friendly, though, when I was working. That's a big part of the job behind the counter. I smiled and chatted and let them think about what it would be like to touch me. How many times was I asked about my tattoos? Ooh, what constellation is that? And I'd pull my shirt down to show my shoulder and the Seven Sisters in the sky. They were hunted by men, I'd tell the leering customer, sunny as can be. Even after they were turned into stars, the men still wouldn't stop. Cool, the customer would say, and maybe drop some change in the tip jar.

It wasn't until Roman started at the paper that I learned Wolfe worked for the Davenports.

"Are you sure?" I asked Bella.

Bella nodded.

"Okay," I said. "But that doesn't explain how you know her."

"Please, Ash," pleaded Bella. "I can't talk about it."

"Can't talk about what?"

"I promise, it's not a big deal. It's just . . . Please understand."

I wasn't feeling particularly understanding. "Fine," I said, standing up.

"Please don't tell Roman," she said.

"Tell him what?"

"About Kiera."

"Why wouldn't I tell Roman? Why does that matter?"

"Just don't, okay?"

"Fuck that, Bella. Roman's my partner. If I want to tell him I'm going to tell him."

"No!" shouted Bella. "I'll tell you if you promise not to tell him."

Why did I agree? I suppose because I figured it was a bunch of stupid Bella-drama. I figured, whatever it was, Roman wouldn't care.

I sat back down.

Bella hesitated. "Okay," she said finally. "So, Wolfe works for the Davenports, right? They're going to buy my house. For like, a lot of money. More than I'd get from a regular sale."

"You're selling your house?"

Bella nodded. "But not yet. And it's not guaranteed. They have to get approval first."

"Approval from who?"

"The town, I think. I don't know the details. But it's all on the down-low and if it doesn't go through, I'm fucked."

"Why would you be fucked?"

"Because I took out a second mortgage and I can't pay it off without them."

"When did you do that?"

"After I got sick. I couldn't work and I didn't have any insurance."

"What about the money your mom left you?"

"She didn't leave me money, she left me the house. I don't even have the money to fix the fucking bathroom."

"Okay. But why can't I tell Roman?"

"Just don't, please?"

"Why?!"

"Because they don't want anybody looking too closely until it's approved."

"It's just a fucking house, Bella. People sell them every day."

"I'm not talking about this anymore. Seriously. Kiera knows we're hanging out. That's why she was pissed."

"She doesn't want you to hang out with me? How is that any of her business?"

Bella looked down. "It's, like, entirely her business. It's the only reason she's in town."

"What do you mean?"

"She's friends with you because Wolfe wants to keep an eye on Roman."

I opened my mouth to protest, but of course it immediately made sense. My skin felt itchy. I thought of all the secrets I'd told her. All the shit I'd talked about the people I love. I pulled out my phone.

"Ash, you can't tell her I told you. Not yet." Bella started to cry. "I need this money, Ash. Please. Kiera says it's only a couple more weeks. Or maybe months, until the deal goes through. Can you just . . . pretend?"

I rubbed my eyes. No, I could not pretend. But maybe, I started to think, I could make this whole thing work for me.

CHAPTER FORTY-SEVEN

"I knew it," said Tara, quietly. "I knew she was lying about those texts from the girl in Virginia Beach. Why did she have to lie? Why not fucking *talk* to us about it?"

Roman didn't say the obvious: that she knew they'd all freak out. Did it even matter anymore? It was clearly their fault she'd been sneaking around. He was too much of a pussy to have a conversation about moving, and Tara . . . Well, his mom admitted she'd threatened to try to get custody of Mason if Ashley even tried.

They'd pushed her to do what she'd done, whatever that was. They had to live with that.

"We have to figure out where that money came from," said Roman. "That's a lot of money. That much cash? And there could be more. She could have a fucking storage locker full of cash for all we know."

"There has to be something in her phone," said Tara.

"I agree. Unless she, like, had a second phone. A burner."

"Jesus," said Tara. "How did we miss all of this?"

"I want to talk to Bella again," said Roman. "She's a fuckup but she loves Ash."

"She didn't love her enough to keep her out of trouble. She didn't love her enough to come talk to us."

Larry called the next morning.

"Don't worry," he said as soon as Roman picked up. "I'm not asking you to come back. Although I could use an ETA. It's pretty fucking hairy around here."

"I'll talk to Wolfe next week," Roman said. Noncommittal but somehow concrete.

"That's what I'm calling about," said Larry. "I'm hoping you can talk to him today."

"Not yet," said Roman. "We still don't have a cause of death and—"

"Listen, he just called me. He wants me to go to the town judge and testify about your wife's cell phone."

Roman didn't bother correcting him.

"Why would Wolfe call you about that?"

"Apparently Sergeant White wrote up a warrant request to get her information from the sky."

"The cloud."

"The what? Yeah. From her phone."

"I know," said Roman.

"He talked to you?"

"Felix did, yeah."

"And you're okay with it?"

"Of course I am," said Roman. "Her phone is missing. It's a fucking murder investigation."

"A murder investigation? That's not what the chief said."

"What did the chief say?"

"Well, he didn't say exactly, but I was under the impression we were looking at an overdose."

"Why does everyone think that? She didn't even have drugs in her system."

"Oh," said Larry. "When I looked at the original report it said there were drugs found—"

"In her pocket. Yeah. But she didn't actually do them. Felix thinks they might have been planted."

"I haven't heard anything about that."

"Have you spoken to Felix?"

"No. I've spoken to the chief."

"Well, the chief has his head up his ass. He's got the first murder in his town in years and he goes off to a fucking conference."

"If you gave permission, I'm not sure why Wolfe would want me involved."

"How does he want you involved?"

"He says the Davenports are concerned that some of your reporting could be in the cell phone. He said they're concerned about revealing sources."

"Bullshit," said Roman. "It's not my cell phone, it's hers."

"That's what I said."

"How does Wolfe even know about the warrant request?"

"It's a small town, Roman," said Larry.

"What are you going to do?"

"Well, I'm not positive," said Larry.

"What did you say when he asked?"

"I said I didn't think it was necessary. Since it wasn't your phone. But he kept saying the family was concerned. How did he put it? Something like, *we'd appreciate you speaking for the paper.* And then he told me Judge Navarro was expecting my call."

"But you called me."

"I did."

"Why?"

"Because it felt odd. I wanted to see if Wolfe had called you first."

"He didn't."

"Have you spoken to him at all?"

"My mom and I went to his house yesterday. It turns out, Ashley was friends with his stepdaughter."

"He has a stepdaughter?"

"He does. And he's been keeping her under wraps."

"I'll be honest, Roman," said Larry after a pause. "I don't really want to be involved in this."

"Neither do I, Larry," said Roman.

"If your wife was murdered . . ."

"She wasn't my wife, Larry."

"What?"

"It doesn't matter. Continue."

"I don't feel real comfortable stepping into a murder investigation."

"Okay, but can you tell Wolfe that?"

Larry didn't speak for a moment. "I'm going to call the chief again."

"Good idea," said Roman. "In fact, tell him I'd like to talk to him, too. Maybe I'll stop by."

An hour later, Roman walked into town hall, which housed the police station, the court, the historical society, the tax accessor, and the mayor's office. His plan was to ask the chief point-blank if he was considering Ashley's death a homicide, but as he walked past the town clerk's open door, someone called his name.

"Roman!"

Evelyn Conover poked her head into the hallway. "I've been hoping you might come by. Did you get my message?"

"No," said Roman. "Sorry."

"Oh please," she said, "don't apologize. I can only imagine what you're going through."

Roman gave her a polite smile. "Thanks."

"Everybody's at lunch," she said. Evelyn was Tara's age, and worked part-time at the clerk's office. The mayor brought her on to fill in when the longtime clerk, Linda Eisner, took time off to care for her husband, who was in the last stages of lung cancer. Afterward, she and Linda decided to job-share. Roman had written about the change for the paper and remembered the mayor being extremely proud of the "progressive arrangement."

"Come on in," said Evelyn. "I'll give you the folder I've been holding."

"Folder?"

"On that Hudson View property?"

Roman followed her into the tiny office, dominated by a heavy wooden desk that would probably need to be destroyed to be removed. A radio in the corner played the classic rock station out of Poughkeepsie.

"It wasn't where I thought it would be," she said, fingering through a set of files in a vertical organizer atop one of the filing cabinets. She pulled out a thin manila envelope and handed it to him. "Somebody must have put it in the wrong cabinet."

"It's okay," said Roman, trying to figure out how to get the information he needed without raising her suspicion. "I feel like it's been a hundred years since I was thinking about this."

"I know," she said. "I'm sorry. You know I usually try—"

"No, no," said Roman, smiling. "It's not your fault. I just mean with everything going on. I'm trying to get organized again. Do you have that original request?"

"I mean, I don't have anything in writing," she said. "Ashley just came in and asked."

"Ashley?"

"She said she was helping you on something for the paper."

"Oh," said Roman, pretending like he knew what the fuck she was talking about. "Of course. Sorry."

"Oh, please don't apologize," she said.

Roman opened the folder. The first piece of paper was a copy of a property deed for 65 Hudson View, Adamsville, NY. Bella's house. He unfolded the legal-sized document and set it on the desk, lifting the pages carefully until he came to the signatures. The first was stamped and dated March 23, 2002, signed by Robyn Abernathy. The final page was stamped November 13, 2018, signed by Bella.

The other paperwork in the file was a photocopy of a property survey, indicating where the lines between Bella's property and her neighbors were drawn. The stamp on the top left said it was performed by Salinger Land Surveyors on December 2, 2023— last year. In the bottom corner was another stamp: "RECEIVED: WinGate, LLC," and a signature Roman recognized: Nicholas Wolfe.

CHAPTER FORTY-EIGHT

On the rare occasions Roman entertained the idea of moving, the conversation always came down to one easy roadblock: money. First and last month's rent plus a security deposit—if they even approved us, given his salary and my entirely freelance income. And speaking of salary, could Roman find work somewhere else? I knew it was possible, but I also knew it would take doing. It would take him deciding it was a priority; and I'd never been able to convince him it should be.

Still, I wasn't going to stop looking, and when I saw the Associated Press job, I bookmarked it, and started working on the application. But even if Roman got the job, there were all kinds of other expenses we'd have to manage: some sort of U-Haul to carry what we had, and buying the furniture we couldn't take—like the dining room table, which belonged to Roman's grandparents and which Tara was never going to give up. And speaking of Tara, pre-K was only half-day, so unless I could make my schedule at the studio match Mason's school—which seemed unlikely—we'd need at least some help with child care for another year.

It didn't all come together until I confronted Kiera. She'd been texting me for days, probably worried that Bella had done exactly what she did after I saw them at Walmart, and told me the truth—or at least part of it. I finally texted back and told her to meet me at the Mexican place by Gold's and be ready to talk.

I got there early and found us a table in the back corner. She arrived wearing sunglasses, like it was a spy movie or some shit. She sat down and neither of us said anything at first. The waitress came by and I ordered a beer; Kiera did the same.

"Is Kiera even your real name?" I asked.

"You don't remember me?"

I raised an eyebrow.

"I went to high school here for a year," she said. "When my mom and Nicholas were married. I got kicked out for doing coke and they sent me away."

I did have a memory of some girl a couple grades above me getting expelled, but it was vague.

"Okay," I said. "So why are you here now?"

She told me what she probably thought was a sob story: the pandemic killed her budding career in PR. She'd gotten engaged, then dumped, and her mom's new husband said she couldn't live with them in Palm Beach.

"He's a fucking Republican," said Kiera. "Mr. Bootstraps."

She went on. Her real dad was an electrician in Queens, where her mom had grown up, and she'd crashed with him for a while, but didn't get along with his girlfriend. She said she couch-surfed and house-sat afterward, "trying to rebuild my network."

"Everything is freelance these days," she said. "Even if I get a great gig, it's temporary. Most of the girls have family money so they don't care. But I have to hustle like crazy and the only way to network is to be out and do you realize a fucking glass of wine is twenty-five dollars in the city these days?"

I gave her the wrap-it-up finger.

"Fine. Fine. My mom must have talked to Nicholas. He called and told me he'd lease me a car the next day and buy me an apartment in the city if I helped him with this thing."

"What thing?"

"Listen, I'm sure you're pissed. I mean, yes, he told me to, like, befriend you, but I feel like we have a connection."

"Tell me what the fuck is going on. Why would Nicholas Wolfe want you to be friends with me?"

She dug into her purse and pulled out a brochure. "Read this."

The brochure was glossy, printed on heavy card stock. "Luxury & Luck" was written in script across an image of a heavily made-up, cleavage-baring woman rolling dice as she leaned over a craps table. I opened the fold and inside was a photograph of a modern house—or maybe it was a hotel—overlooking the Hudson River. More pictures showed an infinity pool, a spa, a dining area, stunning bedrooms and bathrooms with floor-to-ceiling windows and stone soaking tubs. "An opulent, members-only oasis with exclusive access to the only floating casino in New York," read the inside text. "Try your luck, then return to comfort like you've never experienced." On the back, at the bottom left corner, was a website: www.WinGateHudson.com.

"What is this?" I asked.

"As you know, New York legalized gambling last year." She paused. I wanted to hit her. "Only a couple places have licenses so far, but the Davenports found a loophole. They're outfitting one of their yachts into a floating casino and nightclub. It'll go up and down the river—Manhattan to Kingston. And the plan is to have boutique hotel-spas along the way, with drivers all set to take you to and from the boat. They want them super-close to the docks in each town, and they want a quiet place with a view. If it works, they've got like a billion in investment lined up. Not just here—some cities in Europe, too. Bella's place is going to be proof of concept."

I squinted. "The Davenports want to put a hotel on Bella's property?"

"More like a private club, but yeah."

"Is that . . . legal? It's residential."

"Exactly. This is where I come in. Well, actually you. Well, actually Roman. Nicholas got the planning board members and the mayor to agree to the zoning change. It'll bring in tax dollars, it'll be tasteful, blah blah. But, according to him, normally, something like this would go up for public comment."

"Nobody in this town is going to agree to that," I said, starting to understand. "The neighbors will freak out."

"Right. So, they can't find out. The meeting to officially make the change is July 31."

Six weeks away. "How did he get the mayor on board? And the people on planning?"

Kiera shrugged. "I don't think it was that hard. The mayor's old—she's not gonna run again. Now she can retire to Florida. I don't think the planning board even gets paid."

"He bribed them."

"I don't know the details. He just needs to make sure nobody finds out. He wasn't worried about the old guy at the paper, but he was worried about Roman."

"Why not bribe Roman, then? Or befriend him? Or fire him?"

"Nicholas thought that firing him would invite too much scrutiny. I guess he'd written something else about the Davenports and Nicholas didn't want him to, like, get pissed off and start digging more. And he didn't think it was safe to try and bribe him."

"He'd tell you to fuck off."

"That's what Nicholas said. I tried talking to him a couple times—at the Turkey Trot last year, and once again when I happened to see him picking up a take-out sushi order. But he doesn't go out much. Nicholas thought I should try something else."

"And I made it easy," I said.

Kiera shrugged. "You needed a friend. It was good timing."

"You're a fucking bitch."

"Fine," she said. "So, what now?"

I took out my phone and took a picture of the brochure before Kiera could snatch it back.

"Now, you tell your stepdad he's going to pay me or I'll tell Roman."

"How much do you want?"

I did some quick math in my head and decided on a number that would make moving possible even if neither of us had a job for six months: "I want fifty thousand dollars."

It was that easy. Kiera texted me the next morning and told me to meet her in the parking lot of an abandoned bowling alley just outside town. She handed me an envelope.

"There's nine thousand in here," she said, and before I could protest, *she continued. "Nicholas says to tell you that if he takes more than that out at once it'll raise red flags at the bank."*

I wondered if she could see my hands shaking. Part of me wondered if this was all a setup. What better way to silence Roman than to get me on video accepting a blackmail payment. Keep quiet, or we press charges against your son's mom.

"Meet me here next week, same time. You'll get the same amount every week until the meeting. That's fifty-six thousand. Six extra for being patient."

But I only got two more payments.

CHAPTER FORTY-NINE

Bella looked high when she opened the front door. Roman pushed past her.

"What the fuck!" she exclaimed.

"Why is Nicholas Wolfe ordering property surveys of your house?"

Bella's eyes widened. She bit her lip.

"Tell me!"

Bella sat down and started rocking back and forth, holding her head. The story she told was insane, but made perfect sense. She was the most desperate, least connected homeowner on the best block in the town where the Davenports had the greatest chance of ramming through a zoning change. She was the perfect target. She gave him all the details: she'd been on WinGate's payroll as a "web designer" for almost a year. They gave her health insurance and $4,000 a month, and while she didn't have it in writing, Wolfe had promised her $1.2 million for the property once the zoning went through. More than twice what she'd get if she tried to sell it herself. All she had to do was keep her mouth shut.

"Why did you tell Ash?" he asked.

"She saw me and Kiera arguing at Walmart. She wouldn't stop asking. She said she was going to tell you something was up if I didn't tell her what I knew."

"Why are you still working at Walmart if you're getting all this money?"

Bella hung her head. "There's some people there I like. It's somewhere to go."

It was so fucking sad.

"Did Wolfe tell you Ash had to be gone to keep your deal?"

"What? No!"

"Why should I believe you? She died *at your house*! Someone planted drugs on her. You've got access to drugs, obviously."

"I know it's my fault that she died," Bella said quietly. "If I hadn't told her about Kiera, she wouldn't have blackmailed Wolfe."

"Ashley wouldn't blackmail anyone." But as soon as he said it, he knew he was probably wrong. Blackmail perfectly explained the cash. "But Wolfe wasn't at your party, Bella. Neither was Kiera."

"I don't know what to tell you," said Bella. She looked miserable. "You can't think I killed her. I loved her."

"I'm calling Felix," said Roman. "You need to tell him all of this."

"It's not going to bring her back," whispered Bella.

Roman glared at her. "Your fucking deal is done no matter what, Bella. If you think I'm going to let Wolfe win . . ."

"Why do you care! Why do you hate me! You have *everything*. Well, you did, at least. Ashley chose you. You have a career. You have a family that loves you. I have nobody."

"Cry me a river, Bella."

Roman dialed Felix. His phone went to voicemail. A moment later, a text popped up:

> busy—will call later

But Roman couldn't wait. He texted back:

> wolfe was the one paying ash

The phone rang. It was Felix.

"Where are you?" asked Felix.

"I'm at Bella's house. Wolfe has been paying her, too. Ashley found out and she went to Wolfe and—"

"Hold on," said Felix. "Slow down. I can send someone over."

"No," said Roman. "You're the only person we're talking to. Wolfe probably has Scott and the chief and everybody else in this fucking town in his pocket."

"Okay," said Felix. "But you're going to have to hold tight. I'm at the hospital right now. We got called to an overdose in the CVS parking lot. Paramedics revived her and she says she got the drugs from Bryce."

"Jesus," said Roman. "Is it somebody I know?"

"Maybe," said Felix. "She works at the bank."

Roman's blood felt like it was suddenly running with electricity. "Lisa Marrone?"

"Yeah," said Felix. "I got Judge Navarro on the phone and he signed off on a warrant. We're about to pick Bryce up. I'll be in touch as soon as I can."

Roman ended the call and looked at Bella.

"Did Bryce know Ash was blackmailing Wolfe?"

Bella nodded. "That's why he wanted to talk to her that night."

CHAPTER FIFTY

I should have been more careful about the whole situation. After I made the second deposit, and told the lies about my dad and my "aunt," it felt safe, somehow. Both were totally plausible ways of coming into money. People sold all kinds of expensive things on Facebook. There were literally RVs for sale for eighty grand. Surely lots of the sales were at least partially cash.

I wanted to tell Roman. I almost did, a couple of times. I almost convinced myself that he'd see that what I was doing made a kind of sense. Who was it really hurting to let a fancy hotel go up Hudson View? A bunch of snotty ex-citidiots who were gonna be pissed about their view and their property values? They'd be fine. It might even bring the value up if they got celebrities to stay, which, judging from the vibe of the brochure and the membership fees, was what they were going for.

Sure, it was appalling that Mayor Sloane and the assholes on the planning board were engaging in blatant corruption, but what was the alternative? If I told him, Roman could blow the whole thing up with a single Facebook post. They'd all step down in disgrace, but even if Roman convinced The New York Times that this small-town corruption was worth their while, the Davenports would probably come up with some spin about its being the mayor's idea to keep the zoning decision on the down-low; that she thought once the revenue came in and residents' taxes went down everyone would thank her. Then Roman would be out of a job and spend a year asleep, and once again Mason would have a parent whose behavior he had to make excuses for.

No. This was the best way. All I needed to do was get through a month. Then, even if the AP job didn't pan out, I figured, Roman would quit the Advocate in disgust and agree to the move. Tara would beg, but Roman would have seen the light and be able to tell her that he was making this choice because it was the best thing for his family. Not her family; his family. We'd promise to get Mason bunk beds and tell her she could come visit whenever she wanted.

What I didn't count on was Bryce. We hadn't seen each other as much since Bella and I started hanging out. Our little fling ran its course by the end of May. It was clear to me that he was in no way working as a photographer, unless you counted taking pictures at parties where he sold—and did—drugs. And he seemed less interested in me, too. When we were out together he was always looking around like there might be someone better to talk to. The last time we hooked up was at his grandma's apartment. It was awful. I cried in my car afterward. What the fuck was I doing? I hadn't heard from him in almost three weeks when he appeared outside Gold's after my Wednesday morning class.

"So," he said, "a little birdie told me you came into some cash."

"Oh really," I said. "That's news to me."

I couldn't look him in the eye. I unlocked the car and threw my bag in the backseat, but when I went to open the front door, he pushed it shut.

"You're lying. Don't lie to me."

"Fuck off," I said, pulling the door open again. "You don't know what you're talking about."

He let me go, but not for long. The asshole starting following me, and five minutes after I met Kiera the next time, he texted saying that if I didn't meet him in twenty minutes at the Fir Point parking area he'd call Roman and tell him "everything." I had no idea what he actually knew, but I agreed to meet him. On the way there, I downloaded a recording app to my phone, and kept it on when he hopped into my passenger seat.

"She give you another nine thousand?" he asked.

I must have looked surprised that he knew the number.

"Good," he said. "That's about what I need."

"You're not taking it all."

He pulled a handgun out of his waistband and set it on his leg.

"Yes. I am."

"What the fuck, Bryce? Since when do you have a gun?"

"It's a dangerous world, Ash," he said.

It was so strange. We'd been really close for a little while. We were thousands of miles from home and our togetherness in Hawaii had felt more than serendipitous; it had felt significant. Like an inflection; a validation of both our choices to make dramatic life changes. He told me that traveling had made him feel small at first. Who was he *to get all this attention? But as he moved from city to city, surrounded almost entirely by strangers, he began to trust himself. He began to, as he put it, "grow into my power."*

Each of us, he said one night as we were walking on the beach beneath a white moon, are powerful forces. We're all power. All energy. We just have to embrace it. It felt so true. I was happy in Hawaii. I was thriving. I'd created an identity entirely separate from anyone or anything in Adamsville. I hadn't thought of these facts as having anything to do with my power as a person, but I loved that idea. Yes, I remember thinking. We are young and we are powerful! We can make our lives whatever we want!

So much for that. Five years later we were back home, both broke and desperate. Him with a gun and me with someone else's cash and the smell of our fear filling the car.

"You don't have to do this," I whispered.

"Do what? Fucking survive?" He opened the glove compartment. "Is it in here?"

It wasn't.

"You can have half," I said.

"I need it all. I'll take half next time."

"There's no next time," I lied. "You'll have to go straight to Kiera."

"We'll see."

I didn't feel like I had a choice. I opened the center console and gave him the envelope.

"I'm serious," I said. "That's it."

He got out of the car.

The next Friday night, after Mason made it clear he wanted Tara to put him to bed instead of me, Bella texted. Her timing couldn't have been more perfect.

> i know i'm a fuckup but i love you. i could use a friend.

I bought it. Because I could use a friend, too. For an hour or so, it was almost like old times. We sat out back and watched the boats. She was the only person I could talk to about Virginia Beach. I asked her what she was going to do once the house sold and she admitted she didn't have a plan. Matt Biaggi came by and dropped off some weed. Bella jumped a little when he called from the side gate. After he left, I realized why: the next person to stop by, the person she'd actually been expecting, was Bryce.

"Are you following me again?" I asked.

"Nope," said Bryce.

I looked at Bella. She looked at the ground. I stood up, knocking over the rickety aluminum patio table, spilling my plastic cup of hard seltzer. I felt it splash on my ankle. I'll admit it, I was scared.

"Fuck you both," I said, voice shaking. I started walking backward, and then I started to run.

CHAPTER FIFTY-ONE

Roman drove them both to Bryce's grandma's and on the way, Bella admitted she'd lured Ashley to her house that night.

"He should have been an actor," said Bella. "I know it was stupid to believe him but he sounded really sincere. He was literally weeping. He said he was leaving town and he wanted to say goodbye. He said she'd stopped returning his calls. I had *no idea* he knew anything about Kiera or the money."

What was the point of getting mad?

"But she left, Roman," Bella continued. "He showed up and she was scared of him. She fucking ran."

"And what did he do?"

Bella was silent.

"Bella, what did he do after she left?"

"He left, too. But not right away. He didn't, like, run after her."

"Why would she come back?" Roman asked, not really expecting Bella to have an answer.

"I don't know," said Bella. "I didn't see her again. Kevin came home and brought, like, a ton of friends."

"He says he didn't see her either."

"I know," said Bella. "But we were all pretty fucked up."

There were two town police cars at the Washington Arms. Roman turned off the car and as they stepped out, they saw Scott Kingsley walking Bryce out the front door of his grandma's, in handcuffs.

"Did you kill Ashley?" shouted Roman, his voice cracking.

Bryce looked up, his eyes wild.

"Step back, Roman," said Scott.

"Ask him where he was the night she died," said Roman, advancing. He wanted to grab Bryce. He wanted to tear his eyes out.

"Back up!" said Scott. He held out his arm.

"Do your fucking job! Somebody killed her. He killed her!"

"Roman!" Felix jogged toward him from the apartment. "I need you to go home."

"You need to talk to Bella," said Roman. He was breathing hard. "Bryce lured Ashley to her place that night. She left and he went after her."

"Stop," said Felix. "I promise you, we will do this the right way."

"Felix!" Chief Hawkins shouted from the apartment door. "I need you."

Roman dodged Felix and ran. The chief was holding a plastic evidence bag. With Ashley's phone inside.

Roman sat in a hard plastic chair in the hallway outside the police station for five hours. He texted his mom and John saying that they'd arrested Bryce and he was trying to get information from Felix. When Tara called, he filled her in on what Bella had told him, and said he'd be home late.

"Do you want company?" Tara asked. "I could come sit with you."

"I'm okay," he said.

"I love you. Mason loves you."

"I know. I love you both, too."

As he sat alone, Roman tried to imagine why Ashley would have come back to Bella's house that night. When he put together all he'd learned about what was going on in her life, it felt like she was split into two people. One, carefully planning a future with her family, secretly preparing a job application and engaging a real estate agent. The other, almost nihilistic: doing hard drugs, having an affair with a dealer, blackmailing the most powerful person in town. Which one was the real Ashley? Would he ever know?

Eventually, Felix emerged from the back half of the police station and told him that Bryce was being transferred to county jail and that, so far at least, his story matched Bella's.

"We found a gun and enough packaged drugs to charge him with intent to sell," said Felix. "But he's cooperating about Ashley. He says Lisa Marrone mentioned she'd deposited a bunch of cash; I'm sure Lisa will lose her job. He says he followed Ashley and saw her with Kiera and figured that's where the money came from. He threatened her with a gun and she gave him what Kiera had given her, which was nine thousand dollars. He says she told him that was it, but he suspected he might be able to get more. She wouldn't answer his calls so he manipulated Bella to get Ashley to her house so he could talk to her. But, he says, she left and he didn't follow her."

"But somehow he got her phone."

"He says she left it at Bella's and he picked it up."

"Does he have an alibi for the rest of the night?"

"We're working on confirming that."

"So, he stalked her and he threatened her and he stole from her, but he didn't kill her. How convenient."

"He's not going anywhere, Roman. If he killed her, we'll find out."

"Have you talked to Kiera? And Wolfe?"

Felix paused. "One thing at a time, Roman."

"Ash was blackmailing Wolfe. Bryce could have been working with them, too. They all had reason to want her dead. So did pretty much everybody connected to this hotel shit. You're going to have to talk to the mayor. The fucking chief could be involved."

"I know, Roman. I know."

It was after dark when Roman finally got home, but Mason was still awake.

"Daddy's home!" shouted the boy. "Will you put me to bed, Daddy? I already brushed my teeth!"

"Sure, mister," said Roman.

"Me and Gerty and John had pizza for dinner. We saved some for you."

"That's really nice of you. I'm definitely hungry. Why don't you run upstairs and pick a book and I'll be right behind you."

"Can we do the poop book?"

"Of course."

"Hooray!"

Mason ran up the stairs, and John and Tara closed in on him with concerned faces.

"Bryce says he didn't do it."

"What does Felix think?" asked Tara.

"I'm not sure," said Roman. "But they've got her phone. Maybe there's something in there."

"Did you have any idea all this was going on with her?" asked John.

Roman shook his head.

"Your mom told me what Bella said about the floating casino."

"Daddy!" Mason hollered from upstairs.

"Go," said Tara. "We'll be here."

Roman climbed the stairs to his son. He helped him change into his favorite pajamas, the ones with the monster trucks on them, then he read the poop book—three times. Roman flipped off the bedside light and helped Mason get comfortable among his stuffed animals.

"Will you sing your song again? The one about the airplane?"

"Of course," said Roman. He cleared his throat and did his best to remember the words. By the end of the second chorus, Mason was asleep. But Roman stayed with him, looking at his eyelashes, his lips, the mole on his nose. His profile was the same as it had been the day he'd come home from the hospital, weighing barely five pounds. He was the most beautiful thing Roman had ever seen. And now, lying here, warm against his son's back, he felt his body flood with gratitude. Gratitude! Ashley was dead, and still, something existed that could make him feel lucky. He could have been here every night, putting his son to bed. What if he had? What if he'd trusted his love for Mason and Ashley enough to say, *yes, let's go somewhere else.* She wouldn't have needed money from Wolfe. Maybe she wouldn't have started getting high and hanging out with Bryce and Kiera and Bella. Maybe she wouldn't have run into whoever sent her down that cliff.

CHAPTER FIFTY-TWO

John helped Tara wipe up the kitchen and put the pizza they didn't eat into Tupperware. They puttered around a little, waiting for Roman to come down, but finally decided he must have fallen asleep with Mason.

"You wanna head up?" asked John. "Or I could make some popcorn and we could watch a movie?"

Tara wrapped her arms around him.

"I love you," he said. "I wish I could make all this go away."

She pressed into him, smelling the dried sweat of a day working on the back of the house. Her house; and he was doing the work for free. Just because of her. They hadn't had sex since Ashley died, and suddenly, she wanted to. She put her hand on his crotch and looked up. He raised an eyebrow, cracked a little smile, and she nodded. They climbed the stairs.

She woke up the next morning at seven. Typically, Mason would come in to get her around then, but she figured he must be looking at his books in bed, or maybe he was with Roman. She lay awake, listening to the birds. The ceiling fan above her wobbled, making the pull-chain tick-tick against the light fixture. If Ashley had gotten her way, Tara's future would be one without Mason's hopping onto her bed every morning; a future where she didn't get to sing her grandson to sleep. What had she done to deserve such a cruel fate? Ashley had needed her and she stepped in and four years later Ashley was going to punish her for it?

But that danger was gone now.

"Whatcha thinking about?" asked John. He turned his face to hers and looked at her with sleepy eyes, crease lines from the pillow across his cheek.

"Nothing."

"I could fuck you again," he said.

She smiled. "You could."

She was ready, and it was quick. When the orgasm rose up through her she cried out softly and thought *yes, yes, my life is beautiful.*

Tara got up to pee and when she came back, she laid her head on John's chest.

"It's hard to believe somebody really killed Ashley," she said.

"I know."

They lay there in silence, and Tara heard the door above them open. She sat up, preparing for Mason to come in. But his footsteps ran past their bedroom and down the stairs. Roman was with him. She heard her boys' voices but couldn't make out what they were saying. She started to get out of bed, but John put his hand on her.

"Give them a little time," he said.

"Okay."

She lay back down.

"Mason is going to be okay, Tar," said John. "When we were fishing the other day, he was happy. Really. He was splashing and skipping rocks. He even helped me bait his line. He's getting braver. I know it'll be hard. This is traumatic for him. It's never going to be the same. But I truly think he's going to be okay. I think he's going to thrive."

Tara looked up at him. "Thank you," she said. "I know it's not Scarlett or Dawson, but I hope you know how much it matters to Mase—to me—how you are with him."

John smiled. "It's easier with Mase. There's all this shit between me and my kids. All the shit with their mom. It's like a fog. Sometimes I feel like I'm acting with them. Like it's a fucking job interview."

"Ashley said that to me once," Tara said. "She said she felt like I was watching her all the time. Judging how she was with Mason. She was right. I felt like I knew better than her. I liked pulling rank. And honestly, I didn't care if it made her feel bad. I thought I was a better parent. No wonder she wanted to leave."

"It's not your fault," said John. "Think of what would have happened if you hadn't been around to step up with Mason. That little boy would have been *neglected*. And he's a fucking champion. He's the best kid I know. And that's all you. I'm sorry, but fuck Ashley if she didn't see that. She's gonna take him away from you? From this place where he has roots? She's gonna drag him and Roman to some shitty beach town where she knows one fucking lesbian with a yoga studio? Why? Because she's bored? No way. Mason is better off with us."

Two days later, Felix came to the house. Mason saw him pull up and seemed to know it was about his mommy.

"Can I watch TV?" he said.

Tara got him a granola bar and sat him in front of *Bluey*. She kissed his head.

"Maybe we can get ice cream later."

In the kitchen, Felix told them that the chief had agreed to ask the medical examiner to expedite Ashley's full autopsy.

"He wants to do the right thing. I think he knows how bad this could be."

"Do you think he's involved?" asked Tara.

"I don't have any evidence to suggest that."

"That's a bullshit answer," said John.

"Have you talked to Wolfe and Kiera?" asked Roman.

"I went to the house."

"And?"

"Both directed me to their attorney." Felix paused. "Right now, what I have are texts between Ashley and Kiera. They don't say anything explicit about money, but they arranged three meetings in the last month. The first two are less than an hour before she deposited the cash into the bank. And after the third, Ashley gets a text from Bryce. She actually recorded the conversation between them where he threatens her and takes the money. The recording implicates Kiera—they talk about getting the money from her—but the judge wouldn't sign off on a warrant to arrest her. He called it hearsay."

"Because Wolfe is probably pressuring him," hissed Roman. "Or outright paying him."

Felix sighed. "We need more," he said. "Wolfe and Kiera won't come in to talk if we don't compel them, and even then they could stonewall us. Right now, all I have is Bella and Bryce's story that Ashley was blackmailing them. I believe them, but I can't trace the cash and the meetups were in places without surveillance cameras. I'm still waiting on the cell company for location data."

"What about looking at Wolfe's bank account?" asked Tara. "If he withdrew a bunch of cash around the same time, that's something."

"I need a warrant to get into his accounts," said Felix. "And even if the withdrawals matched, they could argue that's circumstantial. Honestly, I think Bryce is the most likely suspect. No one saw her after she left Bella's and his alibi is weak. I think she probably didn't leave. I think she started to walk away and Bryce stopped her. They argued and maybe he pushed her."

"But what about the drugs in her pocket?" asked Tara.

"Maybe she bought them right before and planned to use them later."

"You said they were wiped clean," said Roman.

Felix nodded. "I know. That still doesn't make a lot of sense to me. But it's possible she rubbed the bag against her clothes or something. It could just be a fluke."

"Are you going to charge him?" asked John.

"I can't do anything until the autopsy comes back. We need to know exactly how she died."

"How long will that take?" asked Roman.

"Hopefully less than forty-eight hours. As soon as I know, you'll know."

CHAPTER FIFTY-THREE

The four of them stayed home the rest of the day, rotating between the TV and the kitchen and the yard. John started tearing out the rotted sill, and Tara and Mason found a box of brownie mix to make. Roman sat outside on the porch for a while, picking at his nails and trying not to think about what the people in the hospital basement were doing to Ashley's body.

He texted Bella several times but she didn't text him back. He hadn't heard from her since she'd agreed to talk to Felix. She was probably feeling sorry for herself. Her big money deal was likely over now. She'd have to sell her shitty house for market rate like the rest of them, or live with what she had. And what she'd done.

After dinner, Roman got a text from Matt:

> hey man, bella was just here and she's acting really weird

> what's new

> lol—this seemed different. call me?

Roman sighed. This was a big part of why he and Ashley had let Bella go as a friend: she was exhausting. He called Matt.

"Hey, man," said Matt. "Sorry to bug you."

"What's up?"

"I didn't want to, like, text about it. Bella asked me if I could get her a gun."

"Jesus."

"She seemed really scared. She showed me these text messages somebody's sending her. Like, watch out, and you're going to end up like Ashley."

"She doesn't know who they're from?"

"It came up as a blocked number. I asked her who she thought it was, but she wouldn't say."

"Did you tell Felix?"

"I don't talk to cops if I don't have to, man."

Right.

"So what did you say?"

"I told her I don't have a gun. I want to help her, but I don't want to mess with that shit. I mean, I was at her house that night, too—for a little bit. What if she's working with the cops now? What if she's, like, got a wire on?"

"Okay," said Roman. "Is there, like, something specific you want me to do?"

"I just thought you should know. She seems really freaked out. And I know you two used to be close."

Used to be. "Do you know any of her other friends? Like from work?"

"Nah," said Matt. "That's why I called you. I think she's pretty fucking alone."

The next morning, Roman drove to Bella's house. Her car was gone and the lights inside were off. He knocked, peered in, saw only stillness. The gate that led to the backyard, the one they'd brought Ashley through on a gurney, was ajar. He looked around. No neighbors were outside, though he knew they could be peering from behind their windows. Would someone call him in for trespassing? He decided to risk it.

The backyard was quiet. He walked around the rusty metal chairs and dented fire pit, but before he could try the back door, someone called out.

"Hello?"

A woman's voice. He walked back toward the gate. It was one of the neighbors: Pia Atkinson. She and her husband, Will, were among the Brooklyn pandemic wave. Will worked in finance and, from what he heard, Pia had been an editor at a women's magazine before having their now seven-year-old twins. He'd seen them around town and at a couple of fundraisers for the progressive county candidates.

"Everything all right?" she asked. She was wearing a sundress, no bra.

"Everything's fine," said Roman. "I'm a friend of Bella's."

"I'm Pia. We live across the street."

"I'm Roman."

"You're the reporter," she said. "I'm really sorry about your wife."

"Thanks."

"Like I told the policeman, I'm happy to do anything I can to help."

"You talked to the police? About Ashley?"

"They were here yesterday. Officer White? He wanted to know if our security cameras keep what they record." She turned back to her house and pointed. "We've got a couple. My husband's in charge of all that, though, and he wasn't at home. I told the officer to come back."

Why hadn't he thought of that possibility? The cameras wouldn't have been able to see the rock, but maybe they could show whether Ashley had ever actually walked off Bella's property that night. And if Bryce followed her. And if Kiera or Wolfe had been there at some point.

"I don't really know your friend, Bella," continued Pia. "My husband and most of the other neighbors really wish she'd sell. I mean, the house is an eyesore. And they worry about all the people going in and out. We all have little kids."

"But you don't worry?"

Pia shrugged. "I'm a little more live-and-let-live. She doesn't bother us. I mean, what happened to your wife is really awful. My husband thinks Bella's some drug kingpin, but that's silly. He's from a whole different world. Mr. Ivy League; thinks he's a bit untouchable. But my cousin died of an overdose. So did a girl I worked with in the city. It can happen to anybody who uses, even just occasionally. I just hope Bella gets some help. I'm glad you're still here for her."

Pia walked back across the street. Roman texted Felix, asking if he was planning to come look at Pia's cameras soon. And then he texted Bella:

i'm at your house

Less than a minute later, she texted back:

can you stay? back in 10

Roman texted a thumbs-up emoji and ten minutes later, Bella pulled into the driveway.

"Where have you been?" asked Roman. "What's going on?"

"Come inside," she said, looking around.

"Are you okay? Matt called me."

They stepped inside and Bella locked the door behind him.

"John was here the night of the party," she said.

"John Manchester? My mom's John? You actually saw him?"

"I saw his truck."

"Are you sure?"

"Positive. He's got that Jets sticker on his door. He denied it, but I'm sure."

"He denied it? When did you talk to him?"

"A couple days ago. I was at the gas station and he was at the pump across from me. I saw the sticker and it just clicked. I'd seen his truck pull up at some point that night. I remember it was loud and I looked out the window. I asked him and he denied it, but he was lying. I could tell. Then I started getting these texts from a blocked number."

She showed him her phone.

> no one will believe you

> keep your mouth shut

> no one will miss you if you disappear

> and unlike ashley, they'll never find your body

Roman's blood flooded with what felt like static electricity. His lips tingled. "You have to show this to Felix."

"He's right though, no one will believe me. I don't have any proof he was there."

"It won't just be your word," said Roman, his pulse quickening. "Your neighbor has security cameras."

Pia instructed her husband to open the file from the night of Bella's party. Their system, apparently, backed everything up to the cloud as long as you paid for enough storage. The camera angle gave them a straight-on view of Bella's front door, but the edge of the yard where the rock and cliff were, was out of frame. They watched Ashley arrive on foot at 7:56, and they watched Matt pull up and then leave just after 8:30. Bryce parked out front at a little before nine, and at 9:16, Ashley appeared again, alone. Roman held his breath as he watched her run past the front door, looking behind her, as if she was worried someone might follow. But it was another fifteen minutes before Bryce came out, lit a cigarette, then got in his car and drove off.

"I saw John's truck later," said Bella. "After midnight. I was in my bedroom."

Will clicked fast-forward and slowed down at midnight. There were half a dozen cars in front of the house. The lights glowed bright from inside. Roman imagined it was loud. Bella was holding herself, leaning in, eyes wide. They scrolled at double speed. At 12:34, a white truck slowly rolled by. John's truck; the Jets sticker on the passenger-side door. He pulled past the house toward the dead end that was the lookout, and the path through Bella's woods to their rock.

"Go back," said Roman, his jaw shivering. "Can you see if anyone else is in the truck?"

They scrolled back and slowed down; John was driving. It looked like he was alone. They let the video play. Four minutes after he drove to the end of the street, he drove away.

"Call the station," Roman instructed Pia and Will. "Tell them you have to speak with Sergeant White immediately. Tell them it's an emergency. Call 911 and have them get him if he doesn't pick up."

His hand was sweating as he pulled out his phone and tapped on John's contact.

John picked up.

"Hey, man, what's up?"

"Were you at Bella's the night Ashley died?"

There was a pause. "What?"

"Were you at Bella's the night Ashley died."

"No. Why?"

"I'm at her across-the-street neighbor. They've got surveil-lance cameras outside and I'm looking at you driving your truck up to the house . . ."

The line went dead.

CHAPTER FIFTY-FOUR

I wasn't sure where I was going when I walked away from Bella's after telling her and Bryce to fuck all the way off forever. Not home; Roman was in the city and it was barely nine. John was spending the night up in New Paltz for an early morning job, which meant it would be just me and Tara and I'd have to either pretend I wasn't a mess or go hide upstairs. I texted Diane as I walked, thinking maybe I could Uber to her bar to hang out. But she texted back that she wasn't working, and she didn't invite me to wherever she was.

I walked toward the center of town. Maguires pub would be open, though I mostly hated it there. All the midlife-crisis men gathered together, red-faced and complaining about women. But what the hell, maybe I could complain with them. Or find a corner to cry. As I made it out of Bella's neighborhood and onto the main road, I heard an engine slow beside me.

"Hey," said John from the cab of his truck. "You headed home?"

"Maguires."

"I'll give you a ride."

I climbed in. The truck smelled like a mix of chili powder and grease and construction dust. John moved a plastic bag with a half-gallon of ice cream sweating inside so I could sit.

"I thought you were staying in New Paltz?"

"I was. We've got a super-early morning on this job. But the buddy I was crashing with brought home a chick and I decided to bail. Figured it's early enough I can surprise Tara with some ice cream."

"Nice," I said.

"Where were you?"

"Bella's."

"Oh yeah? You two friends again?"

"No," I said, too quickly. Did I even have friends anymore? Kiera and Bryce and Bella, Diane, Jen, Daniel, Chris, even Roman—none of them knew what was happening in my life. Tara was probably the closest I had to a friend these days, and I was about to explode her world.

We drove in silence and then John passed the turnoff for Maguires.

"You missed the turn."

"I wanted to talk to you," he said. "I've got an idea for the wedding—a surprise for Tara."

"Okay," I said. "Where are we going?"

"Just somewhere we can talk, where people aren't looking at us."

It made sense. If someone saw us in a truck on a Friday night outside Maguires they'd probably think we were sneaking around. John followed the road beside the freight train tracks along the river toward the edge of town and pulled in at a building I'd passed a million times but couldn't say what it housed. Or if it was abandoned. Maybe it was once an office or a warehouse. The chain-link fence surrounding the building was open and John drove around back to the parking area, which was overgrown with weeds. We were at river level, the inlet swampy with plant life and the sediment that washes to the edge of the water. But John wanted privacy, I guess.

"Do you know this place?"

He ignored my question. We parked.

"Listen, I'm just going to come out and ask: are you planning to leave town and take Mason?"

"What? What did Tara say?"

"You can't take him."

"What do you mean I can't?"

"You have responsibilities here."

"I don't need a lecture about my responsibilities—"

"Roman's not going to let you."

"Wait, have you talked to Roman? What did you say?" Tara acted like she'd let it go, but had she told Roman what she'd seen on my phone that night? He couldn't possibly think I would leave him? Not after all this time. I knew he might be seeing somebody in the city, but who was I to judge? My heart twitched: I didn't have all the money yet, but I had enough. I could convince him. I had to. I needed him to know right now that I was in this with him forever. No matter what he'd done. No matter what I'd done.

I felt for my phone, but it was gone. I must have left it at Bella's.

"What did Tara tell you?" I asked.

"Tara will fall apart if you take Mason. He's her whole world."

"That's part of the problem," I said. "I know she'll be unhappy for *a while, but she lived a life before him. She'll go back to that. You'll get married. She'll be fine."*

"She doesn't want to go back to that."

"I don't know what to say. He's mine and Roman's. Not hers."

"That's fucking selfish," said John, the color rising in his face.

"I know," I said. "And I know it's gonna hurt. But I can't be his mom in her shadow anymore. The way she watches me. I can't do it. I know what she did for me. For Mase. But I'm okay now, and I want to take over."

"So stay here and take over. Get your own apartment. Don't move six hours away."

"I'm think I'm done with this conversation."

"You're not the only one who loves him, Ashley. You're not the only person in this family. You don't get to just blow it up because you feel like it. I'm telling you it's going to kill her if you take him."

"It's not going to kill her. She'll have you. Her new husband. She's only forty-four. Honestly, you guys could have a baby."

"She's not going to marry me if you take Mason," said John, his voice low.

"Did she say that?"

"Not in so many words."

"Well, that's shitty, I'm sorry. But why do you care so much about getting married?"

"My parents were married. Mason deserves that stability."

"Mason does? He's not your kid, John."

"I know," he said, getting frustrated. "That's not the point."

"What's the point then? You've already been divorced once. Mason's actual parents aren't married. Getting married doesn't guarantee anything. Just ask your kids."

"Don't fucking talk about my kids!" he shouted, spit flying from his lips.

"Jesus," I said, and I must have smiled. Sometimes I smile when I'm nervous. And John was acting weird. It was kind of funny how weird he was acting.

"You're a selfish little bitch."

"What?"

He hit me in the face. Closed fist to the mouth. The pain was bright. I tasted blood.

"What the fuck!" I put my hand on the door handle. He grabbed my arm.

"We're not done talking."

CHAPTER FIFTY-FIVE

Roman drove the half-mile from Bella's to his house at twice the speed limit, ripping around corners, blowing stop signs, alarming everyone he passed who was outside enjoying this sunny summer day. His mom wasn't answering the phone. And when he pulled up to the house, John's truck was gone.

"Mason!" called Roman, running into the house. "Mom!"

Silence. Music upstairs. He checked the third floor; no one. The second-floor bathroom door was closed. His mom's phone was playing Stevie Nicks. He banged on it. "Mom!"

She opened the door. Steam came floating out. She was wrapped in a towel and her hair was wet.

"What? Are you okay?"

"Where's Mason?"

"Downstairs with John."

"No, he's not. John's truck is gone."

"Oh. Well, they must have run out."

"Mom, John was at Bella's the night Ashley died."

"What? No, he was in New Paltz."

"No, he wasn't. The neighbors have video. He drove up to Bella's at, like, midnight."

"Okay. I . . . I don't understand. Did you ask him about it?"

"I just called him. First he lied, and then he hung up. And now he's gone. With Mason."

Tara's face went white. "I'll call him."

"We need to call the police."

"Wait, stop. John wouldn't . . ."

"Wouldn't what? Hurt Mason? Are you sure?"

Tara was silent. "No. I'm not sure." She picked up her phone and tried to call John. He didn't pick up.

"Where might he go?" asked Roman.

"I . . . have no idea."

They looked at each other, mother and son. Tara dripping wet, gripping her towel like it might save her. Roman's mind running through every possible place John might go with his son and his mind coming up with nothing but walls and waves of terror, crushing what little rational thought he could manage.

"I'll get dressed," said Tara. "We'll find them."

Roman called Bella.

"Where are you?"

"I'm still at Pia and Will's. We're waiting for Felix."

"Tell him to call me as soon as he gets there. John's gone. And he took Mason."

"Holy shit. Okay."

Roman ended the call.

"I'm calling 911," he said to his mom. "They'll put out . . . an alert."

Tara didn't hesitate. "Do it."

For the first time in his life, Roman dialed 911.

"I need to report a kidnapping. My son has been taken by a man we think is dangerous."

The dispatcher took the address and the details.

"Is this man known to you?"

"Yes, he's my mom's fiancé."

"But you think he is dangerous?"

"Yes."

"Does he have a history of violence?"

"What? No. Wait, maybe. But he took my son without permission. I'm telling you, my son is in danger."

"I understand," said the dispatcher. "I'm sending an officer to your address."

"I don't need somebody here! I need people looking for them! He's in a white Dodge Ram. There's a Jets sticker on the passenger-side door."

"Do you have the plate number."

Shit.

"Mom, what's John's license plate number?"

Tara stared at him. "I don't know."

"It's a New York plate," Roman said to the dispatcher. "His last name is Manchester. John Manchester. Can you look it up?"

"I don't have that ability from here," she said. "The officer may, when he arrives."

"It's gotta be somewhere," Tara said, looking around the bedroom. She opened John's bedside drawer.

"Where does he keep, like, paper stuff, tax stuff?" asked Roman.

Tara blinked. She looked like she'd been slapped across the face. "The closet. There's a file case."

Roman turned on the closet light, found a plastic file box with a handle. He put the dispatcher on speaker, put the phone down. Hands shaking, he pushed through the files. "Taxes 2023" . . . "Kids" . . . "Medical." Finally: "Truck." Roman pulled out the folder. The first piece of paper was a receipt from the Dodge dealer. Brake job. "I've got it!" He read the numbers and letters to the dispatcher.

"Can you put out an APB? He's been gone at least . . ." Roman looked at his mom.

"Thirty minutes?"

"At least a half an hour. You need to find him. My son is only four."

"I understand," said the dispatcher. "I have an officer on the way."

"Please send the alert."

"I'm sorry, sir, I can't do that. The officer needs to make a formal—"

"You have to find him! He's got my son!"

"I understand, sir."

Roman ran down the stairs. If he got closer to the door, would the police arrive more quickly?

His phone made a noise: Felix was calling on the other line.

"Hold on," said Roman to the dispatcher. "Someone's calling."

"I'll be right here."

Roman clicked on Felix. "Where are you?"

"I'm in my cruiser. I just got the call about the surveillance cameras. I'm headed to Bella's . . ."

"No! Come here. John took Mason. We need to get an APB. I think he killed Ashley."

"Slow down," said Felix. "I'm on my way."

For three hours, they waited. Bella drove over, and she and Tara and Roman paced on the porch, praying for the sound of John's truck. For him to roll up with Mason and a load from Home Depot and a confused expression when they all came running. For him to offer an explanation of that night. He'd gone to score. He'd gone to do anything but what they feared. Or he could offer no explanation. Tara didn't care. All she cared about was Mason. If anything happened to Mason it would kill her. And it should kill her. She'd turned Ashley into the enemy. She'd allowed John to see Ashley as a threat.

Felix stayed with them. The APB was out. Police all over the state were looking for John's truck, he assured them. Signs flashed on roadways. An Amber Alert had been issued, pinging millions of phones.

At four o'clock, the radio in Felix's cruiser crackled to life. At the same time, he got a call.

"What's going on?" Roman asked.

Felix held up a finger; he was listening.

"We're on our way." He ended the call and told them all to get in his cruiser. "Let's go."

"What's happening?" Tara asked.

"John is on the Bear Mountain Bridge. He's got Mason. And he's asking for you."

CHAPTER FIFTY-SIX

"He wouldn't do anything to Mason," said Bella.

She was the only one who could speak. Tara felt as if her entire body were made of wet sand. Like chunks of it might fall off if she moved. Roman, in the front seat next to Felix, held on to the grab handle and leaned forward. Felix had turned off the radio. The only sound beside the sirens atop the car was the roar of the wind as they twisted over the mountain. Felix sped past the signs in the little town that said to slow to 30. He sped past the BBQ restaurant and the bagel shop that hadn't made it through Covid. He sped past the Dunkin' Donuts and the Circa 1811 Inn; past the motorcycle repair and the twenty-four-hour gym, toward what they could now see was a sea of red and blue lights, and beyond, the bridge across the mighty river.

At the barricade, Felix rolled down his window.

"I've got the family," he said.

The officer waved them through.

"They've got a hostage negotiator about a hundred feet away," said Felix. "But John's got a gun."

"I'm going to throw up," said Roman. He cracked open his door as they drove, but missed the ground and vomited on the seat.

"Tara, he's asking for you. Do you think you're up to this?"

"Yes."

Felix stopped the cruiser and they all jumped out, Roman and Tara running, Felix behind them yelling, "Let them through!"

Tara had never seen so many men with guns. There were no cars on the bridge. Traffic was stopped in both directions. Lights flashing, cruisers and vans parked at odd angles, flares burning in the middle of the road.

"John!" she screamed, waving her arms, her hair whipping into her mouth. "I'm here! I'm here!"

John was standing in the middle of the bridge on the north side walkway. He had a handgun in one hand and was holding Mason around him with the other. Mason's face was bloated and red with tears and panic. He wasn't wearing shoes or a shirt. She'd left him eating dry cereal in the kitchen while she went to shower. They were going to scoot to the playground, maybe get an ice cream. What story had John told the boy to get him into his truck so fast?

"It was an accident!" shouted John. "I didn't mean to hurt her!"

"I believe you!" Would her voice carry over the wind and the sirens? "Mason! It's going to be all right!"

She tried to move closer, but Felix held her back. John could turn and let go and drop Mason over the bridge.

"I didn't want her to take Mason from you. That wasn't right! He's yours. He's ours."

"I know!" It was a lie but it didn't matter.

"Tell him to drop the gun," said Felix.

"Drop the gun!" she shouted. "Let's go home."

"Mason!" shouted Roman behind her. "Daddy's here! Gerty's here. It's going to be okay."

"We're right here," she called. "John, please, let Mason down."

"This isn't what I wanted to happen," he said.

"I know," shouted Tara. "Just let him down and it will all be okay. I love you. It's gonna be fine."

John loosened his hold on Mason, letting him slide to the ground, but he didn't let go. Mason seemed too terrified to move. John held the boy's wrist in one hand, the gun in the other.

"Please don't hurt him, John," Tara called. "Please! We can make this okay if you don't hurt him."

"I would never—"

A shot rang out and John fell. Mason ran to her and Roman and they caught him together, the boy's silence now erupting in screams and sobs. They held one another, the three of them knot-tight, relief exploding in their bodies.

CHAPTER FIFTY-SEVEN

The order to fire had been issued before Tara and Roman stepped foot on the bridge. *If you've got a clean shot, take it,* was the word direct from the scene commander.

"They don't fuck around when kids are involved," Felix told them later.

Could the cops have let him live? Could they have kept talking a while longer until he dropped the weapon? Tara had loved John, but she didn't care. Mason was all that mattered.

She didn't care what happened to John's body. She didn't care what his kids found out, or how. She didn't care who said what about him or her or Roman. She gritted her teeth through the ambulance ride to the hospital to make sure Mason was "okay." She nodded as the doctors assured her that Mason was physically unharmed, and as the nurse handed them a printed list of child therapists in the area. Bobby picked them up and Roman and Tara both rode in the backseat with Mason, neither wanting to be more than a few inches from him. The boy fell asleep on the way home. Roman carried him up the stairs and brought him into the bedroom he'd shared with Ashley. Where was he, deep in those dreams? Tara brought Mason's stuffed giraffe from his bed and all three of them lay down together.

The next morning, a reporter from the local Fox station came to the door.

"Hello?" she called from the porch after ringing twice and knocking several times.

Roman looked down from the third-floor window and saw a white news van parked outside and a man setting up a tripod on the sidewalk. He was already shooting B-roll of their neighborhood. Background for when the anchor told his audience that "Fox went to the home of the deceased man and . . ." How would that sentence end?

He watched the reporter in her color-matched dress and jacket, her high heels and glossy hair. She came back down the front steps and looked up. He ducked. There would be more of them. The street would soon be lined with vehicles. Even just the image of Roman's disheveled face, freshly traumatized, would give them something to build a segment or an article around. Any answer to any question would invite another question, yield another paragraph of speculation. Roman didn't have any answers he wanted to share. Neither, he guessed, did his mother. More reporters meant more disruption to Mason's life. If they ignored them, he reasoned, they would go away more quickly.

He was right. They'd stopped knocking by the time Felix came by with information three days later. Tara and Roman put Mason in front of the television and went to the kitchen, the same as last time.

"Her DNA is all over his truck," Felix told them. "Traces of hair and blood on the front seat. It looks like he tried to clean up. He put a blanket over the passenger side."

Roman remembered this. He'd remarked on the woolen throw when they went to the bar to look for Bryce. John told him he'd spilled a Big Gulp.

"The autopsy showed she died from head trauma. And they found bits of gravel, like broken blacktop, in the wound. She wouldn't have gotten that from hitting one of the stumps or rocks on the cliff. The truck had GPS and we've been piecing together his movements that night. It looks like maybe he picked her up in town after she left Bella's and drove her to the old warehouse on Water Street. There's a parking lot there. You can't see it from the road and they don't have security cameras. It's rained, though, and so far we haven't been able to find anything . . . definitive."

Felix continued. "We do have an idea where he got the drugs, though. GPS puts him at a motel about five miles north around 11 p.m. We did some door-knocking and some persuading, and were able to get someone to identify John as the man he sold a bag of pills to that night. What I'm thinking is that he killed her in the parking lot. I'm not sure if we'll ever know whether he planned it or if it was some sort of accident, then he panicked and figured he'd try to make it look like she OD'd and fell at Bella's."

Tara stared at Felix, speechless. But Roman had questions.

"Why not just leave her in the parking lot? Why risk driving around?"

"It was risky, but it almost worked. Chief was ready to call it an overdose."

"But you weren't."

"We were all just doing our jobs. It looked like one thing to him, looked like something else to me."

"Thank you," said Roman.

"We haven't found her wallet," said Felix. "My guess is that it's in the river. I've requested a dive team, but I don't know if we'll get approval. There won't be charges, so they might not be willing to extend the resources."

"What about Bryce?" Roman asked.

"His gun was unregistered, and he's facing drug charges," said Felix. "He hasn't posted bail. My sense is his grandma is going to let him sit in jail for a while, though she did hire an attorney. He doesn't have a record, so he may well get off with a fine and probation. Depends on the judge. And the lawyers."

Larry came by the house a few hours after Felix.

"I just had a long meeting with the chief," said Roman's boss. "It was off the record, but he's aware of everything you found regarding this hotel thing. At the moment, there's no clear evidence of illegality. But that doesn't mean we ignore it."

Roman raised an eyebrow. Maybe Larry hadn't forgotten the role of the press entirely.

"Here's my proposal," Larry continued. "We go to Wolfe with what we know. You've got the survey with his signature on it. You've got the checks Bella has been getting from WinGate. We ask for an explanation. On the record."

"And if he declines? Or lies?"

"We call the mayor, and the people on the planning board."

"They'll lie, too."

Larry sighed. "Probably. They've probably already come up with a perfectly reasonable explanation. They'll probably say they simply forgot to send out the notice for a public hearing. Or they remembered but one of the clerks forgot."

"And then what?"

"And then what, what?"

"We just let them get away with it?"

"Well, they're not likely to get away with it entirely," said Larry. "The cat's out of the bag. I don't expect you to keep this to yourself, even if we can't actually publish anything. All you have to do is talk to one of Bella's neighbors and they'll take it from there. They won't get their little clubhouse. At least not in Adamsville."

It didn't feel like enough. Maybe it was a stretch to blame Wolfe and the Davenports for Ashley's death, but Roman couldn't help thinking that if she hadn't gotten access to so much money so quickly, she might not have made the plans she made. And if she hadn't made the plans, Tara wouldn't have been so scared, and if Tara hadn't been so scared, John wouldn't have felt the need to protect her by taking away the source of her fear. If that's even what happened. He'd never really know. And he had to live with that.

CHAPTER FIFTY-EIGHT

Tara refused to enter the bedroom she'd shared with John, so it fell to Roman to purge his mom's ex from their lives. Roman spent an afternoon gathering everything John owned. It wasn't much: razors and shaving cream; his deodorant and nose hair trimmer; the dish he kept coins in; the bedside drawer crammed with business cards and toothpicks and gum wrappers and a tube of lube. Roman winced and dumped it all in a trash bag. Most of John's tools lived in his truck, and the police had that, but what Roman found in the shed he put in a box. In the upstairs closet, behind the file case they'd found his papers in, Roman discovered a shoebox with half a dozen watches in it. Some looked old, maybe family pieces. Should he put them aside for John's kids? Roman realized he wasn't even positive how old John's kids were. What he knew was that John had said their mom didn't want them to see John with his "new family," so they were not allowed to visit. But Roman had no idea if that was true.

He found John's ex, Lindsay, on Facebook and messaged her,

saying they were taking his things out of the house and asking if the kids might want anything. He mentioned the watches and tools specifically. Lindsay wrote back minutes later.

> We don't want any of it. We just want to forget him.

Roman put John's clothes into black contractor bags and took everything to Goodwill.

The next day, he put on a collared shirt for his Zoom interview with the Associated Press. He set up his laptop in the living room, and dragged a chair to the corner by the side window with the one live plant in the house. The day before, he'd emailed Denise Witt saying that he would still like to do the interview, but that he thought she should know what was going on in his life. He sent the write-up from the local Fox station, the only one that mentioned John as the primary suspect in Ashley's murder. Denise emailed back and said she was looking forward to speaking with him. One of the first things she asked when he logged on was, "Do you want to write about it?"

The question shouldn't have surprised him—this was an interview for a job where he would write news feature stories, after all—but it did. *Did* he want to write about it? The question felt important. What would Ashley encourage him to do?

"I don't know," he said. "Not right away, at least."

"That makes sense," she replied. "I only ask because I want you to know that this is the kind of role that would allow for something like that. Police shootings, the family court system, guns, mental health, the ongoing trauma of the pandemic—we want to tell all these stories."

How would Ashley react to the way Denise broke down the destruction of their family so neatly into a list of topics? She'd probably be charitable, because Ash was usually charitable. Maybe she'd think about it and say, *she's not wrong.* Maybe she'd say that Denise was good at her job; a lot better than Larry.

"There is one story I'm thinking about," he said. "In small towns, municipal planning boards have a ton of power. They decide zoning changes and capacity, and they're not elected. Sometimes they don't even have any real expertise in building or real estate or law. And most small towns don't have their own newspaper, which means nobody is watching. So, if some big developer comes in and wants to ram something through, it's easy to get approval, and by the time people find out it's too late to stop the wheels turning."

"Okay," she said. "It's an interesting topic. Do you have a specific example in mind?"

"I do."

Denise emailed the next day with an offer: a two-year contract with a $95,000 annual salary and a hell of a benefits package. He'd been making $45,000 at the *Advocate.*

After they put Mason to bed that night, Roman told his mom that he'd gotten the job in Virginia Beach.

"Of course you did," said Tara, her face rigid and weird. Roman thought he understood what his mother was feeling. She was happy for his success, and terrified of what it meant for her; for the hours and days and years that stretched lonely in front of her. She knew that her need to be Mason's favorite had caused Ashley to want to flee, and caused John to stop her. His mother hadn't said the words, but Roman suspected that she would walk around the rest of her life knowing that if she'd been able to let go just a little bit and trust that Mason had a big enough heart to love them all, Ashley would be alive and her grandson's life would be whole.

He imagined that, like him, Tara lay in bed at night wondering what John had said to Mason that afternoon when he grabbed him and ran. What had the boy felt as they drove over the mountain? What would he remember of the minutes on the bridge? What would he remember of the sirens and the gunshot and the blood and the man's head exploding just inches from his own? The man he'd loved.

But Roman was ready to forgive. He could see, even if his mother couldn't yet, that what John had done was nobody's fault but his own. John was a man trying to protect a fantasy. They were simply the unlucky people he'd hooked his dream to.

"Will you come with us?" asked Roman. "To Virginia Beach?"

Tara covered her face with her hands and began to cry. She nodded vigorously.

"Thank you," she said. She stood up and came to him, put her hands on his face. "I love you, Roman. I'm so sorry for what I've done to your family. I will spend the rest of my life trying to make it up to you."

"You're my family, Mom," he said. "You were Ashley's family, too. And you're Mason's family. I know you didn't mean—"

He stopped. He couldn't say the words. Were they even his

to say? Tara would have to wrestle with Ashley's ghost herself; he couldn't lift that burden. But he could do the one thing his mother had always wanted from him: he could recognize that she loved him. That she'd bent her life for him. And that all the love she'd showered on Mason was, at least in part, an expression of her love for Roman.

"I love you, too," he said, wrapping his arms around her. He told himself: *do not let go. Hold on as long as she needs.*

Before he fell asleep that night, Roman texted Wolfe and asked for a meeting.

"Our house and the land it's on are worth eight hundred thousand dollars," he said, back in the lawyer's pristine kitchen the next morning. Kiera was there, too. She sat cross-legged on a barstool, silently chewing her nails. In his pocket, Roman's phone was set to record. "I'll sell it to you for seven hundred thousand if you give me cash within a month. You put in a hundred thousand and you can sell it for over a million."

"And you won't write about the hotel?" Wolfe asked.

"What hotel?"

Wolfe considered. "Fine."

"One more thing," continued Roman. "You're going to buy Bella's house for what you promised her."

"It's not worth half that much if we can't develop it the way we'd planned."

"Not our problem. You have thirty days."

Kiera followed him to the front door.

"Ashley loved you, you know," she said. "Listen. Let me just say this. She told me about your dad. And your mom. She said—"

"Stop," said Roman, his face hot. He'd failed Ashley in a million ways, but he did not have to listen to this girl who came into her life just to use her. Whatever Kiera had to say, she could keep it to herself. "I don't need you to tell me about Ashley."

He emailed Denise and accepted the job. That evening, he drove to Bella's and told her what he'd done.

"You don't have to sell if you don't want," Roman said. "I just figured, while I had him, I'd see what I could get."

Bella hugged him. They went out back and smoked a joint. The sun was going down across the river, but the beauty was gone from this spot. Ashley hovered. Roman hoped she was happy to see them together.

"You could come with us," Roman said. "I mean, you could get an amazing condo in Virginia Beach for half what he's gonna pay you."

"Nah," said Bella. "Thanks. But I think I'm going to Hawaii."

ACKNOWLEDGMENTS

Thank you first and foremost to my agent, Stephanie Kip Rostan, and my editor, Kelley Ragland. For ten years, you've held my hand and had my back, and I will be thankful forever.

Thank you to Jaclyn Manzanedo, my childhood friend who just happens to be an expert in dead bodies. Thank you to Erin Donaghue, who provided crucial editorial (and emotional) support and guidance.

Thank you to my friends Laura McHugh, Lori Rader-Day, and Amy Gentry for keeping me sane and on track as I wrote this book.

Thank you to the Cornwall Public Library, the Newburgh Free Library, and the people at 2 Alices Coffee Lounge for providing a clean, well-lighted place to write. And thank you to Adam Penenberg and Mary Quigley for giving me a happy home with the amazing students who study journalism at NYU.

Thank you to Joel, Mick, Lori, Susan, Marshall, Natalie, Libby, and Jerry. The pandemic sucked, but I'd be happy in our bubble forever.

This book—which is in large part about how difficult parent-hood can be—is dedicated to my parents, Bill and Barbara Dahl. I couldn't dream up better role models. Thank you for the loving home you gave me and Sue.

ABOUT THE AUTHOR

Julia Dahl is the author of *The Missing Hours, Conviction, Run You Down,* and *Invisible City,* which was a finalist for the Edgar Award for Best First Novel, one of *The Boston Globe's* Best Books of 2014, and has been translated into eight languages. A former reporter for CBS News and the *New York Post,* she now teaches journalism at NYU.